Breakaway

Kelly Jamieson

This book is a work of fiction. The names, characters, places, and incidents are products of the writer's imagination or have been used fictitiously and are not to be construed as real. Any resemblance to persons, living or dead, actual events, locale or organizations is entirely coincidental.

Breakaway
Copyright © 2015 by Kelly Jamieson

ISBN: 978-0-9918532-7-4

All Rights Are Reserved. No part of this book may be used or reproduced in any manner whatsoever without written permission, except in the case of brief quotations embodied in critical articles and reviews

Cover Design and Interior format by The Killion Group
http://thekilliongroupinc.com

PRAISE FOR BREAKAWAY

"Breakaway is the perfect summer read! I simply couldn't get enough of this story, and note to the author, I want more! There are not too many stories that center on my most favorite things, Hockey and the players are an all time favorite for me. Add a little bit of humor, a lot of sex, and a little drama and you have the making for one of my all time favorite stories."~*Just Erotic Romance Reviews*

"I love hockey and I really felt like I was there, experiencing everything that Remi and Jason were experiencing. The chemistry between Jason and Remi is off the charts. I was expecting the sex to be numerous and graphic, well, it's more loving, touching and real. You can feel the emotions, feel the touches, taste the kisses and see the tears. I highly recommend Breakaway to any reader that wants a loving, touching and emotional rich story between two opposites that realize what they want and need in their lives is the complete opposite of what they thought they wanted or needed." ~ *Night Owl Reviews*

"I loved this novel. It was hot and real, and it ran the gamut of true human emotion to provide a fulfilling, emotional love story. Don't miss this one!" ~ *The Romance Studio*

"Breakaway by Kelly Jamieson is a wickedly hot romance about a teacher and an athlete who meet, rapidly fall in love and then have to deal with the consequences of his past. The characters are extremely likeable; they share great dialogue and smoking hot chemistry. I fell in love with Remi and Jason's story and found myself unable to put their book down; Ms. Jamieson's writing is very addictive." ~*Two Lips Reviews*

PRAISE FOR THE NOVELS OF KELLY JAMIESON

"Kelly Jamieson delivers a blazing passionate read that tugs at the heartstrings!" **Carly Phillips,** *New York Times* **Bestselling Author**

"seductive and bewitching from the very start … Softly romantic and wickedly provocative" *RT Book Reviews* **on Rule of Three**

"Kelly Jamieson now has a permanent place on my keeper shelf and I can't wait to see what she writes next." **Joyfully Reviewed**

"Ms. Jamieson once again gives the reader a richly detailed story that is brimming over with sexual tension, intoxicating desires and intriguing carnal needs that is edgy and psychologically intense…" **The Romance Studio**

"…I love Kelly Jamieson's books and the way that she depicts her characters…" **Sizzling Hot Book Reviews**

DEDICATION

To all the readers who love my Heller boys as much as I do and keep asking for more…thank you all!

CHAPTER ONE

"It's a classic case of empty nest syndrome."

Remi frowned at her best friend. "How can it be empty nest syndrome when I'm not even a parent?"

Delise waved a hand. "It's the same thing. You've been raising those two kids for the last five years. No, actually you've been raising those kids since they were born. Your parents were hardly ever around. So it totally makes sense that you would feel depressed now that they've moved out."

"I'm not depressed." Remi slumped lower into the soft cushions of her couch.

Delise laughed and patted Remi's knee. "Yes, you are. And you're making the rest of us miserable too. Emily told us you stopped by her place to make sure she was okay the other day and interrupted her and Caleb…"

Remi pursed her lips and folded her arms across her chest. "She was sick."

"That was a week ago."

"I was worried about her."

"She's an adult."

Remi regarded her friend glumly. "I know."

"You just want someone to take care of. I know, hon. And you can't keep dropping in on Jasmine and Ethan."

Remi's stomach tightened. "I've only visited them a few times."

"She just moved out a couple of weeks ago."

"You know I'm worried about her. I think she's making a big mistake moving in with Ethan."

"She's a big girl. She has to make her own mistakes."

"I know, but—"

"I know what you think of her jerk-off boyfriend, but she loves him. If they want to live together, fine. She's twenty-one years old."

Remi nodded "But—"

"You're just such a mother hen, you can't help but worry about them." Delise patted Remi's knee again and Remi scowled. Was she being that much of a pain in the butt to her friends?

Sure, she'd been a little at loose ends since her brother and sister had moved out. Kyle had started college this year and Jasmine had just moved in with her boyfriend. She just had to adjust to things. Then she sighed. The truth was, she did feel lost and alone. Her whole life had been looking after her younger siblings and without them there always needing something, she almost felt like she didn't really exist anymore. But she'd been trying to keep busy with work and after school projects and…pestering her friends. She gave Delise a crooked smile. "I'm sorry."

"Don't apologize! We love you. We just hate seeing you so blue. Some day you're going to be a great mother."

Yeah, right. With no man in her life, motherhood seemed a sadly far-off dream.

"But right now," Delise continued, "You're young and single and now totally free. You should be out having fun!"

"Sure."

Delise grinned and stood. "Which is why we're all going out tonight. You, me, Emily and Sarah."

"We are?"

"We are. And I brought over something to get us started." She walked out of the living room and Remi rose too and trailed her friend into the kitchen. Delise opened the refrigerator with easy familiarity and pulled out a bottle of champagne.

Remi's eyes widened. "Where did that come from?"

Delise grinned, eyes dancing behind her funky eyeglasses. "I snuck it in." She peeled away foil and untwisted the wire cage, then pointed the bottle away from Remi as she eased the cork out. A satisfying pop and a whisp of smoke and the champagne fizzed out. "It's time to celebrate, girl! You can finally have a life of your own! Glasses?"

Remi blinked, then moved automatically to the cupboard where the champagne flutes were. Champagne? What was she celebrating? Her little brother was barely making it through his freshman year of college and her younger sister had just moved in with a man she'd suspected more than once of cheating on her. Remi was pretty sure he had. The scumbag.

"I don't exactly feel like celebrating." She held out the glasses.

"Oh, come on! I know you're worried about Jasmine, but you have to let go! She's a big girl who will have to learn from her mistakes. You just need to change your attitude!"

"I'm living alone for the first time in my life." It hit her then that she did in fact live alone. All alone. No more kids to worry about, to bail out of scrapes, to sacrifice sleep and money and a life of her own for.

Well, until they came running back out of money, brokenhearted or in trouble of some kind.

"But that can be a good thing! Just think—you're free now to do whatever you want! Whenever you want." Delise poured champagne carelessly and it frothed over the top and ran over Remi's fingers in cold foamy rivulets. "Or *who*ever you want." She winked.

Delise was right. She did need to let go. She needed to push aside those worries that Jasmine was going to get hurt or that Kyle was going to flunk out of college and spend the rest of his life working at Burger King.

"You're right. I'll try." She clinked her glass against Delise's. The sparkling bubbles nipped at Remi's nose and throat as she drank and she laughed.

"So. Where should we go tonight?" Delise picked up the bottle to refill the glasses.

"I don't know." It had been a while since she'd been out with her girlfriends. A long while.

"We'll go to Rouge." Delise answered her own question. "It's the hottest, most happening place in town. And you're going to find the best looking guy there, pick him up and bring him home for head-banging, screaming sex. And it won't matter—because you live alone now!"

Remi laughed at the outrageous plans. Like that'd ever happen! But she supposed she was willing to go out. It would be good for her. "Okay!" She forced a smile, drained her glass and held it out for more.

"I'll call Emily and Sarah and tell them where we're going. They said they'd meet us there."

"Wow. You guys have this all planned."

Delise shrugged, mouth curved into a smug smile. She tossed her long spirally auburn hair back over her shoulder. "I had to. If I left it up to you, you'd stay home marking papers or something. On a Saturday night!"

Remi grimaced. Yeah, that was usually what she did on Saturday nights. Or pretty much any night lately. "You're so right." She reached for the champagne bottle. "My life *is* boring. I need to have some fun."

"True that." Delise toasted her again. "Let's go find your sexiest outfit for you to wear tonight."

"Uh. That might be a problem. I don't exactly have a sexy wardrobe."

"Hmm." Delise tapped her index finger against her lips. "Okay, then—let's go shopping!"

"I can't go shopping!" Remi glanced at her watch. "It's nearly dinner time…"

"Remi. You don't have to cook dinner for anyone. Time doesn't matter. The stores are open for two more hours. Let's go!"

Remi stared at her friend, fighting her reflexive resistance to anything spontaneous and carefree. A lifetime of being responsible, of being the dependable older sister, the mature, reliable one everyone counted on, had worn grooves in her that were too deep to disappear in an hour. A day. Maybe ever!

She drew in a long deep breath and straightened her shoulders. "Okay. Let's go shopping."

Pulsing techno music wrapped around Remi and Delise as they descended a long red-carpeted staircase into the dark nightclub. Ornate lanterns on red walls provided discreet light and mirrored columns reflected it back around the room, creating light and shadow, glitter and darkness. Remi and Delise walked into the front area of the club where well-dressed patrons crowded around a long glass and stainless-steel bar. Emily and Sarah waved from a small table near the back, which led to a second level where more gorgeous people lounged on red leather banquettes.

When Sarah looked up at Remi, her jaw went slack. "Remi! Holy cow!"

Emily's reaction was similar. "You look incredible!" She studied Remi's gold sparkly camisole top, short black skirt and stiletto heels. "Where'd you get that outfit?"

"Diva." Remi looked down at herself and bit her lip, wishing she could slouch down into her seat. The low-cut top revealed generous cleavage—not that she had that much cleavage, but the mega-push up bra Delise had talked her into was doing a fine job of lifting up the girls. She tugged at the short skirt and shifted in her chair.

"Doesn't she look hot?" Delise demanded with a satisfied smile.

"She does!"

Delise dropped her small purse on the table. "We went shopping. I helped pick it out."

"Good job, Delise," Emily said.

"I thought it would help with the uh…shift in mindset."

Emily and Sarah grinned.

"So here we are, four single girls out for a night of fun. Now that Remi lives alone, she can do whatever she wants, whenever she wants, with whoever she wants, and that starts tonight! We're going to find her a hot guy to have some fun with."

"No, we're not." Her cheeks burning, Remi picked up a small plastic drinks menu. "What're you two having?"

"Mojitos," Emily answered. "Yum."

"Sounds good to me." Remi dropped the card and discreetly pulled at the bodice of her top.

"Stop it!" Delise gave her hand a smack. "You look great! Stop fidgeting. You'll just draw more attention to yourself."

Remi blinked and dropped her hands to her lap. Delise was right. She needed to act like she dressed this way all the time.

Another quick glance assured her nothing inappropriate was being revealed and she sat up straight.

A waitress appeared to take their order. When she'd left, Delise turned in her chair to scan the crowd, moving to the throbbing music. Flashing red lights lit the dance floor, shifting with dancing bodies. On a catwalk, three gorgeous girls in tiny shorts and bikini tops swung their long hair in sexy choreography. Remi couldn't take her eyes off them. They were so fit, so confident in their beautiful bodies, so graceful.

"That guy over there," Delise said in Remi's ear. Remi dragged her gaze away from the dancers to a group of three men standing at the bar. All three of them were good-looking, clean cut, nicely dressed.

"I'll go invite them over." Delise rose from her chair.

Remi started to grab her arm to stop her, then paused. What the heck? Picking up guys in bars wasn't her style, but it wasn't as if she was a twenty-eight year old virgin, for god's sake. She'd had boyfriends and relationships. There was nothing wrong with talking to some men and maybe making new friends.

She tapped her foot to the music while she awaited her drink, aware of Delise talking to the men out of the corner of her eye. Sure enough, all three followed her back to the table and a search for extra chairs ensued. Soon Remi sat sandwiched between two guys.

She pulled her shoulders in and reached for the drink the waitress set in front of her. Lord.

"Hi," the guy on her right said. "I'm Elton."

"Remi." She smiled at him. His gaze dipped to her chest. Her lips tightened.

"Nice to meet you, Remi," he said, still looking at her cleavage. She sighed.

"I'm Dave," the man on her left said. "This is Tiger."

Remi blinked. Tiger?

The girls all introduced themselves and Remi sucked back her tangy cocktail. The lime puckered the inside of her mouth, but it was cold and wet and she was feeling very warm, despite the scant fabric of her new top.

"We're celebrating tonight," Delise announced to the men.

"Oh, yeah? What?"

"Remi's new life."

Remi wanted to slide under the table. She forced a tight laugh. "It's not really a new life," she explained. "My sister moved out recently and now I live alone."

That didn't even begin to explain the huge change that had just occurred in her life, but whatever. She didn't need to share every detail with strangers.

"Cool," Elton said. He leered at her. "Party at your place tonight, huh?"

She rolled her bottom lip in and seared Delise with a look. She was so dead after this. Delise grinned.

Remi tried to make conversation with Elton and Dave. She really did. But all Dave wanted to talk about was the stock market, which she knew next to nothing about, and all Elton was interested in was staring at her boobs.

Remi ordered another drink along with everyone else. The music grew louder, the dancing more frenzied.

"Wanna dance?" Elton invited.

"No thanks." She smiled politely.

"Aw, come on." He stood and tugged her hand. She tried to resist, but his grip was tight and rather than make a scene, she let him lead her onto the dance floor.

Holy mother of cake, what a mistake. Elton danced like he was doing the funky chicken, elbows up and out, flapping like wings, feet shifting erratically. Her face burned as she cast glances at the other patrons on the dance floor. Nobody paid any attention to them, wrapped up in their own dancing or wrapped up in their partners' arms.

Remi smiled brightly at Elton, waiting for the song to end. When it did, she stood on tiptoes. "I'm going to the ladies' room!" she said into his ear. He nodded and she quickly exited the dance floor.

She passed the catwalk where the go go dancers shook their booties. A group of men at the end of the catwalk watched them with smiles on their faces. Remi spared a glance and then a second glance at the group of big, good-looking and uh…big men. The five of them created quite a sight, with their massive shoulders, expensive-looking suits and neat haircuts.

She returned to the table moments later to find only Elton sitting there.

"The others are dancing," he said. "Wanna go dance again?"

"No thanks." She smiled and picked up her drink.

They sat there for a moment, Remi trying to think of something to say, and then Elton stood and said, "Excuse me. I see someone I know."

He disappeared into the crowd around the bar and Remi sighed. She didn't know what was worse, sitting there with a man she had absolutely no interest in—or sitting there alone. Painfully alone.

Ah well.

She dipped her straw in and out of the cocktail, studying the people. In her sexy new clothes, she definitely wasn't out of place. Many girls wore similar outfits. Rouge was the hottest bar in Chicago, an upscale place to see and be seen.

When the others returned to the table, breathless and laughing, Delise said, "Where's Elton?"

"He went to talk to someone."

A frown creased Delise's forehead. "Well," she said, head swiveling one way, then the other. "We'll have to find someone else for you."

"It's okay, Delise!"

"No, it's not." Delise pouted. "We're finding a hot guy for you tonight if it's the last thing we do."

"I'll find my own guy!"

Delise rolled her eyes. "No, you won't."

"I will, I promise. I'll…go for a walk. Right now." She stood. "After I get another drink."

Delise shook her head, but subsided back into her seat. "Fine."

Delise didn't believe she would try to pick up a guy. She knew her too well. Remi grinned as she squeezed between some bodies at the bar to order another mojito.

Drink in hand, she twisted and turned through the crowd of warm bodies and mingled scents of Armani, Chanel and Prada, the darkness lit by lights flashing in time to pulsing music. She glanced back at the table and saw Delise watching her with narrowed eyes and raised chin. She couldn't help but be amused by her friend's determination, even though she wanted to shake her head. She waved a hand at Delise and moved on through the crowd.

Near the catwalk she paused again to watch the dancers, admiring their defined abs, long lean thighs and sexy moves. Then she spotted Delise coming toward her. Remi's eyes flicked around. That group of stunningly gorgeous guys still stood over there, laughing, each of them holding a beer. She moved toward them.

What was she going to say? This was crazy.

She paused beside the men, and put a hand on the forearm of the one closest to her. He looked down at her—waaaay down. He had to be six foot three at least, and considering she was five foot three—okay, a few inches taller than that in her new heels, but still—he was in another layer of the atmosphere. He lifted a brow.

"Excuse me," Remi said, heat sweeping from her collarbones up over her throat and into her face. "Can you do me a really big favor?"

Jase looked down at the tiny little blonde standing there with her hand on his arm. Was she even old enough to be in the bar? Amusement tickled inside him. He was used to girls hitting on him, went with the territory, but this little pipsqueak teeny-bopper blonde was hands-off material. Not even close to his type, anyway.

"Favor?"

She nodded, smiled with pretty white teeth and tipped her head. "My friend is determined to fix me up with someone. If you'd just talk to me for a few minutes, maybe she'll leave me alone."

"Talk?" His lips quirked. "You want to talk?"

"Well." She licked her lips and blinked rapidly. "Whatever. Just fake it. You know." Her eyes darted to the side, then back. She gave him a bright smile.

She was kinda cute, in a Reese Witherspoon sort of way. Heart-shaped face, small mouth, big eyes. Her chin-length blonde hair flipped out at the ends and long bangs grazed her eyelashes.

She pressed her lips together and gazed up at him and those big eyes were like turquoise pools, liquid and shiny. He couldn't help but smile. It was a new pick-up line, one he hadn't heard, but he didn't have it in him to tell her to take a hike. He turned toward her and bent his head. She was so little, he'd have to crouch to talk to her. "Sure," he said. "Let's talk."

He shifted his body so they stood apart from the other guys, who were giving them amused glances. They could think he was hooking up with blondie here, it didn't bother him. He was a free and single man again as of this weekend, free to do whatever he wanted, including pick up little blonde pixies in bars if he wanted to.

Which he didn't. He almost laughed at the thought. But those big blue-green eyes made it kinda hard to say no to her.

Relief shone in her eyes and her smile beamed. "Thanks." She rolled her eyes. "My friend gets an idea in her head and there's no stopping her."

"Why is she so determined to find you a man?"

She gave her head a little shake, then lifted her drink, closing her mouth on the straw in a tiny pursed-lip suck that shot heat straight to his dick. Jesus.

"She's crazy." She laughed. "My little sister moved out...well, it's a long story."

"Go ahead." He took a swallow of his beer. Hell, it was almost done. "Wait. I need another drink. How about you?"

"Sure."

He caught the eye of a pretty waitress dressed in a low cut, skin-tight black dress. She was more his type—tall, great rack, long dark hair. She hurried over with an inviting smile. "Another of these." He lifted his bottle. "And another..." He looked at uh...hell, he didn't even know her name.

"Mojito," she said.

"I'm Jase," he said, not bothering to watch the waitress leave, even though he knew the tight dress showed off a very fine ass.

"I'm Remi. Nice to meet you, Jase." Her sweet smile pulled at something unexpected inside him.

"Where were we? Oh, yeah, your little sister."

"Oh. Well, my parents died about five years ago. My brother and sister were both teenagers, so I've looked after them since then. My brother started college this year and my sister recently moved in with her boyfriend. My friends think I need to start having more fun now that I'm on my own."

"Wait a minute."

She lifted a brow.

"If your brother and sister were teenagers five years ago, how the hell old were you?" He frowned.

"I was twenty-two."

"No way. You look like you're about eighteen now."

She laughed. "I know, I get that a lot, dammit. I'm twenty-eight."

Huh. Only a year younger than him.

The waitress returned with their drinks. Remi set her empty glass on the small counter near them and reached for the purse hanging over her shoulder. He waved a hand.

"Don't worry about it. She'll just put in on my tab."

"No, no. You don't have to buy me a drink. Really, I just want to get Delise off my back…"

"It's fine," he said firmly, waving her money away. "I got it."

"Oh. Okay. Thank you."

She picked up the full drink and did that sexy little pull on the straw with her pretty mouth.

"So you're a free woman." Just like he was now a free man.

"Whatever." She waved a tiny hand. "Jasmine's twenty-one, it's not like I had to baby sit her. But it feels a little weird to not have two kids at home to look after. I've never lived on my own."

Her bangs lowered and the corners of her eyes creased.

"You don't want to be alone?"

She lifted a shoulder. "I don't know. Delise thinks we're celebrating tonight. And I guess…I should be happy. I will have more freedom to do whatever I want."

"But you don't seem happy."

She looked a little lost for a moment, staring past his shoulder. Then she focused those glowy turquoise eyes on him and smiled again. "It's just hard to let go. My brother's been partying his freshman year away at college. And my sister's boyfriend is a jerk. I can't help worry about them even though they're on their own now."

He studied her for a moment. "You like being needed." Her eyes flew open wide at his words. He smiled. "That's okay. I think it's very cool that you care that much about them. But maybe you need a distraction. Something fun to take your mind off them."

"Like I am tonight," she said. "But Delise thinks I need a man to do it." She rolled her eyes.

"Having a fun night at Rouge is a good start."

"Except I wasn't having much fun." She wrinkled her little nose. "This place is cool, but not really me."

"Me either." Yeah, when the other guys had wanted to come here after the game, he'd agreed because, hell, he could go out and do whatever he wanted now without having to worry about Brianne, but the edgy, agitated, almost desperate-to-have-fun vibe in the room made him feel tired.

"Where would you rather be?" she asked.

He pursed his lips. "There are a few places in Wicker Park I like. They play live music, sometimes the bands are just starting out, but they're pretty good."

"Oh, like Underground and Lucky's. Yeah, I know those bars."

"How about you?"

"Mmm. I like Blue Moon. They make awesome martinis and they have great jazz music."

"Yeah! I like that place too."

"But actually…" She looked down at her drink. "I really just like staying home."

He laughed. "You know what? So do I."

They stood there smiling at each other. Then Remi looked at her watch. "Well. I should get back to my friends."

"Yeah."

A sharp nudge to his shoulder made him flinch. "What?" He turned to Griff, who'd just elbowed him.

"Look who's here." Griff jerked his chin. Jase followed his gaze and saw…Brianne.

Fuck.

Stunning as usual, she stood nearly six feet tall in her three inch spiky heels, wearing a purple dress that looked like it was wrapped tightly around her body in complicated layers. The deep V in the front showed off what he knew to be expensive implants. Long dark hair hung in curls and waves nearly to her waist.

One corner of his mouth deepened. He sighed.

Remi said, "What's wrong?"

He turned his gaze back to her. "Hey, don't go back to your friends just yet."

"Uh…"

"Now it's your turn to do *me* a favor."

Her lips parted and her bangs moved again with the lift of her eyebrows.

"My ex-girlfriend just walked in," he said in a low voice, bending closer to her. "Stay and talk to me so she doesn't uh…get any ideas about getting back together."

Remi stared at him.

"You owe me." He gave her his most appealing smile. It usually worked. And it did.

She smiled too. "I guess I do."

He shifted a little closer to her. Just to make it look like they were together. She smelled incredible. Like spring flowers. Light and fresh and pretty. He inhaled, feeling a strange urge to bury his nose in her hair.

"We could go upstairs," he said. "And sit down for a while."

"That would be great." She made a face. "My feet are killing me in these heels." She extended a leg and he looked down. And lust kicked him in the gut.

She had fucking great legs. For someone so small, they were long, slender and perfectly shaped, with delicate ankles. The shiny black shoe with the skinny heel and pointy toe almost made him drool. He loved shoes like that. Especially in bed.

With black stockings and black lace underwear.

What kind of underwear did Remi have on under that sparkly little top? She had some sweet fucking cleavage that made his dick stir.

Jesus, what was he thinking? He gave his head a shake. "Come on." He took her hand in his, so small it almost slipped right out of his grip, and led her toward the stairs that climbed to the next level.

"Going upstairs, guys," he told his buddies as he passed them.

At the top of the stairs, the music a little quieter, the lights more subtle and glowing, he surveyed the couches and low tables. The place was full—what were the chances they'd find an empty banquette?

They moved through the bar, hand in hand, and then a couple stood.

"You leaving?" Jase asked and they smiled and nodded. Another sexy waitress appeared to clear their empties and Jase and Remi took a seat.

"Aaaah." Remi let out a long sigh. Then she laughed. "I'm not used to wearing heels like this."

Jase wasn't sure if he'd ever seen Brianne without heels. Kinda funny.

He admired Remi's legs again, the short skirt riding up higher on firm thighs. Sweet. He shifted sideways, leaning one elbow on the padded back of the banquette so he could face her.

"So…your ex-girlfriend. You don't want to see her?"

He shrugged, his gut tightening. "Rather not."

"Things didn't end amicably?"

He pushed out his lips. "Uh, no. She was a little upset." Her tears and pleading flashed through his mind and he winced.

"So you're the dumper…not the dumpee, then."

"Yeah." He huffed out a laugh. "But I felt like crap. She's a nice girl."

"What went wrong?" She tipped her head, blue-green eyes fastened on his with focused attention, and sipped her drink.

He sighed. "She wanted to get married. I didn't. I figured it was better to break up now than to let things get too far and have her disappointed."

"I'm sure she was already disappointed."

"Yeah, I guess." He shifted on the couch. "She'll get over me."

"Why do you say that?"

He looked at her. "I'm not that great a catch. I have this feeling she loved me for more than just uh…me."

Her brows drew down and her bangs tangled in her long lashes. "I don't know what that means. Was she after your money or something?"

He shrugged. "Or something. I don't know. I don't want to accuse her of being shallow. Like I said, she's a nice girl."

"Hmm."

What was she thinking? He could see her mind turning over. Enough of this conversation about Brianne. She was the last thing he wanted to talk about.

"Jase!"

Dammit. He looked up at Brianne and forced a smile. "Hi, Brianne."

She stood there all super-model tall and gorgeous, frowning and flicking her eyes back and forth between him and Remi. Her frown deepened.

The air thickened around them and he felt Remi tense. He set a hand on her bare forearm and slanted her a glance. Her eyes were wide and worried and she nibbled her bottom lip.

"I…uh…can leave…" she began, but he clamped down harder on her arm.

"That's okay, honey."

"You said there wasn't anyone else." Brianne stabbed him with an accusing stare.

"There wasn't."

Remi tried to pull away from him and he held on tighter, dragging her across the leather seat easily—she weighed like a hundred pounds—and up against him. She shot him a startled glance.

"Brianne, this is Remi. Remi, Brianne."

Brianne's dark eyes shot sparks and then she swiveled on a spiky heel and stalked away.

Whew.

"Thanks," he muttered into Remi's ear. "I thought for a minute there she was going to make a scene."

"That was your ex-girlfriend?"

"Yeah. Brianne Haskett."

"Jesus. She's a famous model."

"Well, yeah."

"You dumped *her*?" Remi's voice rose. She squirmed next to him so she could look up at him. This close he could see the green and blue flecks in her turquoise eyes, the long eyelashes that brushed her bangs every time she blinked, the perfect smooth texture of her skin.

"Yeah."

"Oh." Silence. More silence. "Well, I guess we're even now. I should get back to my friends."

"Stay."

She blinked up at him. Her soft body squirming in his arms had every nerve ending in his body tightening. He felt the room shift around him, slip out of focus, her face the only thing crystal-clear. The fresh flowery scent of her, the way the red lights turned the flicked-up ends of her hair pink, combined with the deep gratitude he felt for her just being there and saving him from an ugly scene with Brianne, made him want to pick her up and carry her out of there.

So he said, "Why don't we go somewhere quieter?"

CHAPTER TWO

Remi pulled back from Jase on the red leather banquette. "What?"

He looked at her, eyes heavy lidded, mouth curved into a sexy smile. He still had his hands on her, those big, strong hands, and a moment ago she'd been plastered against his hard chest. The air around them buzzed with electricity and she squeezed her thighs together.

"Let's go somewhere quieter. Maybe that jazz club. This place is too…frantic."

"Uh…" Remi's mind worked furiously. What the hell was going on here? This was supposed to be a fake flirtation to get Delise off her back. Okay, and Jase's ex, the freakin' gorgeous supermodel Brianne Haskett. He'd dumped a model, but he was flirting with her? Plain little Remi? A boring, responsible school teacher? Whaaaat?

It had to be a joke.

She laughed.

He frowned.

She laid a hand on his chest—oh sweet loving lord, what a nice chest it was, hard and muscular and warm—and gave him a playful shove. "Don't be silly. We don't even know each other. We're just doing each other a favor."

He blinked, brows still joined above his slightly crooked nose. It was cute, that crooked nose in an otherwise heart-stoppingly handsome face—square jaw, high cheekbones, melting chocolate eyes. A little scar above his left eyebrow was also endearingly imperfect.

"Well, yeah," he said. "But I like talking to you. And it's hard here, with the loud music and all these people."

Her mind skittered off in a thousand different directions. He was serious. He liked talking to her. Warmth blossomed inside her and spread through her body, tingling through every nerve ending. Oh no. She recognized that feeling. It was…attraction.

She liked talking to Jase too.

She put the straw of her drink to her mouth and sucked hard, downing the rest of her mojito. The drinks she'd had so far were creating a pleasant buzz of warmth and well-being. She looked at Jase.

"I came with my friends."

"Me too." He paused. "You need a distraction. Remember? So you don't worry about your brother and sister."

They looked at each other. Heat grew. Tension shimmered. When his eyes dropped to her mouth, everything inside Remi went hot and liquid and aching. Her eyes widened and she licked her lips.

His eyes got even darker and his lips parted.

Remi reached to set her empty glass on the low table in front of them. She missed and it hit the floor with a *thunk*. They ignored it.

"You're not my type," Jase said.

Huh? She blinked. "Okay, then." She started to stand but he grabbed her hand and tugged her back down, almost onto his lap.

"I mean…you didn't used to be my type. Hell." The corners of his mouth turned down. "I sound like an idiot. I *am* an idiot."

Her heart softened. She relaxed onto the couch, his arm around her waist, and it felt sooooo good.

"You're not an idiot," she said with a little laugh.

"Yeah, I am. Bah." He shook his head, mouth tight. "What I mean is, I'm not normally attracted to cute little blondes."

Cute little blonde? Yeah, that was her. How she wished she had mile-long legs and big boobs and full lips like Brianne Haskett. Stephanie Seymour. Laetitia Casta. All those other Victoria's Secret models who looked like that.

No, she was teeny weeny, skinny, flat-chested, with wispy blonde hair.

But Jase seemed to find her attractive.

She tilted her head to one side and regarded him through a rum-and-lust haze. "You're kidding. Right?"

"No. I mean..." He looked confused. "I'm not kidding about not usually being attracted to cute little blondes. But you're...cute."

She laughed. Shook her head. Wished for another drink.

The crazy thing was, he was exactly the type of guy she was attracted to. Not just physically—big guys had always appealed to her, maybe because she was small—but she also liked his smile, his wide mouth and how it tilted up at the corners even when he wasn't smiling, the fact that he was gorgeous but wasn't all hung up on himself and the most important thing—he'd dumped a supermodel!

Dammit. What the hell was going on here? She looked around a bit frantically, now hoping Delise would show up and rescue her. But Delise was nowhere in sight. And Jase was right next to her, touching her, his big body radiating heat. He smelled good, like he'd just showered, a fresh masculine scent of shampoo and men's shower gel, and a faint shadow of beard shaded his jaw. Yum. She wanted to bite him.

Whoa. She blinked. Her mind was in the gutter. What kind of responsible, big sister/school teacher was she?

He put a big hand on her cheek, cupping it, and she melted into a liquid puddle of lust on the red leather banquette. "You're sweet," he said, almost sounding surprised. "Okay. We'll just stay here for a while. We can talk here."

She nodded.

"You're a free woman," he said with a sexy smile. "And I'm a free man. We should both be celebrating. Why not together?"

She took in a long, slow breath. "Why not?" She smiled back at him.

"Here's the deal," he said. "I'm not ready to settle down. I like you. We could have fun together."

"We could." Oh lord. What had she just said? She closed her eyes briefly, then focused on him and firmed her lips. "I'm not ready to settle down either. I just got my freedom. I've had enough responsibility. All I want is to have some fun."

Even as she said the words, a small niggle of guilt wormed its way into her conscience. Was it true? Was that really all she wanted? She'd been mature, responsible, dependable for so long…did she even know how to just have fun?

She wanted to find out.

"Perfect." His thumb traced over her bottom lip. He was watching her mouth again and it was so hot and sexy everything inside her contracted hard. She knew her panties were damp. She knew it. "Let's have some fun, Remi."

And he kissed her. His mouth was warm, his lips firm on hers and when his tongue licked over her bottom lip she moaned helplessly.

Delicious pleasure rippled through her in waves and she put out a hand and rested it on his arm, the wool of his suit jacket soft and warm beneath her palm. Her skin tingled and tightened and that heavy liquid ache between her legs intensified.

His fingers slid around into her hair, cupped the back of her head and held it while his mouth moved on hers, slow, soft, lingering. Her heart beat so fast she was afraid it was going to explode in her chest and she whimpered. Her breasts swelled and she ached to press them against him.

He drew back. "Sorry. I kinda forgot where we are." His voice was husky and sexy.

She sat there dazed and foggy, blinking at him. Where were they? Oh, yeah. In the middle of a hot night club. Music throbbed and the lights pulsed and flickered around them.

"I…I need another drink."

"Good idea." He turned and looked for a waitress and sure enough one hurried over right away, although she gave Remi a look that could have sliced her open. Was the waitress jealous? No way!

Feminine pleasure curled inside her and she smiled and sat back.

"So." Jase looked at her, his eyes intent, face a bit flushed. She'd turned him on. With a kiss. That was so freakin' hot. "What do you do for a living, Remi?"

She opened her mouth to tell him—and then closed it. It sounded so boring. The word "boring" echoed in her mind, what Darryl had called her when he'd given her that ultimatum. The word had stabbed into her heart, mostly because she knew it was true.

"Let's not talk about stuff like that." She crossed her legs. "We don't need to know personal details, right? We just want to have fun."

His eyes squinted at her a bit, then he smiled, too. "Right. Okay." The waitress brought their drinks and they somehow managed to find other things to talk about and laugh about as Remi sipped another mojito and Jase drank his beer, their talk and laughter punctuated with small touches of fingertips on the back of a hand, a stroke down a bare arm, the brush of legs as they shifted on the banquette.

"What things do you like to do in your spare time?" Jase asked her

She frowned. "I definitely need to take up some new hobbies." She tipped her head. "I think I'd like to redecorate my house. And travel." She perked up a little. She'd always wanted to travel. She could do that now. "Yeah, I definitely want to travel."

"Where would you like to go?"

"Hmm. Europe. Especially the Mediterranean. And somewhere for a hot beach vacation. Have you done that?"

"Yeah. Last year I went with some friends to Turks and Caicos. It was awesome."

"Oh wow."

"We rented a villa on the beach. White sand, turquoise waters…kinda like the color of your eyes."

She blinked, warmth spreading through her. "Oh."

"You have gorgeous eyes."

"Thank you."

An hour passed as they talked and smoldering awareness grew, a haze of heated desire floated around them. Remi quivered, pressing her thighs together, her belly fluttery, her pussy clenching. When their eyes met and held, attraction tugging them toward each other, another kiss had her melting against him.

"We need to leave here," he murmured into her ear and his breath there gave her tingly shivers. "I can't keep my hands off you much longer and I'm going to embarrass you."

Weak and trembling with need, she nodded. She felt the same. It took everything she had not to climb onto his lap and press herself against him.

She rose unsteadily. "I'll go tell my friends we're leaving."

"I'll meet you at the coat check."

Pressing a hand to her stomach, Remi found Delise at the table, still with Tiger.

"Where have you been?" Delise asked. "Please tell me you met someone."

"Oh, yeah. I met someone." Remi bit her lip. "In fact, we're leaving now."

Delise's eyes popped wide as dinner plates and Remi almost laughed. "What! Who is it? Where is he? Where are you going?"

"I…uh…don't know where we're going. Maybe…my place."

Delise stood up so fast her chair almost fell over backward. "What! Remi! You can't take a strange man home with you!"

Remi tipped her head to one side and frowned. "Isn't that what you wanted me to do?"

"I didn't think you'd actually do it!"

"But…" Remi blinked. "But, Delise…"

"It's dangerous, Remi." Delise looked around. "Where is he?"

"He's meeting me out front. He's a nice guy, Del. He's not dangerous." Only in that he made her panties wet.

"How do you know that? Jesus, Remi."

"I…" Disappointment started to dampen her happy buzz. "But, Delise…" She leaned closer to her friend. "I want him."

Delise's mouth opened. "Oh." She stared at Remi. "Good god, Remi. Well, hell. Okay. Keep your cell phone on and with you at all times. All times. Got it?"

Remi gave a jerky nod.

"Because I'm going to be phoning you. And if you don't answer, I'm sending the police. Go to your place. Don't go to his place. Nobody will know where you are there." She put a hand to her mouth. "This is still crazy. He could be a serial killer and once you get in a car with him…"

"Ssssh. I'm not that stupid." Remi smiled at her friend. "I know this isn't the kind of thing I usually do, but I want to have fun tonight. I like him. He likes me."

Delise's face softened. She put her hands on Remi's upper arms and squeezed. "Okay. But remember…I'm calling."

"Yeah, yeah."

Remi hugged Delise and then turned and hurried toward the front of the club, looking for Jase. He stood near the entrance, a long black coat loose over his suit, hands in the pockets. Her breath stuck in her throat at how gorgeous he was. She fumbled in her little purse for her coat check ticket, then Jase held the new silver trench coat Delise had made her purchase earlier while she slipped her arms into it.

"Let's go." She turned to him with a smile, lifting the ends of her hair out from the collar.

"Where are we going?" They climbed the red-carpeted stairway to the door, one of his hands on the small of her back.

"My place."

"Okay. We'll have to take a taxi. Unless you…"

"No. I came with my friend."

"Me too."

The frosty March night air greeted them as they stepped out of the club onto the sidewalk of East Van Buren, beneath a green canopy. The small street lined with older buildings was relatively quiet, and Jase took hold of her arm to lead her toward Michigan Avenue. "We'll get a cab on Michigan."

The windows of the office towers climbing into the sky around them glowed golden, and tiny white lights twinkled on the bare trunks and branches of the trees lining the street. Jase was right. As they rounded the corner a yellow cab appeared and he lifted a hand. They climbed in and Remi gave the driver her address.

"Is it far?" Jase asked, his hand warm on her bare knee.

She glanced at him. "No. Lincoln Park."

"Oh. I've only lived in Chicago a few years."

"Oh, really? Where did you live before?"

"Canada."

"Oh." Curiosity pinged inside her. They'd agreed they didn't need to know a lot of personal details about each other, but that was such an unexpected answer she wanted to know more. She studied him. "Why are you in Chicago now? Your work?"

"Yup." He reached out and touched her hair. "What about you? Have you always lived here?"

"My whole life. The house I live in is the house I grew up in. When my parents died, we inherited it, and it was lucky because it was paid for. We didn't have much money, but at least we had a roof over our heads."

"That must have been hard for you. You were what…twenty-two, you said?"

"Yes. I'd just finished college, was just starting my first job."

"And you had to look after your little brother and sister."

"Mmm." She hitched a shoulder. "I did what I had to do."

His eyes grew a bit distant. "I couldn't have done that when I was twenty-two. Hell, I couldn't do that now."

She laughed. "Well, hopefully you won't have to. Are your parents still living?"

"Oh, yeah. Alive and well."

"In Canada?"

"Mmmhmm." He focused back on her, his gaze warm and intent. She quivered inside.

"And do you have brothers and sisters?"

"Three brothers."

"Whoa! Four boys! Your poor mother!"

He grinned. "She's a tough lady."

"Are you the oldest?"

"No. My brother Tag is older. Matt and Logan are both younger."

"That's cool. Must have been a busy house with four boys." She eyed him. "Are they all as big as you?"

"Bigger." He grinned.

"That's not possible."

"Well, Matt is about the same size as me. I might have a few pounds on him yet."

She was intensely curious about the woman who'd given birth to four boys as big as Jase and how she'd raised them, but that was way more personal than they needed to get, so she shut off that train of thought.

The taxi pulled up in front of her two-story Victorian style house, and Jase reached for his wallet to pay. Remi started to protest, but he waved a hand and gave the driver some bills, including enough for a generous tip.

She led the way in her front door, flicked on a light and looked around at her home, wondering how it looked to Jase. She lived a simple life. Although Jasmine had been working at a full-time job for several months now and money was easier, there hadn't been a lot left for luxuries from Remi's teacher's salary over the years. But Jase bought drinks and handed out money easily, wore clothes that were clearly expensive and the watch she'd noticed on his wrist was a stainless steel Baume & Mercier. She didn't know what he did, but he obviously had money.

"This is nice." He surveyed the living room. The house was old, but Remi loved it, loved the character in the big baseboards, the mullioned windows, the original brick fireplace and hardwood floors. "It reminds me of my parents' home in Winnipeg."

"Winnipeg? That's where you're from?"

"Yeah." He slid his coat off and she stepped toward him to take it and hang it up. Nerves tightened and twisted inside her. She'd never done this—never brought a man home like this. She and Darryl had dated for months before they'd had sex and then it had to be quick and planned so as to avoid Kyle and Jasmine. What were the rules? Were there rules? Should she offer him a drink?

"Would you like a drink?" she inquired after hanging his coat in the closet. She stroked a hand down the sleeve of the exquisitely soft black wool fabric before closing the closet door.

"Your coat?"

"Hmm?" She stared at him.

"Are you going to take your coat off?"

She looked down at herself. "Oh!" Her cheeks heated and she gave a lopsided smile. "Yes, of course." She quickly removed the pretty new coat that she shouldn't have spent so much money on and hung it in the closet next to his.

"C'mere." He held out a hand and she hesitated, then walked toward him and took it. "You're nervous."

"No, I'm not."

He laughed softly and pulled her closer, his hands on her hips. She trembled.

"It's okay. Let's have a drink, sit down and talk some more."

"Okay. I have beer or wine…or champagne."

"Champagne?" He lifted a brow.

She moved away from his touch toward the kitchen. "Delise brought it over earlier. To celebrate." She shook her head, smiling.

"Well, we should finish it." Jase followed her. "That stuff doesn't keep."

"Okay." She found two clean champagne flutes and poured the bubbly wine into them.

He touched the edge of his glass to hers before lifting it to his lips. "To Remi. All on her own now. Ready to have fun."

She inhaled. Exhaled. Sipped her fizzy wine. Jase took her hand and led her back to the living room. They sat down on the slip-covered couch.

"Tell me about Winnipeg."

He grinned. "Do you even know where it is?"

She nibbled her bottom lip. "Canada."

His laughter warmed her insides. "Very good. Actually it's not that far from here. Just north of North Dakota. It's a nice city. Not as big as Chicago, of course. Bet you didn't know it was once called the 'Chicago of the north.'"

"I didn't know that." She watched him talk, sipped her wine.

"Back at the turn of the century, Winnipeg was growing fast. There were a lot of skyscrapers built—well, at the time they were considered skyscrapers. The architects who designed them were trained in the Chicago School style. Those buildings are still there, in the Exchange District. In fact, a lot of movies are filmed there because the buildings and streets still look just like they did back then. It's a neat area."

"Really? That's cool."

"Yeah. Winnipeg has stood in for Chicago in a few movies."

"Like what?"

"Um…Shall We Dance, with Richard Gere and Susan Sarandon."

"Get out! Really?"

"I kid you not."

She wanted to know why he'd left, why he was here in Chicago, but didn't want to ask.

"Do you miss your family?"

"Yeah. I see my brothers once in a while." He gave her a funny grin. "And my parents visit sometimes, when they can." He paused. "You must miss your parents."

"Well, I do. But to be honest, they weren't around that much, even when they were alive. They were both doctors and they did a lot of work in Africa."

His brows rose. "Wow. Africa."

"Yeah. It was very noble of them. They felt a…a 'calling', I suppose. But they'd be gone for months at a time."

"Let me guess. Leaving big sister Remi in charge."

"Yeah." Her mouth twisted into a crooked smile. "And then they were killed in a small plane crash in Somalia."

"Ah. That's crappy."

She nodded. "Yeah. But we did okay."

"I see that." He stroked a strand of hair back off her face, sending heat sliding down from his touch.

"Let's talk about happier things."

"How about….let's not talk."

CHAPTER THREE

Their mouths met and clung in a long, slow kiss. When they drew apart, their eyes met. Jase's breath stuck in his chest, his heart thudding painfully. His eyelids felt heavy and then, like two magnets, he and Remi fell on each other, their mouths meeting again, this time hard, hot and hungry.

She wrapped her arms around his neck and practically crawled onto his lap, their tongues sliding, teeth nipping. She tasted goddamn delicious, sweet and sparkly like champagne, with a hint of mint from the mojitos. His hands grabbed her hips and pulled her closer and then she was on his lap, sideways on the couch. He shifted his body, gently lowered her to the couch and moved over her. He kissed her again and again until they both had to break for air, panting.

She licked her lips, staring at him wide eyed. "Wow."

"Yeah. Wow."

And they went at it again, deep, seeking, open-mouthed kisses. His hands stroked her everywhere he could reach, over her hips, her waist, up the sides of her ribcage, thumbs resting just beneath her breasts, then down to thighs bared by her skirt which had ridden up indecently high. Her skin was satiny warm and her body jerked when he found the sensitive spot at the back of her knee.

He was acutely aware of how tiny she was compared to him, worried that he might hurt her, so he took care and didn't let his weight rest on her as he leaned over her to kiss her. She squirmed beneath him, arching into him, and he lifted away from her.

"What?" she gasped.

"Are you okay?"

"Yes." She blinked at him. "Of course I'm okay. Why are you stopping?"

Instead of answering, he just kissed her again, starving for more of the taste and feel of her in his mouth. Their tongues played, her hands wandered up and down his back, then slipped under his suit jacket. Through the thin cotton of his shirt he felt her warmth and he wanted nothing between her touch and his skin.

He sat up again and tore his suit jacket off. Goddamn suits and ties, he'd never understand why they had to wear these things on game days, but apparently they had to look professional. He fumbled at his throat with the knot of the tie, like a noose around his neck, and when he'd loosened it, he popped open the first two buttons of his shirt. Ah. So much better.

He took a deep breath and leaned back down to Remi, kissing her again. Now her little hands tugged at his shirt and found their way beneath it to his skin. He groaned at the pleasure of it.

His dick was so hard it hurt. He wanted to press himself into her softness, but held himself back, again conscious of her size and his size and the difference in their size. They kissed on and on, hands roving, bodies writhing, skin heating.

Damn, had to feel more of her, and he rose up to slide the tiny straps of her top down her arms, dying to see the curves of her breasts. She helped him by hitching her shoulders and then he peeled the sparkly top down to her waist revealing the—thank you, Jesus—black lace strapless bra. He blinked at it, at the delicate curves between the lacy cups, and his mouth watered.

"So pretty," he murmured. "I love black lace."

"That's good."

He tipped his head. "Do your panties match?"

She huffed out a soft laugh. "Find out for yourself."

"Mmm. Okay."

And the top and the skirt came off too, both down over her hips and legs, leaving her lying on the couch in her lingerie and yes, her panties were black lace too, a tiny triangle held on by a slender black ribbon over each hip. Her skin was incredible—creamy smooth everywhere, her body dainty and perfect.

He had to just stop and stare, breathing hard.

"Jase?" She put a hand out to him and he lifted his gaze to her face. Uncertainty shadowed her eyes, her mouth soft and pouty.

"You're so fucking gorgeous," he muttered. "I have to look at you."

Her eyes widened, then drifted closed and the corners of her mouth tipped up. "Thank you. I'm not…"

He lightly rested his fingers on her mouth. "Don't even say it." He didn't know how, but he knew what she was about to say and he didn't want to hear any comparisons between her and anyone else, because there was no comparison. Jase himself was a little taken aback at how stunningly beautiful he found her. His heart stuttered in his chest. Jesus.

He swallowed, then explored her curves with his hands, taking them on a joyful tour of smooth thighs, the dip of her waist, the swell of her breasts. He longed to see her nipples, to taste them too, but he wanted to keep the black lace on as long as possible.

He bent his head and pressed a kiss to the softness of her stomach and it quivered beneath his mouth. His tongue gave a gentle lap, his lips a tiny suck and he breathed in the fresh flowery scent of her skin before he lifted his head. She groaned and slid her hands into his hair.

He pressed a trail of kisses down over her lower belly, noting the tiny fine golden hairs just above the black lace, wanting to see what was beneath it, digging deep for patience. He pressed his mouth over the black lace and inhaled again, her scent now warmer and layered with feminine arousal. It made him so goddamn hard he growled. Her hips lifted beneath him and when he raised his head and looked down at his big hands holding her small hips, he shook. It was like holding a doll, tiny and perfect, but terrifying.

"Uh…" He reared back again.

"What? Now what?"

He shook his head, his brains fuddled a bit. Maybe they shouldn't be doing this.

He shoved a hand into his hair and sat up straight. Remi struggled up onto her elbows, a frown pinching her brows together. "What's wrong?"

His gut clenched, his dick throbbed, his balls pulsed. Hell.

"I don't want to hurt you."

She gazed at him. "We agreed. We're just having fun. No strings attached. Right?"

"I don't mean like that. I mean…physically. You're so little."

His heart thudded and he heard it in his ears as he waited. And waited.

She sat up, all pretty ivory curves and black lace and golden hair. He gulped.

Then his heart stopped. Literally stopped, as she climbed onto his lap, straddled him and went to work on his tie. She yanked it off over his head, fingered open the buttons of his shirt, one, then another, then another, until she spread it wide across his chest.

She sucked in a breath as she did so, eyes glued to his pecs, and he sat there, arms at his side while she palmed his chest. Christ, it felt good.

He lifted his arms and flicked open the button at each wrist so he could shrug out of the shirt, but his mind was spinning at the touch of her fingers sliding down lower over his abs, then to the fastener of his pants.

"Remi…"

She lifted her head. "Don't tell me to stop."

"But…"

Then his heart lurched again and resumed its racing rhythm as she covered his erection with her hand and pressed. His cock twitched hard. "Ah!"

"You don't want me to stop," she murmured, getting to work on the zipper. "I can tell."

"No…I…Jesus."

She tugged at his pants and she needed him to lift his hips to get them off, but he didn't move. Trying to keep his body from exploding with lust, he sucked in a deep breath. "What are you doing, Remi?"

"I'm not breakable. Yeah, you're bigger than I am, but I'm not fragile." She leaned down and pressed a kiss to his chest. "I want to do this."

"Maybe we should…take it to a bedroom."

"Good idea."

She slid off his lap and stood, a tiny goddess in black lace and stiletto heels, and when she tugged his hand and tried to pull his two hundred plus pounds off the couch, he smiled.

He rose to his feet, holding his pants with one hand and her hand with the other, and let her lead him to her bedroom.

She clicked on a lamp beside the bed and he smiled in approval at the gold duvet cover. Four pillows on the bed. No cushions. He walked across a patterned carpet in shades of gold, brown and green, and stopped beside her.

Hunger for her rose in him, need slamming into his balls, sensation prickling over his flesh. But still he held back.

She studied him, then moved toward him and he lifted his arms to take her into his embrace. Then the room flipped upside down as he felt a foot at the back of his knee, knocking him off balance, taking him out, and with a sharp exhale he landed flat on his back on the bed.

He stared up at the ceiling.

"What the…?"

And then Remi was on top of him, straddling him with those smooth slender thighs, her hands brushing over his chest. Her eyes sparkled and her mouth curved into an impish smile.

All the blood in his body raced to his groin, leaving him light-headed and throbbing, his sole point of focus the throbbing between his legs and the woman kneeling right there, her hair lit by the lamp into a glowing golden halo, her softness pressed against his hardness.

"How'd you do that?" he croaked, reaching for her hips.

"Tae kwon do." She leaned over him to kiss him, at the same time rubbing her lace-covered breasts across his chest.

He wanted to know more, but coherent thought spun out of his mind, possibly through his ears, which was why he could hear nothing but a faint buzzing sound, and his eyes closed. He gave himself up to the sensation of her mouth on his, her tongue sliding into his mouth, her small hands all over his naked torso, her body against his as she stretched out over him.

He clasped her hips as pleasure licked up his nerve endings just like her tongue licked his mouth. Her palms rubbed over his nipples, sending tingles shooting through his body.

Then she squirmed down his body and dropped to the floor between his spread legs. She grabbed his pants and tugged, one side, then the other, inching them down his hips.

"Mmmm."

As usual, he wore no underwear and his erection sprang up, thick and hard and hot. He opened his eyes and looked at Remi gazing down at him open mouthed, wide-eyed.

"You're big everywhere," she breathed, reaching for him. Her small pale hand on his flushed cock looked hot, and it felt so fucking good. She stroked him up and down, studying him with avid eyes, and when she licked her lips, he groaned and lifted his hips, pushing deeper into her hand.

He wanted to flip her over and strip the black lace off her body, but once again he hesitated. Sure, she knew martial arts, but she was still tiny and he was still big and heavy. So he slowly sat up and gently moved her off him.

She frowned at him as he laid her down on the gold duvet, her skin glowing in the lamplight. He stroked a hand over one curved hip, trailed a finger between her breasts, down the groove of her abdomen to her navel.

"Jase."

"What?"

"You're still holding back."

His forehead tightened. "What do you mean?"

"I mean…" She sat up. "You don't have to be gentle with me."

"But…"

She cupped his face with one hand and looked deep into his eyes. "I need more than that." She held his gaze for several thumping heartbeats.

"What are you…you mean…?"

She nodded meaningfully. Hell, he couldn't be rough with her. She was a little doll.

"If you won't do it to me…" She lowered her lashes. "I'll have to do it to you."

He felt his eyes widen. His lips parted. His dick lurched. But as much as a turn-on as it was to have a woman threatening to dominate him, it wasn't going to happen.

She raised an arm and flexed it. "Look. I have muscles."

He turned his gaze to her biceps. His lips lifted. "Yes. Yes, you do." Tiny, but her little arm had a defined bulge. "Wanna arm wrestle, baby?"

She grinned. "What do I get if I win?"

"You get to fuck me."

"Mmmm." He moved over her and she lay back down on the bed and slid her arms around him. "What do I get if I lose?"

"I get to fuck *you*."

"How about we just skip the arm wrestling and get right to the fucking?"

Holy shit, she was so hot she was making him sweat. "Sounds like a plan."

He had to see those tits, taste them, feel them, so he slid a hand behind her back and flicked open the strapless bra, then grabbed it with his teeth between her breasts and dragged it off her body.

He tossed it aside and she made a noise low in her throat. He gazed down at her. Her breasts were perfect—round and sweet and soft on her chest, lying there beneath him. He filled one hand, and yes, it filled his hand. Who needed more than that? He liked breasts, any kind of breasts, but he'd never gotten the attraction of enormous boobs. For him, it was all about the feel, the softness, the round shape, the way the nipple puckered and tightened and begged to be sucked.

His mouth watered. Pretty pink nipples all tight and hard. He bent his head and kissed the tight tip, ran his tongue over the bumpy texture and sucked it into his mouth. Sweet and hard, he suckled at it, cupping the other breast, the nipple poking his palm, then he switched and tasted the other one.

Fuck. He was so hard he was going to burst. He groaned.

Remi writhed beneath him. "Harder," she whispered. He paused, resumed his sucking with more force and then he scraped his teeth over her nipple and she cried out. Her hands fisted in his hair and tugged —Jesus, that sent sparks shooting straight to his dick—and he did it again and again. Her body shook and shuddered, hips lifting and electricity sizzled over his skin.

"Christ, Remi."

The way she responded to him, like he was the hottest guy on the planet, sent his arousal zooming into the stratosphere. A fiery wave of heat cascaded over him, all his blood rushing to his cock and leaving him light-headed. His balls drew up so hard against his body he feared they might never come down. He had to be inside her, fucking her, now.

Remi trembled and shivered and shuddered with the need to come, arching against Jase, her arms wrapped around him as tight as she could hold on. Her legs lifted and he fitted himself between them, his cock hot and hard against her belly. She moaned.

She throbbed between her legs, her pussy hot and wet and aching for him. She whimpered.

Burning with pleasure, pulsing with need, she arched her back. He shifted up, his mouth leaving her breasts where he had left tingling magic and sensual shivers and she loved, loved, loved the feel of him against her, how hot and hard and big he was.

This couldn't be happening.

But it was.

She sank into the bed, absorbing the feel of Jase's fever-hot skin against hers, the weight of him, the taste of him when she opened her mouth over the skin of his shoulder. She licked him, sucked him, kissed him, drawing a long groan from him.

"Fuck me," she whispered.

"Jesus." He rose up, took his cock in his hand and pressed at her entrance. She wanted him inside her, but he felt so big, the blunt round head of his cock pushing at her. She reached down between them, pushing her fingers inside herself. She was wet. So wet. She rubbed the moisture around her pussy to ease his way in and he paused, holding himself over her.

Her fingers brushed over her clit, swollen and sensitive, and she moaned.

"Oh, Remi." He stroked up and down with the head of his cock and she felt him get slicker and wetter, sliding, and then he tried pushing into her again.

"I love that," she moaned. "I want you inside me."

"Wanna fuck you, baby." He pushed deeper, a fraction of inch at a time, agonizingly slow, tortuously sweet. He stretched her, filled her, hurt her with a delicious pain and she widened her thighs and lifted her knees to take him deeper.

"You're so small," he muttered against her neck. "So tight. Don't want to hurt you."

"Hurt me. Please."

He went very still above her, half buried inside her. Her heart thudded, her pussy clenched and Jase groaned again. "Fuck, baby. Oh, fuck. I can't hold back."

"Wait!"

He went motionless, gasping for breath. "What!"

"Condom."

He took a breath, then another, and then rolled off her onto his back. He covered his face with one hand. "Goddammit."

"You have to use one."

She rolled toward him and put a hand on his chest. Jesus, she was probably crazy to be doing this, having sex with a virtual stranger, but not using a condom was out of the question. She might be a tiny bit drunk and a whole lot in lust, but common sense tapped its way through to her consciousness.

"I don't have one."

Now she flopped onto her back beside him.

"You don't have a condom?" She couldn't believe that! A good looking guy like him, newly single, didn't have a condom?

"I didn't plan on something like this," he said defensively, his hand still on his face. "Don't you have one?"

"No." That was almost laughable. When would she ever have sex?

She was on the pill, so she wasn't worried about getting pregnant, so maybe…no. "No glove, no love," she said. Then an idea popped into her head. "Hold on." She rolled off the bed and scurried out of her bedroom, down the hall to Jasmine's room. She'd packed everything she owned today, but maybe…just maybe… She hurried into Jasmine's bathroom and flung open the medicine cabinet. Empty. Yanked open a drawer. A box of tampons, a stick of deodorant, a tube of lip balm…Remi dug through the contents of the drawer. A shower cap. She frowned at that and tossed it aside. And…yes! Condoms! She held up the packets triumphantly, slammed the drawer shut and ran back to her bedroom.

She held them up between two fingers as she approached the bed and Jase raised his head. "Thank Christ," he muttered. "I did not want to call a cab to take me to the nearest Walgreens."

She laughed and tossed the packets on the bed and he reached for one, ripped it open and rolled the condom onto his penis with proficient expertise.

Then he grabbed her and rolled her under him and she laughed breathlessly.

"Okay, where were we?" he murmured against her lips.

"You were about to hurt me."

He groaned. "Oh, yeah." And he thrust hard. She cried out, digging her fingers into his shoulders, arching her spine, her head going back. He pressed kisses to the side of her neck and drove into her, his cock hitting her cervix and making her senses leap. Pleasure-pain streaked through her, flames and chills, sizzling and shivering.

She met his every thrust, loving the heavy weight of him on her, the thick fullness of him inside her, the deepest penetration. "Jase, oh Jase. God."

She lifted her head and sank her teeth into his shoulder and he jerked hard. "Christ, Remi." He cock twitched inside her.

And he pulled out.

"What!" She curled up, gazed up at him, at his chest heaving, face gleaming with sweat, eyes dark.

"You have to come first."

"Oh." She let out her breath on a whoosh. "Oh."

He covered her pussy with his hand, cupping her, and she pulsed against him. Then he stroked with his fingertips, parted her folds and found her clit. She jumped as he touched the sensitive nerve endings, fell back onto the bed and closed her eyes. He stroked and rubbed, slicking up more wetness, and she quivered and strained against his touch. "Yes." She tried to breathe. "Yes." The faint buzzing started, the very beginning of an orgasm, spreading from his fingers down her thighs, deep inside her, building, twisting, coiling tighter, hotter, higher.

More. She needed more. She needed that deeper touch, that driving pressure.

"Inside me." She reached for his hips. She dug her fingers into the sides of his buttocks, hard and muscular, pulling him to her. Again he thrust into her and this time the penetration combined with his fingers on her clit sent her spiraling out of control, over the edge, flying.

She grabbed his ass and cried out and he held himself still against her. She felt him inside her, felt the spasms of his cock as he poured himself into her. He came inside her in long, hard spurts, holding his weight off her body, his face buried in the side of her neck.

She pulsed around him in tiny convulsions of pleasure. "Oh dear god." She held him tight. She'd just had the best sex of her life with a man she barely knew. Boring? Practical? Predictable? Ha! She'd just entered a new world, one where she was wild! Wicked. Wanton. Free.

Jase might have dozed off. He felt like he was floating, aware of his hand on the sweet curve of Remi's backside, warm and firm, his other hand tangled in her hair. The softness of her bed cushioned his body and the scent of Remi and her sheets mingled with the warm scent of sex. He drifted on a haze of sensual pleasure. Wow.

Who would've thought the little blond pixie would be such a tigress in bed? She was little but strong, her appetite for sex matching his, head on, full frontal, burn the sheets up.

Christ, she was hot.

He hardened against her and she shifted and murmured drowsily.

He rolled her to her back and kissed her, softly at first, then hotter, harder as she began to respond, fingers digging into his shoulders. Their tongues licked, mouths kissed and sucked and slid.

"Baby, you are so hot." His mouth slid over her cheek and jaw. "So fucking hot."

"Mmmmm." She tipped her head back so he could kiss her neck and he tasted her with his tongue, so sweet, sucked her flesh gently into his mouth, then licked again. She shivered in his arms. "So are you."

"Hot for you."

She smiled then, opening her eyes. "Oh, please."

"What?" He frowned at her.

"You can do better than that."

She was teasing him, the little witch, eyes sparkling, mouth curved appealingly. He shook his head. "Okay." He nuzzled between her breasts. "Your breasts are perfection. I love your nipples, how little and sharp they are, how sensitive…" He nipped at one with his lips and she gasped. "How pretty."

"Oh." Her eyes drifted closed and he sucked on the other nipple.

"You make my balls feel like they're going to explode. My cock is so hard I could take a slap shot with it."

She giggled. "I can't quite picture that. You're big, but not that big."

He laughed too, then rolled to his back, taking her with him, and laid a small smack onto her pretty ass.

Her head jerked up. "Hey!"

"You deserve a spanking." He gave her another tap on the butt. "For making fun of me. I was trying to be sincere."

She moaned. Whoa. Kinda sounded as if she liked those little love taps.

Her body stretched out over his felt so good, soft and warm and silky, and she rolled her hips against him. She was turned on. His dick surged. This was gonna be fun.

He lifted her easily by her hips, holding her above him until she was positioned over his cock, which sought out her pussy like a divining rod, quivering and throbbing. Then he lowered her onto him, slowly, again cautious of how big he was and how small she was and how this position would make her take him even deeper.

Eyes closed, she moaned and whimpered as he filled her. Hot wet velvet closed around him, so goddamn sweet he almost couldn't bear it, the look on her face pure ecstasy, her hands coming up to cup her own breasts and squeeze. Ah, hell.

He shoved into her, fucking her sweet pussy in a frenzy of lust, but then he stopped, gasping for breath. He needed to make sure she was coming. Had to.

He reached between them and found her clit with his thumb, fingers tangled in the tiny puff of curls there.

"Yes," she whispered, still caressing her breasts. So hot. "Yes, right there."

He fought back his own rising orgasm, ready to detonate if she moved even the tiniest…bit…god.

Remi was close. So close. Everything inside her pulled up and tightened and twisted in near painful ecstasy.

She heard bells ringing.

She rode Jase, sliding her hands into her hair, her breasts rising, Jase's fingers working magic on her clit. So close.

The ringing sang in her ears again. "Jesus," Jase said. "Is that your doorbell?"

"No. Don't be silly."

She shifted forward, frowning, trying to pick up that feeling again.

A loud pounding reverberated through the house.

"It *is* the door," Jase gasped, hands on her waist.

Remi paused, breathing hard. "No. It's my heart. Feel it." She took his hand and pressed it to her left breast and he made a noise deep in his throat.

The hammering sounded again, this time accompanied by shouting voices.

Remi paused again. Dammit! Now it was gone, the elusive orgasm. Although, it *was* her third of the night.

What was going on?

"There *is* someone at your door!"

"There can't be." She squinted at the clock beside the bed. "It's three A.M. Who would…?" She clapped a hand to her mouth. "Oh my damn!"

"What?" Jase's brows snapped together. He was still hard inside her.

Remi's mind scrambled. She rolled off Jase and off the bed, eyes darting around the room for something to put on. She scooped up Jase's shirt from the floor. It was so big she couldn't find the armholes and she started toward the door as she fought her way into it.

"Remi, who is it?" She glanced over her shoulder to see Jase climbing out of bed too, and the sight of his body, all bronze skin and incredible muscles, slowed her feet and distracted her for a couple of heartbeats. He grabbed for his pants and started jumping into them as he crossed the room.

Remi hurried down the stairs to the front door, which vibrated under intense, rapid percussion again. She heard a feminine voice calling, "Remi! Are you in there? Remi!"

She peeked out the window and saw—oh god—Delise standing there with two uniformed police officers. Blue and red lights flashed from a car parked at the curb in front of her house. Remi thunked her forehead against the door, hand on the deadbolt, and drew in a long breath. This could not be happening. Could. Not.

She twisted the lock and opened the door just as Jase arrived behind her, chest bare, pants undone, hair standing on end.

The police and Delise burst into the small foyer.

CHAPTER FOUR

"Remi! Oh, thank god, you're okay!" Delise turned to Jase and her mouth parted and she blinked. "Uh…."

"Delise, I'm fine."

Remi turned to the police officer, her cheeks scorching. "I'm so sorry, officers, everything is fine."

"Uh huh."

Remi stacked one bare foot on top of the other, glad Jase's shirt covered her to her knees, and wrapped her arms around herself. "Delise! Was this really necessary?"

Delise snapped her mouth shut and swiveled her gaze to Remi. "I told you I would call you! Where's your cell phone?"

Remi swallowed and rolled her lips in. "Um…in my purse. In the living room."

Delise pursed her lips and planted her hands on her hips. "Remi, I can't believe you! I said I'd call and you'd better answer and…"

"I know, I know, but I forgot all about that and we were…um…kind of busy." She tried to ignore the smirks on the faces of the policemen. "But I'm okay, truly."

"I guess we can go, then," one officer said.

"I am so sorry," Delise said to them. "But I really thought…she'd left with a stranger and we'd arranged…well…thank you."

"Hey," said the other officer, looking at Jase. "Aren't you…"

"No," Jase said firmly, turning away. Remi shot a glance at him as the officers shrugged and left. As she closed the door, she saw with relief they'd turned off the flashing lights. What would the neighbors think? Lord!

She turned back to Delise and Jase, both eyeing each other and giving each other tight smiles.

"I'll go home now," Delise said. "I'm sorry to interrupt you, but dammit, Remi…"

"I know. I know." She held up a hand. "I take responsibility. You did say that and I just forgot. I never thought you'd actually call the police, though!"

"I've been phoning you for the last two hours! I started calling an hour after you left and…well, that was fast work is all I can say."

Jase grinned.

Remi's insides shook and burned. "I'm sorry, Delise."

She hugged her friend, then watched her out the window as she got into her car and drove away. She again turned back to face Jase. "I am so sorry." She covered her mouth with her hands.

"Yeah. Well. Maybe I'd better go."

She wanted to protest, but clamped her mouth shut and followed him back to the bedroom where the rest of his clothes were. She pulled out her thick white terry robe and replaced Jase's shirt with it. Reluctantly she handed the shirt over to him. Silky soft, it smelled delicious, like him, warm male and spicy shower gel.

When he'd finished dressing, having stuffed his tie into his suit pocket, he paused. "I'll need to call a taxi."

"Oh. Yeah."

He pulled out a cell phone and punched in a number—taxi on speed dial?—then she led him to the front door where his coat hung.

This wasn't ending the way she would have liked.

Dammit.

"I'm sorry," she began again, but he stopped her with a finger on her lips.

"Stop apologizing," he said softly. He took her into his arms and pulled her up against him. She went up on her toes and it still wasn't enough, so he lifted her right off the floor and kissed her. "It's okay." Another kiss. "Can I have your number, at least? I'll call you."

Sure he would.

"I don't know," she whispered, loving the feel of him holding her like that. "Apparently I'm not really meant to have fun."

"Oh come on. Everyone is meant to have fun. This is funny. I've never had the cops break in on me while…uh…"

Her cheeks heated again and she wriggled down. He entered her phone number into his cell phone as the lights of a taxi pulling up outside swept over them.

He grinned and shoved his phone into his pocket, cupped her chin in his fingers and brushed one more kiss over her mouth. "Night, Remi. I had fun tonight."

"Me too." She watched him leave through the small window of the door, her heart constricting inside her chest. "Oh, me too. So much fun."

"What do you mean they're not coming?" Remi stared at the principal, a chill sliding over her. "There are two hundred and fifty kids in the auditorium waiting for them."

Jennifer grimaced. "Jemar Fast was charged with drunk driving on the weekend. Not a good role model for the kids."

Remi's brows pulled down and she rubbed between her eyes. "Great. Just great." She'd worked so hard to get the kick off rally for the Stars for Reading program to be held at their school this year, with three members of the Chicago Bulls participating.

"It's not over," Jennifer said. "They found someone else. Three Wolves."

"Wolves."

"The hockey team."

"Oh. Of course. Okay. Better than nothing, I guess." She took in a breath. "I better go make sure they're not destroying the gym."

Two hundred and fifty middle school students in the auditorium near the end of the day probably had a bit of energy to burn. Especially her grade six students Justin and Ryan. Their ADHD made them a handful at times.

"When our hockey players show up, I'll bring them right down," Jennifer promised her.

"Thanks."

Remi hurried down the school hall, past empty classrooms and into the gym. The kids were actually being pretty good, sitting on the bleachers and filling the room with a dull roar punctuated with the occasional scream of high-pitched laughter.

"Change in plans," she said to her fellow teacher Paula Vaughan. "We have hockey players coming instead of basketball players."

"Oh. Okay."

"Okay, everyone, listening!" She paused and waited for the noise to subside, holding a hand in the air. "We're running a bit late, so please be patient. Jemar Fast isn't going to be with us after all." Big groans of disappointment greeted that statement. "But someone else is coming in his place."

"Who is it, Ms. Buchanan?"

"Yeah, who is it?"

Dammit, she didn't even know who it was. "Three players from the Chicago Wolves are coming today."

Cheers echoed in the gym. Huh. Guess the kids knew hockey.

"They should be here shortly to get us started. Has everyone got their book picked out that they want to read first?"

Another burst of cheering erupted and she grinned. She loved it when kids were into books and reading. Some of her students were already avid readers, but others, like Justin and Ryan, struggled with it.

Out of the corner of her eye, she saw Jennifer entering the auditorium with a group of men. Relieved, she prepared to turn the microphone over to the principal to introduce their new "stars" and get things started. If they didn't get going soon, the kids would be beyond control.

Remi went to stand with some other teachers at the side of the gym and watched Jennifer lead the three men to the front where the sound system was set up. Big guys, all three of them…Remi's eyes widened and she straightened. She blinked and focused on the back of one of the men. It looked like…no. She shook her head. Then he turned.

Jase.

Her face went hot, her body got chilled and she fell back against the concrete block gym wall.

He said something to Jennifer and they both laughed. His gorgeous smile flashed. Today he was dressed casually in jeans and a Wolves T-shirt that hugged his broad chest and shoulders. The other two men with him…yes, she was sure they'd been with him that night at Rouge…also wore the same T-shirts.

Hockey players.

Well, didn't he just look like a hockey player? Big and tough, with a crooked nose. Except he had beautiful perfect white teeth—didn't most hockey players lose their teeth by getting hit with a puck or something?

She licked her lips.

Jennifer spoke into the microphone to get the kids' attention and get the rally underway, but Remi barely heard a word she said until she introduced "Jase Heller!" and the kids all screamed and clapped.

Dear god, he was famous.

And she hadn't even known who he was.

No wonder he dated a model. She leaned her head back against the wall and covered her eyes with one hand. She'd slept with him. Her. Remi Buchanan, sixth grade teacher at Abraham Lincoln Middle School. A wave of heat swept over her at the memory of his touch, his mouth on hers, his body inside hers.

Her one wild attempt at being fun and spontaneous and sexy had ended with the police at her door. She chewed on her lower lip. That could have been very bad for Jase. Oh, god.

Jase had taken over the microphone and was getting the kids all worked up into a frenzy over reading books. She focused on him and what he was saying, clamping down on the resurgent lust.

"So you guys can ask us all questions now if you like," Jase said. "Who's got a question?"

Hands shot up and little bodies bounced excitedly on the bleachers. Remi smiled.

"What's your favorite book?" a student asked Jase.

"I have a lot of favorites," Jase replied. "But I really love Tom Sawyer."

A murmur of agreement rippled through.

His hockey buddies shared their favorites too.

"What's your favorite video game?"

Jase tipped his head to think. "Tough one," he said. "Right now I like Hosuko Heroes."

More cheers. The kids were eating it up.

"How many of you play sports?" Jase asked. Again hands reached for the sky and kids jumped up and down. "Wow! That's great! Any hockey players?"

More hands.

"Any girl hockey players?"

Remi laughed and shook her head, but sure enough, several girls jumped up and waved.

The rally continued and then the three athletes stationed themselves at the doors of the auditorium along with the teachers to hand out buttons and score sheets and gift bags with free books to the kids as they filed out.

Remi went over to talk to Jennifer, who was all smiles. "That went great!" she said. "Those hockey players were fantastic with the kids!"

"Yes. They were."

"Come on. I'll introduce you. You'll be working with them over the next few weeks."

Remi nodded, sucking her bottom lip as she followed Jennifer toward Jase. Her heart picked up speed and her head went just a little light as she neared him, tummy tight and fluttery. She'd given him her number, but he hadn't called.

Yet. It was only Wednesday.

Maybe he had no intention of calling her.

Maybe he was going to be horribly embarrassed to see her.

Maybe he was going to regret that he'd volunteered to work on this program.

Remi pressed a hand to her stomach and stopped with Jennifer. Jase was bumping fists with a boy—Remi's student Ryan—who'd stopped to talk to him. She'd never seen Ryan so focused.

Then Jase straightened to his full imposing height and turned and his gaze landed on her. His eyes widened and then a slow smile spread across his face.

She liked that smile.

She gave him a tremulous smile back.

"Remi, this is Jase Heller, Dominic Griffin and Matthieu Lalonde. Gentlemen, I'd like you to meet Remi Buchanan. She's a grade six teacher here at Lincoln and she's the one who was instrumental in bringing the kick off rally to our school this year."

Jase's smile disappeared, replaced by a glower. Oh lord. He was embarrassed. She automatically held out her hand.

Jase took it first. "We've actually met." His face smoothed and that charming white smile flashed.

"Oh, really?" Jennifer's forehead creased and she shot Remi a curious look.

"Nice to meet you, Ms Buchanan," Dominic said, shaking her hand with a grin. Matthieu did the same. Remi hadn't paid that much attention to Jase's companions that night, since all her attention had been focused on Jase, but she was pretty sure they'd both been there too. Her cheeks felt like they were on fire. Did they know she and Jase had…yeah. They must know.

Her whole body blazing, she kept a smile firmly in place. "Thank you so much for coming today. I understand it was somewhat short notice."

"Not a problem," Jase said. "I've been involved in the program for a few years at other schools. I'm glad to do it again this year."

"The kids really seemed to enjoy it," Jennifer said. "I think we're off to a great start."

"So for the next six Wednesdays we'll be back here to work with smaller groups," Jase said. His gaze held Remi's and she resisted the urge to fuss with her hair. Did she have any lipstick left on? Likely not. Usually by the end of a school day she didn't care.

"That's wonderful," she choked out. "We really appreciate it. It helps the kids get more involved when there are role models for them participating."

They made small talk for a few more moments and then Jennifer offered to show the three athletes out, their jackets having been left in her office.

Remi watched them leave, feeling a weight of disappointment settling on her. She left the custodians in the now empty gymnasium dismantling the sound system and putting the bleachers away, and walked slowly down the hall to her classroom, also empty but much quieter.

She sank onto the chair behind her desk.

She'd felt his stiffness. The coolness of his greeting, although he'd smiled at first. He was so freakin' good looking. She couldn't believe she'd done what she had with him. And had so much fun. Watching him with the kids here had been a whole other side to him—boyish and charming and fun. Yeah. He was all about fun.

Which was the opposite of what she was all about. She was all about serious responsibility. Boring.

She sighed and picked up a folder of math quizzes she had to mark that night. She bent to pick up her briefcase from under the desk.

"Hey."

She straightened up so fast she cracked her head on the edge of the desk.

"Ow!" She rubbed her temple, blinded by the pain.

"Jesus, Remi, are you okay?" Jase's voice, heavy footsteps and then his hands on her shoulders.

"Yes, yes. I'm okay." She blinked up at him. "Dammit."

"Sorry. Didn't mean to startle you."

"Th-that's okay." She tried to shake off the pain. "I'm fine."

"I was surprised to see you here," he said slowly, releasing her and stepping back.

"Have you really been involved in the Stars program before?"

"Yeah. This is my fourth year."

"That's…impressive."

"It's important."

"I…it surprises me. To hear you say that."

"Why? Because I'm a big stupid jock?"

"No, of course not!"

"I like kids." He shrugged, now wearing a black leather jacket. A super soft, thigh length black leather jacket.

"I could tell that. They liked you too."

"I didn't know you were a teacher." The glower returned to his face.

"Well, I didn't know you were a hockey player."

"Really?" His brow creased.

She tightened her lips against a smile. "Sorry. I guess you're not that famous."

He looked at her, smiling wryly. "I guess not."

"What's wrong with being a teacher?"

He pressed his lips together. "Nothing, I guess."

A silence stretched between them.

"Well," he finally said. "It'll be fun over the next few weeks. So…I guess I'll see you again next week."

"You don't have to." The words spilled out her mouth. "You can work with a different group. It doesn't have to be mine."

He frowned. "Why?"

"I just thought…we had that one night…thing…and you might be…"

Lord help her, she was stammering like Joey Kupchuk, a boy she'd once taught who had a painful stutter.

"That's okay." After a short pause, he said, "I was going to call you."

She waved a hand, anxious to stop him before he said something she didn't want to hear. "That's okay. It was just one night of fun. Right?"

"Right." Relief lightened his scowl and he gave her a faint smile. "That's right. Okay, then. I'll see you next week. Bye, Remi."

She watched him leave, then sank back onto her chair, her legs soft as butter. Damn. She'd known it was only one night, and now knowing who he was made it that much clearer—he'd never really intended to call her.

"Wasn't that the little blonde you picked up last weekend?"

Jase stared out the passenger window of Griff's car as they left the school parking lot. "Yeah."

"You didn't know she was going to be there?"

"Nope. We didn't get into a lot of conversation." Hell, that wasn't true. They'd talked about a lot of things. Just not their professions.

Griff laughed. "Right on, dude."

"She did not know you were a 'ockey player," Matthieu, also known as Frenchy, said from the back seat in his rhythmic French accent.

"Nope, she didn't know that either."

Jase couldn't believe she was a teacher. He'd picked up a *teacher* in a bar, taken her home and fucked her! Jesus!

"Kinda awkward, running into her again like that." Griff signaled and made a lane change.

"I was going to call her again." Jase still stared out the window. He *had* wanted to see her again. She was adorable, but fuck! A teacher! "But not now."

"Why not?"

"She's a teacher." Griff was probably his best buddy, in Chicago at least, and even he didn't know about the trauma inflicted on him by teachers. "I don't date teachers. Don't want anything to do with teachers."

Teaching was a noble profession. He couldn't judge all teachers the same. Just because a few teachers had made his life hell didn't mean they were all like that. Hell, he should thank Ms Wong. If it wasn't for her, he probably wouldn't be where he was.

"Huh." Griff shot him a mystified glance. "She's kinda cute. What difference does it make if she's a teacher?"

"Never mind. Not going there. Let's go get some food."

"Where should we go?"

"I need a 'amburger," Frenchy said.

"Burgers sound good. How about Benny's?"

Griff tapped his fingers on the steering wheel. "They have vegan food there?"

"Dude." Jase grinned at him. "Shut up about the vegan shit. You know you're dying for a burger."

"I've been doing good this week!"

"It's only Wednesday."

"Yeah, pretty sure they have a tofu burger there." Jase snorted.

"Beans and rice again?" Frenchy asked. "*Câlisse.*"

When they arrived at Benny's, Griff inspected the menu then slapped it down. "Fuck it. Burger it is. With cheese and bacon."

Jase held out his fist.

Griff sighed and bumped knuckles.

"What's with the big vegan push anyway?"

"Chantal is vegan." He named his new girlfriend.

"You've only been seeing her a couple of weeks," Frenchy said. "Dat is a pretty big commitment."

"Too big." He grimaced. "Of course, she doesn't need to know about this."

"She'll smell the beef on your breath," Jase said. "There's no way to hide it. In fact, the odor will come out of your pores. I've heard that."

"Bullshit."

"Also a relationship built on lies is not healty," Frenchy added.

Jase lifted an eyebrow. "And there is that."

The waitress approached, a stacked brunette wearing a tight, low-cut T-shirt. She gave them all the eye. "Hi guys. How are y'all tonight?"

"Great."

"You all play for the Wolves, don't you?"

"Yep."

"I knew it. I'm a big fan." She beamed at them. "Can I get you something to drink?"

They ordered beers and gave her their food orders at the same time. When she left, Griff rose from his seat. "Gotta drain the main vein. Be right back."

Jase watched him leave, then reached across the table for the cell phone Griff had left sitting there. "He'll never learn." He touched the screen. "And still not password protected." He opened Griff's email and tapped in a message, laughing softly. Then he set the phone back.

"What did you do?" Frenchy grinned at him.

"You'll see."

Griff arrived back at the table at the same time as the cute waitress. This was the type of chick he was usually attracted to. But tonight, he kept thinking about a tiny blonde pixie.

Griff's cell phone chimed. He absently picked it up and swiped the screen. Taking a sip of his beer, he read the screen. "What the fuck?" He scowled.

"Something wrong?" Jase casually leaned back in his chair holding his own beer.

"She thinks I gave her some kind of disease…are you fucking kidding me? Wait, what?" He read more. "*Why does it hurt when I pee?*" He lifted incredulous eyes to Jase. "You fucking asshole!"

"What?" Frenchy still had no clue.

Jase collapsed in laughter, almost falling out of his chair. "What did she say? Let me see." He reached for the cell phone but Griff yanked it out of his reach.

Griff told Frenchy, "He emailed Chantal 'why does it hurt when I pee?' She emails back, 'You bastard, you better not have given me something! Go to the doctor!'."

Frenchy cracked up too.

"Fuck you, Heller." Griff tapped in another email back to his girlfriend, while Jase wiped tears. "I'm telling her it was you and you better fucking own up."

"Ah, that was beautiful." Jase mentally patted himself on the back. He didn't prank the guys as much as he used to but it was still good to have some fun once in a while. "I was thinking about putting it on Twitter, but I figured the team might not be too happy about that. So consider yourself lucky."

"I need to learn how to set a fuckin' password," Griff muttered. "The last time he did this, he sent my girl a text that said, 'My ass hurts too much for sex tonight'."

Jase and Frenchy both fell over laughing again.

Try as he might, Jase couldn't get the sexy little teacher out of his head for the next week, until he was back at Abraham Lincoln Middle School a week later, sitting in her classroom with a bunch of sixth graders.

He watched Remi with another group as he sat in a corner of her classroom. He seemed unable to drag his eyes away from her, and his concentration kept drifting off into images of her naked, his hands on her…dammit. He had a hard enough time paying attention without a major hot distraction like her.

He should just ask her out again. He'd wanted to. He'd planned to call her. He couldn't stop thinking about her.

And yet, the intimidation factor was high. Teachers were smart. Bossy. Know-it-alls. Teachers made him feel like a speck of dirt on the ice.

Why he kept thinking about Remi, he'd never know. She was clearly unimpressed with the fact that he played a game for a living. He'd caught that comment about how surprised she was that he was involved in the reading program. She probably thought he didn't even know *how* to read.

A familiar knife twisted in his gut at that thought. He had to get over all that old crap.

Dammit. A teacher.

She laughed at something one of the kids said and at that moment looked up. Their eyes locked on each other across the room. His heart knocked in his chest.

He tore his gaze away from her, sucked in air and tried to focus on the kids he was supposed to be paying attention to. Christ, she'd really think he was illiterate if he couldn't even read a short story with the kids, and she'd really think he was stupid if he couldn't focus long enough to put a few sentences together about what they'd read.

"I cried when Travis had to shoot Old Yeller," Lindsay confessed. Two boys groaned.

"Hey," Jase said. "I cried too. He loved that dog. Don't you think that was a tough choice he had to make?"

Again, he caught Remi's eyes on him and had to refocus.

As the session drew to a close, Remi retreated to her desk and began tidying up. Jase found his jacket and slid his arms into the sleeves, taking his time, picking up some books and placing them on a table, until the kids were gone and he and Remi were alone.

She looked up at him, her pretty face expressionless, as he approached the desk, a book clasped in his hands.

"Is this what we're reading for next week?" he asked.

She nodded, lifting an eyebrow. "Yes."

His face heated. She knew he'd already told her students that. He felt like one of those kids, a kid with a crush on a classmate, practically scuffing his feet on the floor as he hung around on a pretext.

"So, I…uh…" Jesus, she had turned him into a stammering idiot. Why did teachers have that affect on him? He drew in a long slow breath, and forced a smile. She was just a woman. A hot, sexy woman, one whose bell he'd already rung. Repeatedly. Nothing to be afraid of.

He was terrified.

"I'll…uh…see you next week," he said and booked it out of there.

Helping kids with reading, being back in school in the classroom, creating hopefully positive experiences for other kids had seemed like an excellent way for him to deal with his own crappy past and the other years he'd done this Stars for Reading program had been great. But this year…why was he getting all screwed up again?

So he'd nailed a teacher. She was just a woman. It didn't matter if she thought he was big and dumb. It didn't matter what she thought at all.

Remi watched Jase with the kids. This was now the third week he'd been there in her class and the kids seemed to love him, but she was starting to have doubts about his ability to keep them focused. Seeing as he could barely keep himself focused.

He kept staring off into space or, even worse, staring at her, dammit, and Jessie Doherty had to ask him the same question twice, then twitch his shirt sleeve before he seemed to hear her. "Sorry," he said to her with a smile, but it wasn't long before he'd done it again. He rubbed his face, glanced over at Remi, and when he saw her watching, a dark flush stained his cheeks and he frowned at the book in his hands.

With a sigh, she moved over to the group and took control of the discussion about The Chronicles of Narnia, earning a scowl from Jase that tightened her insides. Well, she couldn't worry about him, she needed to make sure the kids were getting something from this.

Two kids hung around after class, Ryan and Jessie.

Ryan started talking about hockey, while Jessie stood there smiling worshipfully up at Jase.

"You ever come to any Wolves games?" Jase asked Ryan.

"No," he said glumly. "My mom says tickets are too expensive."

Jase's smile disappeared. "Yeah. I guess they are pretty expensive."

"Well, I guess I better go," Ryan said.

When he'd gone, Jessie looked up at him. "Are you married?"

He grinned. "Nope."

She nodded and gave a smile that looked way too mature for a twelve-year old. "When's your next game?"

"Friday night." He folded his arms across his wide chest. "You like hockey?"

"I love hockey," she said breathlessly.

Remi sighed. The pre-teen clearly had a huge crush on Jase.

"Cool," Jase said.

Jessie made no move to leave.

"Jase." Remi spoke up. "I need a word with you before you go."

Jessie dragged her feet out of the classroom with a wistful wave at Jase.

Jase turned to face her and her stomach went fluttery. His expression turned wooden. "Yes, ma'am, what is it?"

Remi glared at him. "You know, if you're not into this anymore, we can probably find someone else."

"Do you know how many people are in Ryan's family?"

She blinked at the completely unrelated question. "Um…why?" She frowned at him.

"Just curious."

"He has a brother, I taught him two years ago. And his mom, she's a single parent."

He nodded. "Okay."

"So as I was saying—"

"You don't need to find someone else," he said. "I'm still into it."

"Well, it didn't seem like it," she snapped back. "You kept drifting off somewhere. You weren't even paying attention."

He stared back at her, his mouth tight, eyes narrowed. "I'm sorry. It won't happen again. Ma'am."

"Why are you calling me that?" She set her hands on her hips. "It sounds ridiculous."

"You're the teacher, right? You're in charge."

"I'm not…" She blew out a breath. What was with him? "Okay, we all have days where we have a lot on our minds. I'm sure that's what was happening today for you. But you have to be able to hold the kids' attention."

"I know that."

They stared at each other, the air crackling between them.

"This was supposed to be fun," he muttered.

Her lips parted. Fun? Oh yeah, sure. Fun. His main goal in life.

Oh, why was she thinking like such a stick in the mud? Of *course* it was supposed to be fun. What better way for kids to learn than by having fun? "I'm sorry if you're not enjoying it," she said stiffly.

"Whatever." He grabbed his leather jacket and headed for the door. "See you next week."

She stared after him, stomach churning, heart thumping. What had she said that had made him so angry? She covered her eyes with one hand and stood there for a moment. Damn, having him in her classroom every week was becoming torture. She still felt unreasonably attracted to him, going hot every time she saw him and hotter every time their eyes met. Which happened a lot, because she kept catching him staring at her. With a frown on his face that totally confused her. *He* totally confused her. Dammit.

CHAPTER FIVE

Jase made a call from his cell phone once he got to the car, then headed home to his Lakeshore East apartment. He knew he'd been having a hard time paying attention with the kids, but he couldn't exactly tell her it was because he was distracted by her. By her pretty face, sexy mouth, shiny blonde hair and her breasts so soft and full beneath the silk blouse she wore. He'd had those breasts in his hands, had tasted those sweet little pink nipples…

Damn, he was getting a stiffy again. He hadn't been so nuts over a girl since high school, for chrissakes. But he kept thinking about her, fantasizing about all the things they hadn't had a chance to do in that one night. And the worst thing was, the more time he spent with her, the more he actually…liked her. She was gentle but firm with the kids, knew when she could act silly and make them laugh, knew when she had to rope them all in and get serious. They all spoke to her respectfully but with a warmth that told him they liked her. And hey, respect was important too. He knew how important it was to respect your leader. He'd had coaches that had been the guys' best buddy, but couldn't get shit out of them when it came to performance. He'd had coaches who'd been assholes on a power trip that had the same result. It was the coaches who earned his respect that he'd go the distance for, the distance and beyond.

And to have a teacher like that…those kids were damn lucky.

He'd acted like a jerk and he hated it, but when she'd asked for "a word with him" he'd been sent back through time to his own middle school years and one of the eighty gazillion times he'd been in trouble with one of his teachers. All those old feelings of incompetence, inferiority and anger had surged inside him and he'd taken them out on Remi.

Even though he could see she was a really great teacher.

His fingers tightened on the wheel of his Jeep as he drove home, the sun low in the sky now. But she was still a teacher. Christ. Maybe he should find someone to take his place. Or switch classes with one of the other guys. He'd been confident that working with Remi wouldn't be a problem after their one night, but clearly he'd been wrong. Maybe that was what was causing that tension snapping between them like a rubber band. Maybe she was pissed because of that. But that was giving himself way too much credit and she'd said herself one night of fun was all she wanted.

Agh. He knew enough about women to know that what they said wasn't always what they meant. Why the fuck couldn't they just say what they meant? It would make the world a lot simpler.

He drove into the underground parking garage beneath the high-rise building in which he lived, navigating the concrete pillars and parked vehicles until he arrived at his spot.

He couldn't give up. He was determined to get past this and deal with the old crap that kept surfacing. He was going back to that classroom next week, even if it killed him.

His cell phone rang as he rode the elevator up to his apartment and he thunked his head back against the wall, recognizing the ring tone. It was Brianne. He still had his phone programmed with that Sexy Chick ring tone for her.

He looked at the phone, closed his eyes and let it go to voice mail.

Why did she keep calling him? This was the fourth time since they'd broken up. He hated to hurt someone's feelings, but how much clearer could he make it? They were done. The phone beeped to indicate a voice mail. Gritting his teeth, his listened to it as he let himself into his apartment. "It's me," her breathy voice began. "Please, Jase. Please call me back. I miss you so much. I need to talk to you."

Hell.

"Are you sure you want to work on this committee?"

A week later, Remi was in the principal's office, talking to her boss about a joint parent-teacher fund raising project to support the school's music program. "Of course," she said to Jennifer.

"You've taken on a lot of extra projects lately. Stars for Reading, the anti-bullying task force and now this…"

Remi gave her boss a bright smile. "I like to be busy." She'd been spending even more time after school with some of the kids who liked to hang around too, trying to keep herself from missing her sister and brother and harassing her friends.

Jennifer nodded slowly. "Okay." Then Jennifer's gaze went past Remi's shoulder and a smile broke across her face. "Ling! Hi!"

Remi turned to see Ling, the school's administrative assistant, standing there holding her new baby. She'd been off on maternity leave since having her son two months earlier.

"Did you bring that sweet baby in to visit us?" Jennifer moved from behind her desk and hurried over to Ling.

Ling smiled. Her cheeks glowed from the cold outside and her silky dark hair swung forward as she set the baby carrier on the floor. "We sure did come for a visit. Josh fell asleep in the car on the way here, though." She quickly unbuckled him and dug him out of layers of padding and blankets.

Remi smiled at the baby, snuggled into the seat, with his little thatch of dark hair like his mom's and chubby rosy cheeks. Then his eyes flickered and he blinked at them, and gave a mighty yawn.

"Oh, you're awake. Let's get you out of there so you can say hello to everyone." Ling lifted him out and stood.

"He's beautiful." Remi couldn't take her eyes off the sweet little face. She touched his hair, then his cheek, so smooth and soft.

"Here, you want to hold him?"

"Oh yes!" Remi eagerly accepted the little bundle and held him to her, letting his small weight sink into her arms. "Hello, Josh, you handsome man, you." He smelled like baby powder and she closed her eyes and breathed him in. She felt an ache of longing that went all the way from her heart to her womb, and she opened her eyes to smile down at him, then looked at Ling, who regarded her with a knowing smile.

"You need one of your own," she said.

Remi laughed. It didn't seem likely at the moment, but some day. Maybe. "Is he a good baby?"

"He's so good! He hardly ever cries. And he's slept through the night the last four nights in a row."

"That's awesome."

"He wants to eat all the time, though." Ling grimaced. "He's growing so fast!"

"He'll be big like his dad."

Ling smiled. "I hope so."

"I have to go," Remi said, regretfully. "I have the Stars for Reading program starting in a few minutes." She handed Josh back to his mother reluctantly and her arms felt empty. She sighed, but smiled as she left Jennifer and Ling chatting.

Babies were so sweet and precious and she'd never admitted it to anyone, but she wanted one of her own. A crazy thing to want when she wasn't married and didn't even have a boyfriend. Probably she just wanted to replace her brother and sister with someone else to look after. She rolled her eyes at herself as she hurried down the hall toward her classroom. Except…she'd always loved babies and kids. Hell, that was why she'd become a teacher. She sighed.

Jase was in her classroom when she arrived and she went from soft longing to tingling awareness in the blink of an eye. As he worked with the kids, he seemed more focused this week, though very tense. Which was exactly how Remi felt. Damn. She plastered on a smile for the kids and made it through the reading session. Once again, Jase hung back until they were alone.

Her heart tapped in her chest as she gathered up some papers she was going to take home and looked up at him inquiringly.

He stood there, putting his jacket on, blinking, his mouth tight. She'd kissed that mouth. And he was such a good kisser…

With a mental shake, she tried to refocus.

"Was it better today?" Jase asked, almost sounding…nervous.

"Was what better?"

"Ah…me. I know I've been kind of distracted. But the truth is…Remi, you distract me."

Her heart missed a beat and her mouth fell open. "Me."

"Yeah." He rubbed his face, then blurted out, "I can't stop thinking about you!"

She stared at him, her lungs refusing to expand and take in oxygen. Funny he should say that, since she couldn't stop thinking about him.

"Would you like to go get some dinner?"

She still stared at him. From the pained expression on his face, she wasn't entirely sure he'd actually meant to issue that invitation. "Dinner?"

"Yeah." He lifted a shoulder. "You know. In a restaurant."

Now she almost smiled. "Why?"

"Uh…because we have to eat?" He smiled too, that sexy, boyish smile that was enough to melt her panties. And she did begin to feel a little warm and her tummy did a little flip.

"I don't think so." She broke eye contact and picked up the folder she planned to take home.

"Why not? C'mon, Remi. We had fun that night."

Was that was this was about? He wanted more sex? "I think if you're looking for *fun*, you'd be better off with one of your supermodel girlfriends."

He drew back and his smile disappeared. "What's that supposed to mean?"

"I mean, I'm not really made for fun. Apparently. After what happened the last time." Add to that the fact that he'd said he was going to call her when he clearly had no intention of ever doing that, having dinner with him would be a big mistake.

He laughed. "I told you. That was funny. Maybe not at that moment. I think it's nice that your friend cares that much about you."

And it also showed how out of character it was for her to do something like that, but she didn't want to point that out to Mr. Fun.

"Come on, Remi." His voice was deep and velvety soft. "It's just dinner."

The suggestive and silky tone of his voice made her shiver, made her nipples tingle, made her insides clench.

He reached out and stroked a hand down her bare forearm, lingering at her wrist, his thumb stroking over her pulse there.

"How about the fact that you said you were going to call me and you never did?"

He pursed his lips. "I meant to call you. Really."

She lifted one skeptical eyebrow.

"Really. But then I came here and found out who you are and…" His words trailed off and she regarded him with confusion.

"You found out who I am? How about, *I* found out who *you* are!"

He waved a hand. "That doesn't matter."

He apparently really believed that. She gave her head a shake. "You're a famous pro athlete. I'm a teacher. That doesn't exactly seem like…" She waved a hand back and forth between them.

"You're telling me," he said with heartfelt agreement that only puzzled her more. Lord, the man was twisting her brains up. "C'mon. Let's go out."

"When?"

"Right now. Tonight."

"I can't go out on a school night!"

He laughed. "Why not? It's just dinner."

Why not indeed? He'd dismissed every objection she had, although hadn't really dealt with them to her satisfaction. Remi nibbled her bottom lip. No Jasmine or Kyle waiting at home for her to cook dinner. She had papers to mark but that could wait till later. What was wrong with a dinner out? Other than this guy was the hottest guy on the planet and was dangerous like dynamite. And about as resistible as Vosges dark chocolate truffles.

Why the hell not?

"We could go to Inferno," he said. "The food's incredible there."

It was the hottest, most expensive restaurant in Chicago. She looked down at her black pants and teal blue turtleneck sweater.

"I'm not really dressed for that," she murmured. "Neither are you."

"True." He shrugged. "Not that I care. How about pizza?"

She smiled him. "That sounds great."

They dropped her car off at home and he took her to Mama Sophia's. Over deep-dish pizza and beer she quizzed him about his hockey career. "I don't know much about hockey," she admitted. "But I think it's very rough."

"It can be." He smiled at her. "That's the fun part."

"Do you fight?"

He laughed. "I have been known to throw down. But not often. There was a time back when I was a junior player and I was headed to goonsville. I was big and I liked to protect the other guys, but sometimes I tended to jump in and get physical without thinking about the consequences. I had a great coach, though, who really got me to work on controlling those impulses and to think about things." He tilted his head. "You should come to a game."

"Oh. Yeah. Maybe."

"I'll get you a ticket. I'll get you two tickets and you can bring your friend…what's her name…?"

"Delise."

"Yeah. She didn't seem too impressed with me the other night. I think I should make it up to her."

"It wasn't you she wasn't happy with, it was me." Remi grimaced. "She's the one who wanted me to find a guy that night and get lucky. Then when I did, she freaked out and got all paranoid that I was leaving with a serial killer."

Jase choked on a mouthful of beer. "Good to know she has a high opinion of me."

Remi laughed. "She didn't even know who you were. She would have felt that way if I was going home with the Pope."

"Ha. Be glad it was me. You wouldn't have gotten three orgasms with the Pope."

Now it was her turn to choke. "I didn't get three! We were interrupted…"

"Damn. That's right." His eyes went even darker. "I guess I owe you one more, then."

Everything inside her drew up tight and her skin tingled with warmth. Oooh. Suddenly it was hard to breath. Maybe after this…

"When is your next game?" she asked breathlessly, clutching her beer glass.

He grinned. "Sunday afternoon. Two tickets. Okay?"

"I'll check with Delise."

He nodded. "I'm number twenty-five. Don't forget that."

Remi's cell phone chimed in her purse. "Damn." She grabbed her bag and dug around for it. It was Jasmine, sobbing.

"He's such a jerk!" she cried.

Remi eyed Jase. "Uh…who is, Jasmine?"

"Ethan!"

Remi sighed and leaned back in the booth. "Why? What happened now?"

Sniffling and choking noises came across the line. "I think he's cheating on me."

"Oh." Remi rolled her eyes. There they went again. She'd been waiting for this.

"So I'm moving back home."

"What!?" Remi sat up straight.

Jase frowned at her from across the table and mouthed, "What's wrong?"

She shook her head and put her hand to her forehead. "When?"

"Right now. I'm on my way there. Where are you?"

"I'm…out. Having dinner."

"On a school night?"

Remi rolled her lips in and released them with a pop. "Yep. I'll be home in a while."

"Get home quick. Please, Rem." She sniffled again.

Remi ended the call and dropped her phone into her purse, then met Jase's eyes. "My little sister. She just had a fight with her boyfriend and is moving back home as we speak."

"Oh."

She nodded, and finished her beer. "I'd better go. She sounded pretty upset."

"Damn."

She huffed out a laugh. "Yeah. Damn."

He'd already paid the bill with a platinum credit card and stood to help her with her jacket. "We could go back to my place."

She looked over her shoulder and up at him. Her insides all warm and melty, she really, really wanted to.

"I'm sorry," she said, voice catching. "My sister was crying, and seemed really upset."

He nodded. "I understand. Another time."

Sure. She'd heard that before. He was looking for fun and she was going home to be the responsible, dependable big sister yet again. She'd never hear from him again. She knew how that worked.

He parked in front of her house in his Jeep Liberty. "Do you want me to come in with you?"

"That's okay." She smiled at him. He reached across and took hold of her chin with his fingers, then leaned over and brushed a kiss across her mouth. A soft, melt-your-insides kind of kiss. She blinked at him.

"I'll call you tomorrow. About the tickets. Check with Delise."

She stared at him. "Really?"

"Yeah. Really."

Her heart missed a beat, then pitter-pattered embarrassingly. A thrill skittered through her. "Okay. Thanks."

CHAPTER SIX

Remi and Delise found their seats, row twelve right behind the Wolves bench in the Metro Center, home of the Chicago Wolves. "Great seats," Delise remarked.

"Yeah." They watched the players skating circles on the ice in the warm up, shooting randomly at their respective goalies. "Let the Beat Build" by Lil Wayne blasted energetically from the speakers and the chilled air in the center smelled of popcorn, sweat and artificial ice. A puck bounced off the boards with a bang that made them jump.

"So…what's with you and this hockey player?"

"Nothing."

Delise snorted and tossed her long auburn curls. "Riiiight. And that's why he gave you free tickets to the game."

"We're just having fun."

"Mmm. It looked like you were having fun that night. Did I tell you how cute you were in his shirt?"

"Oh, god." Remi closed her eyes momentarily. "I'm sure the cops appreciated it, too."

"They were having a good laugh about it, I think."

"Well, it turns out Jase is involved in the Stars for Reading Program at my school this year."

"You're kidding." Delise swiveled her head to look at Remi. "You didn't tell me that."

Remi licked her lips. "Yeah, well. I didn't know it until he showed up at the kick off rally. He was a last minute replacement. He acted kind of weird. Sort of brushed me off. Which was okay, because even though he said he'd call, I didn't expect him to. It was just one night."

Delise shot her a who-are-you-kidding look.

"But then last week after class he asked me out for dinner."

"I see."

Remi frowned at the disapproving tone in Delise's voice. "I thought you wanted me to have fun."

"He's a professional hockey player."

"Yeah. So?" Like she didn't know that and hadn't already been over that a million times in her own head.

"Professional athletes are…um…trouble."

Remi scanned the players in white jerseys, the home team Wolves, with their red, brown and black logos, looking for number twenty-five. She couldn't find him. She frowned. "What do you mean by trouble?"

"They cheat on their wives." Delise dipped her hand into the bucket of popcorn Remi held on her lap.

"I'm not going to marry him," Remi said, still looking for Jase. Delise snorted. "He's probably just being nice to me, giving me tickets, because I'm a teacher at the school he's volunteering with." And Remi knew she should just shut up, because the more she went on about how it was nothing, the lamer she sounded. She pressed her lips together and tightened her fingers on the bucket.

A loud horn blew to signal the end of the warm up and the players slowly started leaving the ice. Remi focused on each player as he skated up to the boards, stopped sharply, then jumped lightly off the ice to walk to the dressing room.

There he was! Number twenty-five. Hard to tell, with all the equipment and the helmet. He was definitely one of the bigger players. When he arrived at the boards, he lifted his head and looked directly at her. He must know where their seats were. She smiled and gave a little wave and he too lifted a big gloved hand before disappearing.

She shivered and not just from the cold. He'd looked for her. She hadn't seen him earlier, of course, he'd left the tickets for her at the box office. She wouldn't see him after, either, unless she wanted to hang around for an hour after the game. She and Delise would likely go have something to eat after.

"I've been reading about hockey on the internet," she told Delise. "So hopefully I know what's going on."

"I think it's pretty simple. They score a goal by shooting the puck into the other team's net."

"Well, duh. I got that much."

"There's no half time."

Remi grinned. "No. Three periods. Two intermissions." She picked up her Diet Coke and sipped it. "I guess we'll figure it out."

She wasn't prepared for how fast the players moved, the brutal hits that shuddered the glass above the boards, and the way the puck sometimes missed the net in a blistering shot that sent it soaring over the boards.

"Jesus," Delise muttered. "You could get hurt at one of these games."

Remi'd flinched once too, when two players fought over the puck and sent it flying in their direction.

Jase was one of the players who did the face off thing, trying to get the puck, bending low to the ice, legs wide apart. He seemed to win most of the face offs, from what she could tell. But the score wasn't reflecting that. The visiting team, the New York Rangers, scored one goal and then another.

Remi and Delise exchanged disappointed glances at the score. She wanted Jase to win. Maybe he'd score a goal. According to the team's website, he was one of their top scorers.

And then he got the puck and broke away from the rest of the players, racing toward the Rangers' net all on his own, carrying the puck. The crowd roared and Remi's heart jumped. He drew back his stick and took the shot—oooh, a fake! He did a quick little maneuver and shot to the opposite side of the net, but no! The goalie stretched out a gloved hand and made what seemed to be an impossible save.

The crowd all groaned and Remi slumped back in her seat. "Damn!"

Jase's teammates all skated in after him and they shot the puck back and forth around the net, across the ice, around the net again. "What are they doing?" Delise muttered. "They need to shoot at the net to get a goal."

"I think they're trying to set something up."

Remi caught the amused glances of a couple sitting in front of them and realized how clueless she and Delise must sound. She bit her lip. Hopefully those people didn't know she was there as Jase's guest. She wouldn't want to embarrass him.

And then a Ranger got the puck and Jase took off after him and, to Remi's horror, he smashed the guy into the boards with a thundering crash. The crowd cheered in delight, but Remi put her hands to her mouth. Dear god, he was going to kill the other guy. Or himself. Or both of them.

But they both skated away, although Jase had to adjust his helmet.

Every muscle in her body was tense. Sheesh. She had to relax.

The pace was sizzling, the action nonstop, the tension high. For the rest of the first period, it seemed the teams were skating from one end of the rink to the other and back again. These guys had to be in great shape, although as she watched it seemed to Remi that sometimes they only played for a minute at a time, constantly hopping off the ice onto the bench and being replaced by players barreling over the boards and racing into the game.

When the buzzer sounded to end the first period, the Wolves were still down two nothing.

Remi and Delise stood to go out onto the concourse area and stretch their legs.

"Holy crapsicle," Remi said. "I don't know about the players, but I'm exhausted."

Delise shook her head. "You were playing that whole game with Jase."

Remi frowned. She had been caught up in it. It was exciting—but scary. Thrilling—but stressful.

"Oh my god." Remi clutched Delise's arm

"What?"

"Look over there. It's Brianne Haskett."

"Who? Oh, yeah. I see her. Rumor has it she's going to model for Victoria's Secret."

Remi's stomach plunged to her toes. "Really? It figures."

"Why?" Delise looked at her, eyebrows lifted.

"She's Jase's ex-girlfriend."

Delise's eyebrows flew higher. "Wow."

"I know. Don't say it. What the hell's he doing with me, right? I told you, he's just being nice to me."

"I wasn't going to say that. Geez Remi, give yourself some credit. You're gorgeous too."

Remi tipped her head to one side and smiled at her friend. "I love you. I wonder what she's doing here."

Delise gave a crooked smile. "Cheering on her ex? Wonder if she still has feelings for him."

"He dumped her. Could be." She watched Brianne talk to a group of other women, all of them tall, gorgeous, exquisitely groomed and expensively dressed. She sighed. "Let's go back in."

The drama continued to the third period, when the Wolves scored a goal, making it two-one, then they blew one chance after another to tie it up. Remi sat on the edge of her seat the entire period, cheering the team on, earning amused glances from Delise.

And then, along the boards in the corner near the Rangers' net, Jase was scuffling for the puck with another player. First he got it, then the other player stole it, then Jase, and he whirled around to skate around the net and try to get the puck in. So close! The crowd screamed, Remi clutched her hands together— and another Ranger body checked Jase, knocking him to the ice. Hard.

Another Ranger took the puck and raced out of their end with it, leaving Jase laying on the ice, still.

"Mother of pearl." Remi pressed her hands to her mouth, staring at Jase's motionless body. Then he moved and hunched up onto his hands and knees and Remi's stomach lurched when she saw the blood all over the ice beneath him.

The whistle blew and play stopped while the Wolves all came back to surround Jase. A man in khaki pants, T-shirt and runners came out onto the ice, slipping and sliding his way over to Jase, who by that time was on his feet and skating slowly toward the bench, holding his face.

Remi couldn't breathe, her heart thudded so hard in her chest. The arena faded into a blur and a distant buzz of sound as she watched Jase leave, blood pouring from his face. Another player brought his stick and his helmet, which had been knocked off him.

She looked wide-eyed at Delise. "Oh my damn. I hope he's okay."

A small crease marked between Delise's brows and she set a hand on Remi's arm and squeezed. "He was walking and talking. He'll be fine. It's not like they carried him out on a stretcher."

"Oh god." He was gone now and she had no idea what had happened to him or if he was okay.

The rest of the game was a blur. The Wolves didn't manage to score another goal, ending the game with a loss, but the exciting fun had gone for Remi. When the buzzer ended the game, she and Delise made their way out of the arena, buffeted by the large Wolves' crowd.

"Okay," Delise said. "Where should we go for dinner?"

"Oh." Remi took a breath of the crisp late afternoon air, standing on Grand Avenue. "I don't care."

Delise looked at her sideways and one corner of her mouth deepened. "You okay?"

"Of course! Why?"

"You seem kind of distracted."

"I'm fine. Just wondering how Jase is."

"Uh-huh."

"What does that mean?"

"I thought there was nothing between you."

"There isn't."

"You seem awfully upset about him being hurt. Which is just one more reason why dating a hockey player is a bad idea."

Remi tightened her lips. She knew it was a bad idea. Delise didn't have to keep telling her that.

Delise sighed. "Why don't you just call him?"

They started walking and Remi tucked her big turquoise scarf up higher under her chin against the late afternoon breeze off Lake Michigan. She bit her lip. Should she call him?

"Let's go here." Delise stopped in front of a small Thai restaurant.

They stepped inside and were seated at a small table near the front. They draped their jackets over the back of their chairs and Remi set her cell phone on the table and eyed it between studying the menu.

"Call him."

"I have to give him time to get cleaned up. I'll call him later. After dinner."

Her stomach tight, shoulders tense, she managed to eat half her pad Thai, but she barely tasted it. Focusing on conversation with Delise took her mind off Jase for a while, until they emerged from the restaurant onto the dark street and she remembered with a jolt all the blood and Jase being helped off the ice.

Delise drove her home. "I'm sure he's fine," she said. "Athletes are tough."

Remi made a face and nodded as she got out of the car.

Jasmine sat in the living room watching television, wearing cotton pajamas, her long blonde hair pulled back into a pony tail. "Hey. How was the game?"

"The Wolves lost." Remi unwound her scarf from around her neck. She glanced at Jasmine. Damn. Her puffy eyes and pink nose told her she'd been crying again. "Did you talk to Ethan?"

"Yes." Jasmine sniffled. "He wants me to come back."

"Oh." Remi dropped into an armchair, slip-covered in creamy canvas to match the sofa even though they were ancient and from a different set. "And what did you say?"

"I told him I…I'd think about it." She swiped the back of her hand across her nose. "I love him so much, Remi. I want to go back and try again."

Remi held in her sigh. "Why do you keep going back to him, Jasmine?"

"Because I love him. He swears he wasn't cheating on me."

"And you believe him?"

"Yes."

Remi leaned her head back and looked at the ceiling. "Well, then if you go back, you'll trust him?"

Jasmine bit her lip and tears sparkled in the lamplight. "Maybe."

"Maybe you should think about it before you decide to go back."

"That's what I'm doing. I'm not rushing it."

Remi wished Jasmine would see that her relationship with Ethan wasn't healthy, but she seemed blind to it and got defensive if anyone tried to point that out to her. But maybe taking her time before moving back in with him would give her a chance to think about their things.

The doorbell rang, interrupting her gloomy thoughts. She frowned.

Jasmine sat up straight and put her feet on the floor. "That must be Ethan."

Remi rose and looked at her. "Do you want to see him?"

"Yes. No." Jasmine scrubbed at her cheeks and smoothed her ponytail as Remi went to the door. "I don't know."

Jase walked up to the house, the front window glowing golden through the drawn curtains. In the quiet dark neighborhood, it seemed like a beacon—inviting, homey, welcoming.

He stood on the porch beneath the light and paused.

What the fuck was he doing here?

After the game, the guys were going out and had invited him along. For some reason, going somewhere like Rouge or another hot club with groupies and puck bunnies appealed to him as much as a stick in the eye.

The game had sucked. He'd played like crap, couldn't get anything going and only their goaltender had saved them from getting their asses really kicked.

The face of one person kept floating into his head—Remi. He wanted to see her. He wanted to tell her he could play better than that. He wanted to know what she'd thought of the game. So here he was, like an idiot, standing on her doorstep afraid to ring the bell.

He pushed the doorbell.

He shoved his hands into the pockets of his long coat, still dressed in suit and tie. He hadn't gone home; after the coach had reamed their asses for how they'd played, he'd gotten in his Jeep and driven straight here.

The deadbolt clicked and the door slowly opened.

He smiled at Remi standing there, but her eyes went immediately to his left temple. Oh yeah. He lifted a hand to touch the butterfly tape.

"Hi," he said.

"You're not Ethan."

"Uh…no. No, I'm not." Ethan? Who the hell was Ethan? "Did I come at a bad time?"

"Ethan…" A young girl with puffy red eyes and a pink nose appeared in the French doors to the living room. "Oh." Her face fell.

Jase looked from Remi to the young girl behind her, looking so much like Remi, but obviously distressed about something. "Hi," he said. "You must be Jasmine."

She frowned. "Yes. Who are you?"

He grinned and stepped forward into the foyer, hand outstretched. "Jase Heller. Nice to meet you."

She shook his hand, sending a confused glance toward her sister.

"Sorry, Jasmine, it's not Ethan," Remi said softly. She closed the door.

"I see that." Jasmine's eyes filled with tears and Jase looked at Remi. She gave him a strained smile.

"Come in," Remi invited, leading the way into the living room. She picked up the remote and turned off the television.

"I was watching that," Jasmine protested.

"No, you weren't," Remi said. "You were crying about Ethan. Maybe you could uh…go to bed?"

Jasmine looked back and forth between the two of them. "Oh. Sure." She disappeared down the hall.

"She's still here?"

"Yes." Remi blew out a breath. "But it sounds like she's moving back in with Ethan." She shook her head.

Should he even take his coat off? "I guess I did come at a bad time."

"Oh, no! It's fine. I just got home, actually. Delise and I went out for dinner after the game."

"How did you enjoy it?"

She stared at him wordlessly.

"Well?"

"It was awful!" she burst out.

"Yeah, we played like crap."

"No, I mean…my god, Jase, that is a brutal sport! Look at you!" She bit her lip and eyed his forehead again.

Disappointment filtered down through his body. Here he'd been thinking she'd be all impressed. Instead, she was horrified. Great.

She was a teacher, he reminded himself. He'd gotten past that fact enough to ask her out for dinner the other night after getting to know her and how she treated the kids in her class, but still…she was intelligent, educated. She probably thought hockey was a bunch of goons beating each other up, chasing a stupid little puck around the ice. It was true—he played a game for a living. How could he ever hope to impress her with that?

"I'm fine. It's just a little cut."

"You were bleeding."

"Yup. That happens when I get cut." He grinned again, holding his arms out at his sides. "I'm tough. But if you want to kiss it and make it better, that would probably help."

She didn't move. "I was going to call you. To see if you were okay. And thank you for the tickets."

"Well, then it's good I came over to show you I'm fine." He still stood there in his coat. "And you're welcome."

She rubbed her forehead and let out a short breath. "Okay, good, I'm glad you're okay. Let me take your coat."

He smiled as he shrugged out of it, ignoring the twinge in his shoulder from the hard check he'd taken from Sanders in the third. Probably not good if she knew about that additional minor injury. She disappeared to hang his coat up, then came back, rubbing her palms over her jeans. "Would you like a drink? Beer?"

"Um. Sure, a beer would be nice." He followed her to the kitchen. "Some of the guys were going out after, but I…didn't feel like it."

"Because you lost?"

"Well. Yeah." He was bummed about that for sure. "We haven't done as well as we should have this season and playoffs are almost here. If we don't win our next few games, we might not make the playoffs."

Drowning his sorrows at a rocking club like Rouge again would probably have been a better way to take his mind off the shitty game he'd just played than sitting here in Remi's house. But this was the place he wanted to be.

"Oh." She handed him a beer and kept one for herself. "I guess that's bad."

"Hell, yeah." He sighed as they walked back to the living room and took a seat, side by side. She curled one leg under her. Damn, she looked good in jeans. He wished he could have seen her at the game. "That's bad. That's what it's all about. Making the play offs. The Stanley Cup."

She nodded, eyes soft and warm. "Want to talk about it?"

He did. So he talked. And she listened. She was a great listener and seemed to get his drive, that dark need inside him to fight to the end for the win. Not literally fight. Well, sometimes he did, but it was more a powerful need to battle through and come out on top. Some of her questions amused him, but it felt good to talk about how crappy he felt, how he was letting the team down, how the team was letting down the coach and the owners and the fans—especially the fans.

"So if you win your next three games, you're in?"

"Only if New York loses." He grimaced. "We needed those two points against them. That's how close it is. Dammit. We should have been way ahead at this stage of the season. Ah, well."

"You put a lot of pressure on yourself, don't you."

He considered that. "Yeah. I guess."

"But you aren't responsible for the whole team."

"I'm a part of the team. We're all responsible for how the team does."

"And you hate it when you don't play well."

"Of course I hate it!" He shook his head, the image of his high school English teacher Ms Wong flashing into his head, the damning message she'd beaten into him through that junior year. "I have to be good."

She nodded and he wanted to tell her more, but the stuff backing up in his brain was some kind of stinging shit and talking about it wasn't easy. Which was why he didn't. Ever.

"When's your next game?"

"Tuesday night."

"Oh."

"I'll still be there Wednesday for the reading program," he said. "Don't worry."

She nodded.

"Then we go to New York and Boston." He paused, then the craziest thing came out of his mouth. "You should meet me in Boston."

Her eyes popped open. "What?"

"Yeah. The game's Saturday night. We could go out after. We have a day off Sunday."

"I can't do that!"

"Why not?"

"I…I…just can't. That's crazy."

He shrugged and picked up a strand of her golden hair, rubbing it between thumb and fingers. "It's not crazy. It'd be fun."

She shook her head. "I am so out my league with you. I don't have money for stuff like that, Jase, and I—"

"I'll pay for it," he interrupted. Christ, what kind of scum did she think he was, that he'd invite her like that and not pay for it? "I wouldn't ask you if I wasn't going to pay your airfare and you can stay with me."

"Oh." She nibbled her bottom lip. "That's nice of you, but I can't let you do that. And that's not the only reason. I can't just take off like that."

"Why not?" He lifted his chin. "Why can't you go away for a weekend?"

"Because…because…I just don't do things like that."

"I thought you wanted to have fun? Break loose. Living on your own."

She grimaced. "As you can see, I'm not on my own right now."

"Your sister is an adult."

Her brow furrowed and the lip-nibble continued. "I know. But going on a trip…that's big. I…hardly know you."

"It's just fun, Remi. Right?"

"Yes." Regret shadowed her eyes. "But I can't. You need to go and focus on your game, anyway. It's probably better if I don't come."

He sighed. She was probably right. He didn't know why he'd suggested it. Nobody brought girls on a road trip It was kinda crazy and he'd be busy practicing, then playing. Boston was an in and out game, not really a weekend.

"Yeah. You're right." He tipped his beer and finished it. "I guess I should go." He set his empty bottle on the coffee table and leaned forward for a kiss. He'd wanted to touch her since he walked in the door, slide his hands into that silky hair, feel her peachy-soft skin, get his hands under that black turtleneck sweater, find out if she was wearing black lace underwear again.

Christ, it seemed like ages since they'd slept together. He'd been thinking about her for the last few weeks non-stop. When he'd seen her at the school that first day, standing there all cute and little and big eyes full of apprehension, he'd been happily surprised. When he'd found out she was a teacher, that had just about put an end to the strange attraction he felt for her. But his impulsive invitation out for dinner hadn't turned out so bad. She hadn't made him feel stupid or lacking.

Even tonight. Although she'd been dismayed by the rough game and his little wound, she'd listened to him talk about the game and hadn't made him feel stupid. She'd made him feel good.

He needed more of that. He needed to be with her. Bad. And now her sister was down the goddamn hall.

Frustration rose in him as his mouth covered hers and he fought to restrain the lust that made him want to toss her down on the couch cushions and fuck her brains out.

She tasted sweet and warm, her small tongue meeting and playing with his in a long, drugging kiss that had his head spinning even more than the painkillers they'd given him earlier. He put a hand on her cheek, so tiny and soft, and held her face while they kissed and kissed again.

He wanted to growl. A small noise did come from deep in his throat. He coughed and drew back. "I guess I'll see you Wednesday, then. At school."

She nodded, mouth full and soft, eyes so turquoise blue and clear he wanted to fall into them and drown in them.

"We'll go out for dinner after."

She tipped her head to one side and sent him a slow, so sexy smile. "Okay. Dinner, I can do."

"It *is* a school night," he teased.

She laughed. "Yes, it is."

"And I might end up dragging you back to my place after."

Her eyes darkened to teal blue and she lowered her chin. "Promise?"

His dick hardened. He could have groaned. "Hell, Remi." He glanced through the French doors, and she caught his look and laid her palm on his cheek.

"I know," she whispered. "Wednesday."

He stood and let her get his coat, and then he picked her up and kissed her again at the door, lifting her feet right off the floor so he could fit her to his body. She wound her arms around his neck and kissed him back and his dick surged and hardened even more. "Ah, Remi," he groaned against her mouth.

A throat clearing had him lifting his head to see Jasmine standing there, staring at them open mouthed. He let Remi slide down his body to the floor and grinned. "Just leaving," he told Jasmine. "Night, Remi." He brushed one last kiss across her mouth before leaving.

Outside, he left his coat undone, letting it flap open as he strode toward his Jeep. The chilly March night air would hopefully cool down his overheated body. Jesus. A warm feeling of well-being simmered inside him along with frustration. He'd wanted to see her and he had. They'd talked and somehow she'd made him feel less pissed off at himself, somehow she'd made him feel like it was so easy, they'd win their next three games and be on top of the world. He was on top of the world right now as he walked to his Jeep, the nearby streetlight reflecting on chrome and sparkling off the glass, the neighborhood quiet and dark and peaceful. He took a deep breath of cool night air and let it out. She made him feel on top of the world—but he wished he were on top of Remi.

CHAPTER SEVEN

All through dinner Wednesday evening, all Remi could think about was going back to Jase's place and having hot sex with him.

She clenched her thighs together as she ate, drank three glasses of wine to wet her dry mouth and pushed her food around on her plate—fabulous shrimp, but who cared—trying to keep her mind off Jase's body. Naked. Over her. Under her. Inside her. Her pussy clenched hard at that thought and she trembled.

They emerged from the restaurant on Michigan Avenue, a trendy upscale place that apparently wasn't far from Jase's apartment. Jase put his arm around her shoulders and pulled her in close, then bent to kiss her cheek. His mouth felt warm in the cool night.

Then a blinding flash exploded in front of Remi's eyes. She made a small sound and put a hand up. "What was that?"

"Shit."

"Hey, Jase!" a voice called. Remi couldn't even see who was talking to him, blinking at the spots in front of her eyes. "Is this your new girlfriend?"

She shook her head and looked up at Jase. He didn't answer, just smiled grimly and took her arm, hustling her up the sidewalk.

"What's her name?" the voice called from behind them.

"Who is that?" she huffed.

"Reporters."

"Huh?"

"News reporters. Sorry about that, Remi. I had no idea they were out there."

"Uh…" She sucked in oxygen as she practically ran to keep up with his long-legged stride. "What did they want?"

"Pictures. A story."

"About you?"

"Yeah." He laughed and slowed his stride. "I know it's crazy, but sometimes they follow me around."

Holy crapsicle. She hung on to his arm as they walked around the corner and then into the entrance of the high-rise that housed his apartment.

"Stop."

In the elegant lobby, all marble and glass and brass, she planted her feet in her high-heeled boots and didn't move.

"What's wrong?"

She threw out a hand. "This. This is what's wrong. Look at this place. There are reporters following you around. Paparazzi, for god's sake."

"Uh…"

With his lips parted, thick brows drawn down and that butterfly bandage still on his forehead, he looked adorably confused.

"This is just one more reason why I should not be doing this."

"What is? Why? What are you talking about?"

"Your life. It's crazy. It's…I don't even know. This is just so not me, Jase."

He put his hands on her shoulders, heavy and warm even through her coat. "Remi. It's not that big a deal. I just rent this apartment. It's close to the arena."

"Phhhhht." She couldn't even guess how much an apartment like this cost, but it was probably close to her whole month's pay check.

"And the reporters…well…you get used to it. It's kinda cool. They don't stalk me like I'm Britney Spears or anything. Just once in a while."

She shook her head. Once in a while! She couldn't even imagine that.

"Come on, Remi. Lighten up. It's fun. Right?"

The curve of his lips, the appeal in his dark chocolate eyes, made her soften inside.

"Fun."

"Yeah." He stroked her cheek. "We're just having fun. So some reporters want to take our picture? Why not? You're gorgeous."

"No, I'm not." Not like a model. Those must have been some good shots when he'd been dating Brianne. She pictured the two of them stopping and posing for photographers. She sighed. That was so not her. Her stomach quivered inside. Oh, hell.

"You are." He touched her hair. "It's not a big deal, sweetheart. We just ignore them."

"I just feel…like I'm way out of my depth here."

"That's 'cause you're so short." He grinned and swung her up in his arms. She squealed and grabbed for him. "Even in those hawt do-me boots with killer heels."

He carried her across the floor to the elevators.

"Put me down!" she begged, her words and Jase's footsteps echoing in the lobby. "Seriously, Jase!"

His smile faded when he saw the look on her face and he halted and let her slide down his body until her feet touched the floor.

"I can't do this." She pushed away from him. She took a couple of steps back, clutching her purse to her chest. "Paparazzi, for god's sake." She shook her head, her chest tight with disappointment. This was insane. She could not go around having photographers stalking her and taking her picture. She peeked up at Jase through her eyelashes, her eyes prickling a little. "Could you take me home?"

He stood there gazing at her. "I don't want to." He shoved a hand into his hair.

And she didn't want to go. They'd been having so much fun and she'd been all warm and tingly and looking forward to…oh, hell. She turned away from the look in his eyes. This was so not her world. Her lips wanted to pout with regret and she dragged in a long shaky breath. She waited.

Finally, with a noise of frustration, he stabbed the button of the elevator. "Fine," he muttered. "I'll drive you home." With hunched shoulders, he stood there, waiting for the elevator car to arrive. Then they got in, the doors slid closed and dense silence surrounded them. Her eyes burning even more, her throat tight,

Remi looked down at the pointy toes of her boots and licked her lips.

"I'm sorry," she choked out when the doors opened onto the parking garage.

He gave a jerky nod and strode toward his vehicle, his long legs leaving her behind. She hurried after him, her high-heeled boots clicking on the concrete floor.

"So," he said after they'd climbed in and he'd started the vehicle. He clenched the steering wheel. "What does this mean?"

"I…I don't know."

"'Cause I can't control the media." He stared straight ahead. "We can try to avoid them, but they're always going to be there."

"I know."

"They're really not that bad, Remi. If we hadn't won the Stanley Cup two years ago, most people in this city wouldn't even know who I am."

She nodded and, with a sigh, he put the Jeep in gear and backed out of the parking spot. He drove through the cavernous concrete parking structure, used a card to exit and pulled out onto the street.

She didn't know what to say. Her stomach felt all tight and achy. The drive to her place was silent.

He walked her to her door and paused. "We're off to New York tomorrow. Back Sunday. I'll call you when I'm back"

She watched him walk back to his Jeep through a blur of tears.

"Is this you?"

Jennifer walked into Remi's classroom during lunch period the next day, holding the newspaper.

Remi looked up from her sandwich and the spelling tests she was marking. "Is what me?"

"This." Jennifer held out the newspaper and showed Remi the photograph.

Remi's heart lurched. "Oh. My. Damn."

The photograph was of her and Jase leaving the restaurant, Jase's arm slung around her shoulders pulling her in for a hug, both of them smiling at each other. The caption read "Is one of Chicago's most eligible bachelors off the market already?"

Remi stared at the photo, her breath stuck in her throat, the sandwich in her hand forgotten.

"Are you dating Jase Heller?" Jennifer asked.

"Um…" Jennifer was her boss. Was this going to cause a problem? "Not really. We've gone out a couple of times." Was she supposed to tell Jennifer they were just having fun? Hot, sexy, no strings-attached fun?

"Well." Jennifer grinned. "It's a nice picture."

Remi grimaced. Actually, it was a good picture. She looked kind of pretty, cheeks flushed, smiling at Jase, and of course Jase always looked good. Except the looks on their faces had an air of…intimacy. Like they were in love or something.

Ha. In lust was more like it.

She had to read the article, which to her dismay talked a lot about Jase and Brianne and how'd they only recently broke up—how recently?—and how they'd been such a stunning, elite Chicago couple, rich, beautiful, talented. Although what kind of talent did it take to be a model? Then Remi frowned at her own snarky thoughts.

She buried her face in her hands. Once again, this was just another sign that she was in a world she had no business being in. She might as well have landed on another planet and started hanging out with space aliens for all the familiarity she had with paparazzi, publicity, money and models.

Only every other teacher on staff at Abraham Lincoln Middle School saw the newspaper that day and remarked on the photograph to Remi. By the end of the day she was shaking her head. What the hell had she'd gotten herself into by hooking up with a famous superstar hockey player?

Then came the phone calls from not only Jasmine, who'd moved back in with Ethan, but from Kyle, good lord, away at Illinois State, who'd somehow come across the photo on the internet.

"Don't worry," she assured each of them in turn. "I've only seen him a few times, it's not serious."

And then came the calls from Emily, Sarah and Delise. They arranged to all get together for pizza at Remi's place on Saturday night. "I'll tell you all about it then," she told them.

Jase's cell phone rang with the Sexy Chick ring tone that—dammit—he'd forgotten again to change. Brianne. Shit. He tossed down the clothes he was packing for the road trip.

He debated ignoring it, but then flipped open the phone to talk.

"Who's the girl, Jase?" Brianne demanded immediately.

"What girl?"

"Didn't you see the paper today?"

"Uh…no."

"Nice picture of you two. Isn't she the one you were with at Rouge that night? Didn't take you long to find someone else. I guess it *was* me, huh?" She reminded him of his lame line when he'd broken up with her, telling her it wasn't her, it was him.

There must be a picture of him and Remi taken last night. "Brianne." He closed his eyes. He so did not want to have this conversation. "I told you the truth. I met her after we broke up and it's…it's nothing serious. We're just going out, having fun."

"Right. You bastard." And she hung up on him.

Shit. He tipped his head back and gazed up at the ceiling of his apartment.

Then he called Remi. "Hi, Remi."

"Now what?"

He frowned at the exasperated greeting.

"I gather you saw the paper today?"

"Oh, hell yeah."

Her tone told him that nothing about that made her happy.

"I'm sorry."

"It's not your fault," she replied and he heard a sigh. "You are who you are."

"Is it at least a good picture?" He smiled hopefully.

"Actually it is. But I'm not used to having my picture all over the newspaper. Thank god they don't know my name."

"That won't take them long."

He heard her groan. "I think I heard from everyone I know in Chicago about the picture. And some people not even in Chicago."

"Ah. I'm sorry if it put you in a bad spot. But it's really no big deal."

"Again, not to you."

"I gotta go," he said regretfully. "I have to finish packing and get to the airport. I'll talk to you next week, okay?"

"Okay."

"Oh Remi, he's so hot!" Emily said, looking at the newspaper photo.

"He is," Sarah said, looking over Emily's shoulder. "Very hot. Very…big."

"And don't tell me he's just being nice to you because of the reading program," Delise said in a dry tone. "With that look on his face, he's not just being nice to you."

Emily was intrigued by the paparazzi story. "Like, how many paparazzi were there?"

"I don't know how many there were. It felt like a hundred."

"Really. Wow. He's that famous?"

Remi shrugged. "Apparently." None of them being big hockey fans meant they were clueless.

"I still say pro athletes are trouble," Delise put in.

"She's just jealous." Sarah shot Delise a mischievous look.

"No, I'm not!" Delise paused with a piece of pizza half-way to her mouth. "Okay, maybe a little. I totally get the appeal after going to that game. Those guys are insanely fit and the testosterone level in that building was sky high. Also, Jase is cute. But I still don't think pro athletes are really upstanding guys."

"How can you say that!" Remi shook her head, thinking of the work Jase had done with the kids at school. Oh hell. She was defending him.

"Well, a lot of them don't exactly have good track records. Wives beating them with golf clubs for cheating on them.

Getting accused of rape or abusing their wife. Taking performance enhancing drugs. Or other illicit drugs."

Remi sank her teeth into her bottom lip. "Yeah. Uh…well, that's true." There had been some stories in the news lately. "But they can't all be like that. Anyway, having people stalk you like that is kind of scary." She thought back. It really had frightened her. She couldn't imagine that happening if she'd been out alone. Not that it would, since she was nobody, but at least with Jase there she'd felt somewhat protected.

"Oh." Delise regarded her with sympathy. "That's not good."

"No." She shook her head. "So it's probably not a good idea to see him again."

Delise nodded slowly. "So what should we do? Hit a club tonight?"

Remembering the last time she'd done that and had met Jase didn't make Remi feel much like hitting a club, but she went along with her friends, mostly to keep busy and to keep from thinking about Jase.

After the four day, two game road trip, Jase wanted to go home and crash. But he had business stuff to attend to, laundry to do and oh, yeah, call Remi.

He wasn't sure if he was angry or disappointed about what had happened last week after those damn photographers had descended on them. Sure he was disappointed, because he and Remi had been on their way up to his apartment for what he was sure was going to be some really hot sex. But he was angry too, angry at the paps for screwing up his night, but also annoyed at Remi for letting it get to her. It really wasn't that big a deal, especially if you compared him to big movie stars. Half the time they'd followed him, he'd been pretty sure they were more interested in pictures of Brianne than of him.

Which reminded him—she'd left another message on his voice mail. Why, when she knew he was seeing someone else, he had no goddamn clue. He really needed to call her and have a little chat.

He sat on his couch and held his cell phone in his hand. Jesus. He had to call two women and there was nothing good about either of those calls. He hated having to tell Brianne to get lost, but really, she needed to get over it and get on with her life. And he was afraid to call Remi because he had a rock-like feeling in his gut that *she* was going to tell *him* to get lost.

Which kinda didn't make sense, given the reason he'd broken up with Brianne was because she was getting way too serious. And here he was all freaked out because Remi didn't want anything to do with him.

Get it over with, dude.

So he called Brianne first. Amazingly, he got through to her. He'd thought maybe she'd be on a photo shoot or something.

"Jase!" she answered breathlessly. "Hi!"

She sounded so damn happy to hear from him. He closed his eyes.

"Hey," he said. "How are you?"

"I'm okay. I'm so glad you called!"

"Uh, yeah. Listen. You gotta stop calling me, Brianne."

Silence.

"I'm sorry."

"I miss you so much." Shit. She sounded like she was going to cry. "Please, Jase. Can't we just sit down and talk?"

"We did that already," he reminded her. And hadn't that been fun. "I'm sorry, Brianne."

"I don't understand! How could you find someone else already? You were seeing her before you broke up with me, weren't you?"

"No! Christ, no." But it *was* true that it hadn't taken him long to meet someone. He'd never intended for that to happen, he'd been looking forward to being single and free, and he sure hadn't anticipated getting tangled up with someone else that fast.

"Never mind," she snapped. "Damn you, Jase."

And she hung up.

He tapped the screen to end the call. Yeah, that had gone well.

On to the next call. Of course Remi was at school. He glanced at his watch. It should be her lunch time, so he might catch her. And he did.

"Hi," she said, not sounded nearly as enthused to hear from him as Brianne had. Dammit.

They made the usual small talk and then he said, "Can I see you tonight?"

She sighed. "I don't think so, Jase. This isn't really going to work."

Well, he'd seen that coming. He leaned back into his couch. He wasn't going to be like Brianne, all heartbroken and chasing after her. He had some pride. With his insides burning, eyes closed, he said, "I figured you'd say that. Okay." He paused, not sure what else to day. "I guess I'll see you tomorrow. At school."

"Yes."

"Okay. Bye, Remi."

And again he ended the call. Then he threw his phone, hard, across the room.

It wasn't that easy. Despite her conviction that they were from different worlds and her resolve that they shouldn't see each other again, when he showed up at school on Wednesday, looking all big and handsome and—dammit—a little sad, she went all soft and warm and shaky inside. She couldn't take her eyes off him as he worked with the kids, and more than once their glances collided, then skittered away.

When most of the kids had left and Ryan as usual hung back to talk about hockey, Jase quietly said, "Here." And he slipped Ryan an envelope. Remi frowned.

Ryan opened it and peered inside, then looked up at Jase open-mouthed. "Are these tickets to one of your games?"

"Yeah. There's three. For your mom and your brother too."

A huge smile broke out on Ryan's face. "Holy…I mean, wow. Thank you! I can't believe this! I've never been to a real live hockey game!"

Jase grinned and Ryan dashed out, no doubt excited to get home and share the news.

Remi's heart tilted and warmth curled inside her. She smiled, but shook her head as their eyes met, alone now in the classroom.

"All the other kids are going to be upset that they didn't get tickets."

His eyebrows drew down. "Damn. I didn't think of that. I just thought...he's been doing so well and when he said they couldn't afford to go to a game..." He shook his head. "Shit. Sometimes I don't think things through."

Her throat got a little tight.

"Remi."

He walked toward her, then stood there, gazing at her. "The paparazzi are really not that big a deal."

"It scared me." Although now that she'd had some time to digest it and put in perspective, it actually didn't seem so bad.

He went to a crouch in front of her where she sat, frowning, and took her hands. "Scared you?"

"Yes." She swallowed. "I'm just not used to that."

"They wouldn't hurt you."

"Remember Princess Diana?"

His eyebrows flew up. "Jesus. I'm hardly in the same class as Princess Diana. They don't chase me around like that."

She blew out a breath. "I know." She paused. "Once again, Jase, that just showed that I'm not the right kind of girl for you. I don't live in that kind of world."

"Are you fucking kidding me?" He stared at her. "That doesn't matter. You're smart and beautiful. I'm the one scared spitless of you. Your brains and education."

Her heart tightened painfully. "What?" Was that true? She gazed back at him searchingly.

He dropped his gaze and shook his head. "Never mind."

She touched her hand to his cheek, rough with beard stubble. "Oh, Jase."

He looked at her hopefully. "So can we go out again?"

She surrendered to it. To the feelings swelling inside her, big and soft and warm. To him and his boyish charm.

"Saturday. We'll go do something fun." His mouth curved appealingly. "Just fun. Right?"

She sighed. "Okay."

"Dress warm." Jase had just arrived at her place Saturday afternoon for their date.

"Where are we going?"

"Navy Pier."

"Navy Pier! I haven't been there in years!"

"I've only been there once. It was fun."

"Okay. Sounds crazy, but okay."

"You should know by now, I am crazy. I'm all about the fun, baby."

She laughed. "Let me go put on another sweater."

She returned to her bedroom and exchanged the long-sleeved sheer top she wore for a black turtleneck sweater. She eyed Jase when she returned to the living room. Instead of his usual leather jacket, he wore a ski jacket with a fleece lining, so she chose her black puffer jacket and looped a long black and grey scarf around her neck. She pushed aside her black high-heeled boots and pulled out her sheepskin lined Ugg boots. Then she peered into her purse to make sure she had gloves.

"It's going to be freezing there," she warned him as she locked the door behind them.

"Bah. It's April."

"It's fifty-seven degrees!"

"That's balmy! Wait 'til you come to Winnipeg in January."

Like that was going to happen. Her heart beat a little faster. Intense curiosity to see where Jase had grown up flickered inside her.

They wandered around Navy Pier, surprisingly busy. It was a relatively mild April day. Probably lots of tourists were out. Jase bought her popcorn and they looked in the little shops at jewelry and souvenirs. Then he spotted the shop where you could build your own bear. "Hey," he said, dragging her inside. "I want to build a bear for you."

Okay, he *was* crazy. Laughing, Remi followed him into the store, full of little girls and their mothers. All eyes landed on Jase—big, tall, gorgeous and decidedly out of place. Warmth seeped through Remi and heated her cheeks, but she had to smile.

She selected a furry brown bear, then they had to record a message.

"Remi is 'beary' beautiful," Jase said into the small device, looking at her. She laughed again. The recording was tucked inside. They stuffed the bear, fluffed the bear and then had to dress the bear.

"Oh, no question." Jase surveyed the choices. He reached for a tiny Chicago Wolves uniform. "Has to be this."

Smiling, touched and charmed, Remi nodded. "Of course." And her bear was dressed in the hockey uniform including a tiny stick.

She hugged the bear to her as Jase paid for it and they wandered back outside.

"I know," Jase said. "We have to ride the Ferris wheel."

It was late afternoon by this point.

Remi eyed the huge structure with its gazillion spokes and lights. "I don't know…"

"Come on, Remi." Once again he gripped her hand and tugged her along. She had to almost run to keep up with his long strides toward the Ferris wheel.

They had a gondola all to themselves. Remi gripped the side tightly, closing her eyes as they began to ascend, Navy Pier dropping away beneath them.

"Hey," Jase said softly. "Open your eyes. The view is awesome."

She pressed her lips together, her skin crawling, stomach jumping, but she opened her eyes.

"Are you afraid?" Jase asked, shifting closer to her.

"Um…yes. A little."

He put his arm around her and tucked her close to him.

"There's nothing to be afraid of."

She made a little choked noise. "Oh, no, not at all. We're just…how far off the ground?"

"About a hundred and fifty feet, I think." He calmly gazed around. "Look! Doesn't the skyline look amazing?"

The sun was low in the sky and the buildings of downtown Chicago all gleamed like, tall, slender, silver cubes and cylinders on one side, the lake stretching out endless and blue on the other.

"Yes," she said softly. "It is beautiful." She snuggled into his warmth. The wind up here carried a crisp bite and her cheeks and nose began to sting a bit.

She looked at Jase, his handsome cheekbones reddened from the cold, eyes taking in the view, smiling. She clutched her bear in his Wolves uniform to her and suddenly her throat tightened. God, she liked this guy. So much.

He turned to look down at her, snuggled under his arm, and his smile deepened. "See? It's fine."

They swung over the top and began to descend and her stomach flipped over. "Mmm. Fine."

He laughed. The yellow, red and blue canopy of the merry go round grew larger as they lowered, and then they were swinging back up again. She drew in a deep breath.

"What's that?" Jase pointed. She identified various landmarks to him and by the time they slowed and stopped, she'd almost forgotten she was nervous. At the very top, the gondola swaying gently, Jase tipped her chin up with one gloved hand and kissed her.

His nose was cold brushing her cheek, but his mouth was warm on hers, delicious and ardent. He drew back, rested his gloved hand on her cheek and their eyes met and held, the world spread below them, and time came to a halt. His dark eyes flashed, his lids lowered and they kissed again and she pressed closer to him. He hauled her closer, up onto his lap and the gondola swayed. Remi let out a little shriek, her stomach clutched and she dug her fingers into his jacket. Jase laughed softly and they started moving again. Remi grabbed tighter with a start, making him laugh again.

"Let's go find some dinner," he said after they'd disembarked from the Ferris wheel. She wanted to fall to her knees and kiss the ground, but instead held her bear tightly. "How about that Billy Goat Tavern?"

She smiled. "Touristy, but okay."

"Come on, I'm new in town."

They walked into the lively restaurant.

"What's the biggest burger you have?" Jase asked the server.

"That would be the triple hamburger."

"Okay, I'll have that."

Remi grinned behind her menu. He could probably eat two, the size he was. She ordered a hamburger. Jase sat her bear on the table, propping him up against the wall, making her laugh again. God, she hadn't laughed so much in…okay, ever.

They'd just finished a dinner full of talk and laughter, teasing and flirting, when three women appeared beside their table. "Jase Heller!" one of them said with a big smile. "Can we get your autograph?"

"Uh…" Hell, he did not want to do this, but he was never rude to the fans. "Sure." He cast an apologetic glance across the table at Remi.

"Here." The woman dug in her purse and pulled out a pen. "I don't have anything for you to sign, so you can do it right here." And she pulled down her low cut top so Jase could sign her chest, just above her left breast.

He gulped and tightened his jaw as he tried to sign without really touching her. It probably was no accident when she moved and her breast brushed against his arm.

"I saw you play against the Bruins last week," one of the other women said, stepping up for her autograph. In the same place. "You got two goals."

"Um, yeah." He signed again and turned to the third woman, and when he'd finished signing her chest, she took the pen from him, took his hand, turned it palm up and wrote a phone number on it. Jesus.

"I love watching you play," she purred, making intense eye contact, making her words sound dirty.

Jase swallowed, forced a smile and shot Remi a look. She sat there, stone-faced, mouth tight, hands clasped around her drink. She lifted one eyebrow at him.

The three women seemed in no hurry to leave.

"Can we get pictures with you?"

They pulled out their phones and took turns taking pictures. Then they paused and looked at Remi, as if they'd just noticed her. "Could you take one of all of us?"

Christ. "Sorry, ladies, but that's all I can do. My girlfriend and I are just finishing dinner."

The three women shot baleful looks at Remi and finally left.

"Sorry," he muttered, reaching across the table for her hand. "That never happens."

"Really."

She didn't sound convinced.

"Well, it happens sometimes. I'm sorry, Remi."

"Don't apologize. It's not your fault." But she looked pissed. "And I'm not your girlfriend."

"I had to get rid of them somehow. Let's go." He rose from the table and held out a hand to help her up. They emerged from the restaurant to a flash bursting in front of their eyes.

Oh, no. Not again.

CHAPTER EIGHT

"It's okay." Jase turned her from the photographers. He muttered under his breath. Jesus. What were they doing hanging around Navy Pier, for God's sake? He never would have anticipated they'd be there, looking for someone to photograph. And Remi was already annoyed. "I guess we're done here." Damn. They'd been having such a great day.

"Yeah. I guess."

He shot her a sideways glance, walking down the sidewalk, holding her hand, remembering the last time he'd tried to take her back to his place. "Will you come home with me?"

She stopped. They faced each other. She looked so pretty with that big scarf wrapped around her neck. "Will the paparazzi follow us there?"

"I don't know." He glanced over his shoulder. They seemed to have dispersed. "I don't think so."

"Will you wash that phone number off your hand?"

After a blink of his eyes, he burst out laughing. "Yes."

She inhaled a long slow breath, then nodded and relief slid through him. "Okay."

The elevator pinged and the doors slid silently open. They stepped in and he punched a button for his floor, then as the doors closed, he lifted her against him, effortlessly, and kissed her.

If she'd been standing, her legs likely would have given out, it was such a turn-on to be held aloft like that, against his chest, his mouth hot and hungry on hers. His strength turned her on. His mouth turned her on. His everything turned her on.

They kissed like that, wet, sliding, open-mouthed kisses until the elevator opened onto his floor and he carried her down the carpeted hall to his door. Only then did he gently lower her feet to the floor and she leaned against the wall, panting, while he unlocked the door.

He shoved the door open and they practically fell into the foyer, grabbing for each other, frantic, hot, hungry.

"It's been so long," he panted.

"I know."

He unwrapped her scarf, shoved her jacket down over her shoulders and she wrestled out of it as he got rid of his jacket, tossing it into a pile on the floor. Then he picked her up again, this time straddling him, and she wrapped her legs around his waist as he walked to the bedroom.

She caught a glimpse of his apartment—stunning and modern with a wall of windows overlooking the glittering Chicago skyline, a couple of pieces of black leather furniture and a big screen television—before it disappeared from view as he strode into the bedroom. Dark. Shadowy.

He carried her over to the bed and stood there kissing her, hands beneath her ass. She tightened her legs on him and kissed him back, threading her fingers through his soft dark hair.

Their mouths devoured each other over and over in hot hungry kisses. She needed more. She arched against him, bumping her center into his stomach. He groaned. He shifted her higher. She wrapped her arms around his head while he nuzzled at her breast, but damn, there were too many clothes in the way, her sweater and bra. She let go of his head and reached for the hem of the sweater and he clutched her tighter, shifting his feet to balance better as she straightened and tugged the sweater off over her head.

He made an appreciative noise in his throat as he looked down at her chest. "Very nice."

She remembered that he'd liked black lace, this one very sheer and edged with velvet. Breathless, she looked down at his head as he bent and pressed a hot kiss to her chest between the curves of her breasts. Her heart thudded madly.

"So sweet," he murmured. Then he tipped her back. She squealed and clutched onto him tightly with both arms and legs and he laughed, holding her suspended over the bed.

"Jase!"

He held her like that for a moment, just looking at her, then dropped her to the bed. She gave a tiny bounce and he reached for the lamp beside the bed, a warm glow spreading instantly around them.

He lifted one of her feet and tugged off the sheepskin lined boot, then did the other. Then his fingers went to the button and zipper of her jeans. "Let's get these off." He drew them down over her legs. "Oh yeah, that's pretty." He gazed at her matching panties, sheer black lace and velvet too, and she lay there clad in black lace and nothing else.

He laid his big palms on her thighs. She quivered at his warm touch, her body heating under his attentive gaze as he studied her laying there sideways on his bed.

Which was wide enough to sleep on sideways. The bed was huge, but she supposed a man the size of Jase needed a king-size bed.

"Next time I'll wear white lace."

He grinned. "I like black, but you could wear anything and it'd be hot."

Her nipples tingled and tightened beneath the lace, her breasts swelling and aching. Boldly, she slid a hand down her tummy and cupped her pussy, hot and damp and pulsing.

"Damn." His eyes darkened and he yanked his long-sleeved T-shirt over his head. He quickly got rid of his clothes and fell to the bed beside her, rolling her beneath him, mouth on her again, ravishing and warm and delicious.

He kissed the side of her neck, sending sweet shivers over her body, rolled again so she lay top of him and laid a firm tap on her butt. The sting sent a wave of heat over her and her pussy wept.

She moaned again.

He patted her again with a sharp caress, one cheek then the other.

She hid her hot face against him and his hands gentled on her ass, stroking up and down, fingers trailing along the sensitive crease where cheek met thigh. Then he pushed aside the narrow band of fabric that sat over the crease between her cheeks and stroked there too, up then lower, where he found her wet center.

"Remi, God. You're so wet." He stroked there with his broad fingertips, over her pussy lips, between, then probing deeper inside her. She felt the slickness, and muscles clenched around his fingers. Her clit quivered, her breath suspended. "I love how wet you are. How hot you are." And he withdrew his fingers to lay several more stinging little slaps on her ass.

God, that just turned her body liquid, flames of pleasure licking from his touch over her skin, burning her up. She'd never been with a man who'd known she wanted that, needed that. Even last time, he'd been so afraid of hurting her he hadn't really let loose.

"I love that," she gasped, and then he shocked her even more by tangling his fingers into her hair and tugging her head up. The pull on her scalp tingled and sharp and hot sensations sizzled from her head to the base of her spine. "Oh, god."

"That too?" He held her head and gazed into her eyes. She looked deeply and saw what she needed to see—not hesitation or doubt, but caring and a desire to please her.

"Yes," she moaned. "That too." She licked her lips. His fingers tightened and he tugged her head back even further, arching her back so her breasts thrust out. He lifted up—abs of steel, that man—and kissed each curve, then licked and sucked gently on her sensitive flesh. "Like the black lace," he muttered, releasing her hair to reach for the clasp of her bra. "But I wanna see your nipples. Want to taste them." He flicked it open and she sat up, straddling his hips, and let it fall off her shoulders. She sat, fingertips on those eight-pack abs. His gaze wandered over her, eyes warm with admiration. Her breasts tightened, nipples throbbing, aching to be touched.

And then he did, cupping them, brushing his thumbs across the tight tips, and she let her head fall back, let her breasts fill his palms. Ripples of exquisite pleasure stroked over her, centering between her legs.

"So pretty," he murmured, her sensitive nipples leaping to his touch, needing more. Again as if he knew her body, he grasped them between thumb and forefinger and gave a firm nip.

She cried out, arched more, flames shooting from breast to womb, and he did it again and again until her nipples were hot points of sensation. "Oh, Remi."

His hands went to her waist and he lifted her—actually lifted her—off him, his big hands spanning her narrow hips. He set her on the bed, then moved over her, dragging her panties down over her thighs. She bent her legs so he could pull them off over calves, then feet, then tossed the panties behind him.

Jase stroked his hands down over her calves, her ankles, her feet, sending warm shivers over her, then back up and between her knees and he parted her legs. He kneeled before her and she bit her lip as she studied him through heavy-lidded eyes. His torso was sculpted of gleaming bronze skin and hard muscles, broad rounded muscles over his shoulders, slabs of muscles on his chest and ripped abs. Only a dusting of hair darkened between his pecs and arrowed down toward the thick nest of hair between his legs, where his cock jutted, enormous, dark and beautiful.

He was beautiful.

His lips parted as he gently pushed her thighs wider and her teeth sank deeper into her bottom lip as he studied her. She wanted to squirm, heat cascading over her body, wanted to close her eyes against the intensity of his gaze, but she kept them open.

His fingers hard on her thighs, his hands large enough to almost close right around them, he licked his lips, then bent his head and pressed a kiss to the fluff of blonde hair on her mound. "Sweet," he whispered. He kissed his way to one side, his mouth warm on the flesh of her groin, his breath like a feather, tickling, tormenting. He pressed his nose there and inhaled deeply and she melted into the bed.

"You smell so good." He licked her. "You taste so good."

She quivered and throbbed for more, but let him take his time. He played and touched and explored with big broad fingertips, assertive yet gentle, and with his eyes, hot and avid. When he slid one finger inside her, she arched off the bed and fisted her hands into the bedspread.

"So tight," he whispered. "So tight and hot. You have the prettiest pussy, Remi. So tiny and smooth and pretty."

He laid a firm, closed mouth kiss right over her clit. She quivered. Pulsed. Ached.

And then he tasted her. His tongue swiped up in a long, luxurious lick, up one side of her slit, then the other. He nibbled and sucked at her pussy lips, gently drawing her sensitive flesh into his mouth. She writhed beneath him, eyes now tightly closed, everything centered on the sensation between her legs. She had never experienced oral sex like this. He worshipped her with his mouth, with lips and tongue and teeth, as if he couldn't get enough of her, as if he wanted to eat her alive, breathe her in.

And then he closed his lips around her clit and sucked. She bucked off the bed again, made a low hoarse noise in her throat, turned her head from side to side on the mattress. He sucked and sucked, gently, then more firmly as pressure built inside her, exquisite twisting pressure. Her orgasm ripped through her like wildfire in her veins, her body taut and arching, and she cried out.

"Oh, dear god." Her body limp, she whimpered as he continued to kiss her pussy with soft gentle purses of his lips and nudges of his tongue, so sensitive that every touch sent a barrage of sparks through her. "Stop, please." She reached for him and tried to grab his hair. "I can't take any more."

"Mmmm." He took one last little lick, then lifted his head. "Wanna make you come again, baby. You taste so damn sweet."

"Please." Her chest ached from trying to breathe.

"Please yes? Or please no?"

But he ignored her garbled response, probably couldn't understand it anyway, and proceeded to lick her to another shuddering, mind-shattering orgasm

"I want you to stay," he whispered to her much later. "But I have an early flight to Vancouver in the morning."

She tilted her head and gave him a regretful smile. "Mmm. That's okay."

"I'll drive you home."

It sucked having to get out of bed and get dressed. Once at her place, he walked her to the door.

"Good luck," she said. "I'm cheering for you guys. You can do it."

"Thanks." He paused. He didn't want to leave her. He swallowed. "I'll call you after the game."

"Okay."

He slowly walked back to his Jeep. It was the middle of the night. He didn't want to leave her.

What was happening here? All he could think about was Remi, all he cared about was her and how she was feeling. He hated it that the paparazzi had scared her. It had never bothered him before, but suddenly it mattered to someone else and she mattered to him and…

He climbed into his vehicle and sat there for a moment. Christ. He had to stop thinking thoughts like that. He'd just broken up with one girl because she was getting too serious. He was in no way ready for a serious long term relationship. Hence the break up.

He was going to let loose and have fun in Vancouver like the single guy he was. Road trips were always good for some action.

This place was killing him.

They'd won their Sunday afternoon game against the Canucks. They'd been out for dinner to celebrate and now were hanging out in some glittery club not unlike Rouge, full of beautiful people in designer clothes. A bunch of girls had latched onto the hockey players, literally in some cases hanging off their arms, and Griff and Frenchy and the others were lapping it all up. Oh yeah, they'd be getting lucky tonight.

Jase had politely extricated himself from the clutches of a gorgeous redhead and then a hot blonde, finding himself bored and distracted. He'd had a few beers and didn't want any more. The throbbing music was giving him a headache.

The peace and quiet of his hotel room was calling to him. He wanted out. So he left, to the surprise of his teammates.

Back at the hotel, he sat on the bed with the remote for the television and channel surfed. Nothing appealed to him. He decided to play Nintendo for a while, but when he kept screwing up, he ditched that too. He tossed aside the controller and stretched out on the bed, hands behind his head.

What the fuck had happened to the guy who was all about the fun?

Remi. He'd said he'd call her to tell her how the game went. He'd wanted to call her the minute he got off the ice, jubilant and triumphant, but had to deal with the television and newspaper reporters asking a million questions about heading into the playoffs with such a dismal record lately and the much-needed win and his hat trick. He was always polite and patient with the press. It was important for the team and for the league, so he always tried to give them his best, most thoughtful answers and take the time to chat with them.

He grabbed his cell phone and punched the button that was now Remi on speed dial. She answered right away.

"We won," he said.

She laughed. "I know. I watched it on TV."

"Really?"

"Yeah. Congratulations."

"Thanks." He grinned and relaxed. "Feels pretty good."

"I guess so. See, I told you you'd do it."

"You did."

Again they talked for nearly an hour.

"I wish you were here," he said and then he couldn't believe the words had popped out of his mouth.

"I wish you were here," she replied in a sexy voice. Hell. They were about eight hundred miles too far apart.

"Wanna have phone sex?"

A pause. "I've never done that."

"Get outta here. Really?"

Another pause, slightly frosty-feeling. "And you do it all the time?"

He laughed. "Of course not, I was just kidding." Sort of. "Okay, get ready."

"You're not serious."

"Serious as a missed penalty shot."

She giggled.

"Come on, Miss I Just Wanna Have Fun. Let loose. What are you wearing?"

She laughed again at the cheesy question.

"Um…flannel pj pants and a long sleeved T-shirt."

"Mmm. Sexy. Take them off."

"Jase."

"Right here."

"I can't do this."

"Why not?" Ah, hell. "Don't tell me your sister is back again."

"No! No, I'm alone. I just…"

"Just do it." He put a hand over his fly, testing his erection. Yup, hard as a goal post. "I'm gonna. I'm unzipping my pants right now."

He heard her breathless noise as he did what he was telling her.

"Okay," she said in a throaty voice. "I'm taking my top off."

Jase groaned.

Remi sat in her living room Monday night, papers spread out around her as she marked social studies projects. But her mind kept wandering back to Jase.

Earlier, she'd done a little additional research. About Jase. Google brought up a treasure trove of information—personal information with oodles of photos of him, including sexy photos of him shirtless, advertising for a brand of hockey equipment and aftershave, and many, many photos of Jase and Brianne. Not to mention older photos of Jase and other women. Lots of other women. But he and Brianne had apparently been together for two years.

That was a long time. What had happened?

There were articles about his family—the new "first family" of hockey with three brothers in the NHL and the fourth brother a top draft pick although he now played for a farm team. He'd be in the NHL too, one day.

She also found lots of stats on goals and penalty minutes and things she didn't understand and salary information and—holy crap! Jase made nearly six million dollars last year! She actually felt nauseous when she read that.

No wonder he thought women were after his money.

With a sick feeling in her stomach, she dropped her pen and leaned back into the couch. She wished she hadn't found that out. She did not want to know how much money he made. If she didn't know, he couldn't think she was after his money like every other woman. Because she wasn't. Hell, she wasn't even after him. They were just playing around. Having fun.

She felt unreasonably annoyed, irritation like a persistent itch, at the things she'd discovered on Google. He was rich. Famous. Talented.

Except the last two days she'd actually missed him. Missed him with an aching intensity deep inside that scared the crap out of her. Because she wasn't supposed to be getting emotionally involved. Especially with someone like Jase.

Her annoyance rose, now at herself for missing him when he so clearly out of her league.

God, if Darryl had thought she was boring, what on earth was Jase doing with her?

Besides having phone sex.

Sweet loving lord. She pressed a hand to her stomach. She'd done a few things lately with Jase that she never would have thought of doing before. What was happening to her?

Her doorbell startled her into a straight up position and she blinked, then got to her feet.

Jase stood on her doorstep.

Her heart expanded, softened, accelerated. She opened the door to him.

"Hi." His smile crinkled his eyes and made her melt.

"Hi."

And then they were in each other's arms, kissing frantically. Her arms slid under his leather jacket, finding warm male muscles beneath his cotton shirt. He hoisted her up against him, feet dangling, and kissed her until the room spun around her.

He lowered her to her feet and she clutched his arms to keep herself from falling. "Wow."

"Yeah." His eyes sparkled. "What are you doing?"

"Marking projects." She led the way into her living room and grimaced at the sight of all the papers everywhere. "Uh…sorry about the mess."

He shrugged. "No biggie. You saw my apartment."

"Oh, yeah." She grinned as she picked up papers and piled them on the table, remembering the chaos she'd only noticed as they'd been leaving his place.

Jase sat on the couch and she sat beside him, but he immediately picked her up and set her on his lap and kissed her again, long, deep, kisses.

Her skin tingled and her breasts swelled. She ached between her legs and pressed into him, until sanity intruded into her lust-fogged brain and she drew back.

"Jase." She put a hand on his chest, feeling his heart thudding beneath her palm. "What are we doing here?"

"Making out." He nuzzled her neck.

She pushed on his chest. He was like a frickin' wall.

He lifted his head and gazed at her quizzically. "What?"

She shifted in his embrace. "I mean, what are we *doing*?"

"Fun. Remember?" He held her gaze, then his smile faded. "Aw, fuck."

"Yeah. That's kind of what I was thinking."

CHAPTER NINE

They sat there, silence swelling around them, dense and tense.

"I missed you," Jase finally said.

Remi bit her lip. She'd missed him too, so much, but she was vexed from all the stuff she'd found on-line about him and how this was supposed to be fun and how much fun it had *not* been, missing him like that.

"Remi." Jase put his knuckles under her chin to lift it. "I think I'm falling in love with you."

She stared at him. Her body went stone-still and stone-cold. Her heart suspended beating. He did not just say that.

The look on his face—the hopeful, nervous anticipation—gave her a splintery feeling in her chest. And it pissed her off.

She shoved at his chest with both hands and scrambled off his lap.

"You are not!" she yelled. "Are you insane?" She stood there, hands on hips, glaring at him. "That is the craziest thing I've ever heard."

His eyes shuttered and the cracking feeling inside her intensified to the point of hurting.

"I think you should go," she snapped. "We hardly know each other. This was supposed to be fun. If you can't keep it fun, then let's just forget it."

He set his big hands on the couch cushions beside him and stared at her. She kept her frown firmly in place although the corners of her eyes were stinging. She blinked rapidly.

"I think you're kind of overreacting," he finally said, the words long and stretched out. "What's gotten into you?"

She breathed out through her nose, lips pressed together. "This isn't working, Jase. You live in a different world. I had no idea who you were or what you did or that you make freakin' millions of dollars."

"What does that have to do with anything? And besides, I never knew you were a teacher, either, but I didn't let that stop me from getting to know you."

She took a step backward. What was he talking about? That made no sense at all. "You have something against teachers?" She gave her head a shake at that.

"Forget it." He stood, towering over her. "You're acting weird, Remi. You knew that stuff last week. Why is it such a big deal now?"

"Because you…you said…that!"

He ran a hand through his hair, making the short dark strands stand up in all different directions. He closed his eyes briefly. "I'm sorry. I just wanted you to know…ah hell. This is fucking nuts. What the hell am I doing?"

He walked to the door, still wearing his jacket.

He turned in the French doors, his mouth a straight, grim line, brows drawn down over his eyes. "Bye, Remi."

When she heard the front door close, her knees wobbled. She stumbled to the couch and sat down, her fists clenched. What the hell had that been? Falling in love? Was he crazy? Okay, she knew he *could* be a little crazy. A little impulsive. But that was just too much, too fast.

Except…she really, really liked him. And even though she knew she didn't really fit in with his world, it wouldn't be that hard to fall in love with him too. Some of her anger dissipated, replace by heavy sadness and regret. "Damn."

Much as Jase looked forward to working with the kids at Abraham Lincoln Middle School, he dreaded going there Wednesday afternoon. He was dying to see Remi, but he was terrified too. He pulled in to the parking lot in his Jeep and sat there, hands on the wheel.

He wasn't sure exactly what the hell had happened at her place Monday night. Women. He damn sure didn't get them. And why, why had he made that lame confession about falling in love with her? Once again, he'd blurted something out without thinking about the consequences of it. He'd spent his whole life working on controlling his impulses, and telling a woman he was in love with her was one of the craziest impulses he'd ever had, with huge fucking ramifications. Stupid, stupid, stupid.

He'd never told any woman he loved her. Not even Brianne. Well, okay, his mother, but that didn't count.

He jumped out of the vehicle and walked toward the school. As he neared the entrance, he saw Griff pull into the parking lot. He worked with a different class…maybe he could offer to trade today?

Nah. Couldn't do that. He had to see how Ryan was doing this week with Tom Sawyer. The kid reminded him of him at that age. Ryan was going to face the same struggles he had too. It made him ache for the little dude, but made him even more determined to try to help.

The kids and Remi were in her classroom. She was sitting at her desk and she looked up at him when he walked in and she kept her face from showing an expression, but she looked sad. There was no hiding that.

His heart squeezed. He tightened his mouth.

"Hey, Jase!" The kids all greeted him and crowded around him and he forced a smile.

They got busy with their reading activities and he signed all their forms listing all the books they'd read since last week. Some kids were crazy readers—a list a mile long—others like Ryan had only read one book.

"You finished it?" He looked at Ryan, who nodded, trying not to look pleased. "Good job, dude!" They bumped fists. "Let's talk about it."

Ryan was having a hard time today, Jase could tell. He was unfocused, fidgety; Jase knew the signs. He tried a few times to draw him back, but knew it wasn't going to work today.

Then Remi came over, having noticed his struggles. "Ryan…what's going on?"

No, no. Jase looked up at her and shook his head. He didn't want the kid to get in trouble for something he couldn't help.

"Nothing." Ryan shifted in his seat one way, then the other.

"D'you need to go for a drink of water?" she asked him. "I'll come with you."

Jase watched them leave the class. He wanted to follow. He was worried for Ryan. What was she going to say to him? A memory flashed through his mind. *"Stupid. You're just stupid. Would you just sit still and pay attention."*

He remembered being taunted and teased by other kids, remembered defending himself with his fists instead of his brains and the shitloads of trouble he'd gotten into because of that, which hadn't endeared him to his teachers at all.

He surged to his feet and strode across the classroom, leaving the kids on their own for a moment. He had to get to Ryan. He walked into the hall and stopped. Remi and Ryan stood there and she had her arm around his shoulders. "Did you take your medication today?" she asked softly.

Ryan said nothing, then shook his head.

"You have to take it," she said. "Come on, Ryan. You know it's important."

"I hate taking it."

"We talked about this before. Remember? About how smart you are and how the Ritalin helps you learn. If you miss out on stuff now, Ryan, it'll be so hard to get caught up. That's what it's there for."

Jase stared at them, his heart thudding, his breath choppy.

She'd told the kid he was smart.

His heart expanded till he thought it might burst out of his chest. Jesus. He wasn't *falling* in love with that woman. He was *in* love with her. Head over hockey skates in love with her.

CHAPTER TEN

Remi turned. "C'mon," she said with a smile. "Let's not waste the time that Jase is here…" And then she looked up and saw him standing in the door of her classroom and the look on his face made her knees fold. She almost couldn't walk.

"Hey, Jase." Ryan went up to him. "I…I'll try to pay attention. Let's talk about Tom Sawyer."

Jase's dark eyes met hers, catching her gaze and holding it. An invisible thread tugged between them, drawing her to him. Why was he looking at her like that? Like she'd sprouted pigs' ears out of her head or something.

He kept staring at her even as Ryan went back into the class.

"What?" she whispered, eyebrows raised.

He said nothing, but followed her back into the class. He sauntered over to Ryan and they started talking and she went back to the other kids, but had a hard time dragging her gaze away from him.

Why had he followed her out into the hall? Why did he look so pole-axed?

He was so patient with Ryan, even though Ryan was having a bad day. He made the boy laugh at something, and her chest constricted. She blinked and tried to focus on the other kids. Her throat felt tight and achy and she just wanted this to be over, much as she loved spending time with her students. She was going to go throw herself in Jase's lap in a minute.

She tried to breathe, in and out, until finally the clock on the wall said the reading program was over.

The kids were in no rush to leave, though, talking to Jase, taking their time getting their belongings together. "Don't forget your homework!" she reminded one.

And Jase seemed in no hurry to leave either.

Finally the classroom was empty and quiet except for the two of them.

Jase sat on one of the small desks. She hoped it would hold his weight.

"Thanks," she choked out. "Again. You were great with them. Especially with Ryan."

"He's a good kid."

He was still looking at her strangely. She put a hand to her hair to make sure it wasn't sticking up or something. "Yes, he is."

"You told him he's smart."

She blinked. "Yes. He is. He's a very smart kid."

"He has ADHD."

"Yes." Her brow tightened. "How'd you know that?"

"Never mind. Remi."

"What?"

"Don't push me away, Remi."

Her body went soft and hot and her ears buzzed. She swallowed through a painfully tight throat. And then she was in his arms, climbing up his body, kissing him, feeling the wetness of her tears on his face. "Oh, Jase. This is crazy."

"Yeah, it kinda is." He held her face in his big hands and kissed her so gently, so tenderly, she trembled. "Come home with me."

"Yes."

Remi could not believe Jase had talked her into this.

It was Saturday morning and she was getting off a plane at LAX. Jase's last road game had been last night against the Kings and he didn't have to be back in Chicago for a practice until Monday, so he'd convinced her to fly to Los Angeles for a weekend with him.

Jesus. Who did things like that? Flying to L.A. for the weekend.

Apparently she did.

She couldn't even imagine how much the airfare had been. She tried to put that out of her mind.

She walked out of the gate, pulling her small carry-on which was all the luggage she'd brought, looking around for where to go. Follow the crowd seemed the best plan. Everyone was heading for a set of long escalators. This was all new to her—despite her parents having travelled the world, she never had. New and scary and exciting because she'd always wanted to travel. She'd never been able to, never had the money, never been able to leave Kyle and Jasmine. Even when she'd had the opportunity when they were older, there was always that fear that if something happened to her, like what had happened to her parents, she'd be leaving them all on their own and the fear of doing that to them had been paralyzing.

But here was she was in Los Angeles and her stomach quivered with excitement. She turned her cell phone back on in case Jase tried to call her as she rode down the escalator, then searched the crowd at the bottom for him.

There he was. A smile broke across her face at the sight of him, taller than everyone else, broader than everyone else, dressed in jeans and a grey T-shirt. Bare arms in early April. Awesome.

He spotted her too, sending her a big grin, and caught her at the bottom of the escalator in a big hug.

"Congratulations," she said to him after he'd kissed the wits out of her. "You won last night."

"Yeah." He grinned. He took her suitcase in one hand and her hand in the other and started toward the exit. "I got two goals."

"That's all?" She lifted a brow at him mockingly, and he growled.

"Whaddya mean, that's all?" Then he laughed and lifted her hand to his mouth to kiss her knuckles.

They stepped out into sunshine and warm humidity. "Oh, that feels nice."

"Bring a swimsuit?"

"Yes."

"Good. There's a nice pool at the hotel."

He led the way across roads crazy with speeding cars, honking taxis, limos and noisy shuttle buses to the parking garage. "I got a rental car for the weekend."

"This?" She stopped in front of the sexy black convertible. She gazed across the roof of the car at him.

"Yup. Sweet, huh?"

She smiled. "Perfect."

He put the top down and they were soon leaving LAX, the warm wind tossing Remi's hair around her head, and she sat there with a feeling of warm contentment mingled with excited anticipation. As they drove along Century Boulevard, her cell phone rang in her purse.

With a small frown, she pulled it out. Kyle.

"Hey," she said into the phone.

"Hi, Remi," Kyle said. "How're you doing?"

"I'm okay." She grinned at the thought that he had no idea where she was just then. "What's up?"

"I've got a bit of a problem."

"What is it?"

"I kinda…missed an exam yesterday."

She glanced at Jase, who was glancing at her as he drove. "What do you mean, kind of? You missed it or you didn't."

"Okay, I missed it. It was totally an accident. My alarm didn't go off and I slept in." His words picked up pace. "But if you could call the dean and tell him that I was sick, they might let me re-write it."

"But you weren't sick."

"But if you say I was, they'll let me rewrite it."

She paused and stared at passing palm trees and billboards and big hotels.

"You want me to lie about it for you?"

"Well…yeah. Please, Remi. If I can't write the exam, I flunk the whole course. I'll have to do it all next year. That's going to set me back."

Shit. It was hard enough paying his tuition without tacking on an extra year—term? Whatever.

"I don't know, Kyle." She nibbled her lip. "Are you sure that's all I'd have to do?"

"Yeah. I think so. But you have to do it Monday."

"Let me think about it."

"Where are you, anyway?"

"I'm…uh…actually in Los Angeles."

"Whaat! What are you doing there?"

She sent another sideways glance at Jase, this time smiling. "I'm having a little weekend vacation. With Jase."

"You're still seeing him?"

"Yeah. I'll call you back later. Bye, Kyle."

She ended the call.

"Your brother?"

"Mmm. He has a little problem he wants me to fix."

She told him the story and he frowned.

"He does want you to lie for him. How old is he?"

"Eighteen."

"Shit."

"He's just a kid."

"When I was eighteen, I was earning my own living. I'd been on my own for a couple of years."

"Well. He's in college. I still have to support him while he goes to school."

Jase's mouth twisted. "I suppose. I didn't go to university."

The touch of bitterness in his tone made her shift in her seat to look at him. "That's okay. You had other talents."

He nodded and accelerated fast to merge onto the freeway.

"Didn't you finish high school?" she asked tentatively.

"Yeah, I did. I was playing major junior hockey and I was living in Brandon. With another family. They made sure I went to school, although it was kind hard keeping up with it when we were on the road a lot. But I did finish. I even took a few university courses."

"That's good." It must have been hard to combine school and a hockey career at that young age. Kids that young weren't ready to be living away from home. Yet Jase seemed to have done okay. "Was it hard for your parents to let you move away when you were so young?"

He glanced at her. "I don't know. I never thought about it." He tipped his head to one side. "It was just what we had to do. I guess it probably was hard for them, but…my parents made a lot of sacrifices for all of us so we could be successful."

"That's what parents do."

"Yeah."

She'd bet it had been a lot harder for his parents to let him go than he even realized. "Where are we staying?" she asked, changing the subject. Sunshine flashed and glinted off speeding chrome and glass surrounding them on the freeway.

"The Ocean Front, in Santa Monica."

"Oh. I've never heard of it."

"It's a small place, a boutique hotel, very nice."

She was sure it would be, knowing Jase. More excitement tingled in her veins.

Her cell phone rang again as they were checking in. She moved away from Jase in the lobby, her boots clicking on the bamboo floor. She needed to get out of these winter clothes. Kyle again. She sighed. "Hello?"

"Look, I didn't tell you the whole story when I talked to you earlier."

She slowly walked past white upholstered furniture and palms in chrome pots. "What's the whole story?"

"I was sick yesterday."

"Oh. Why didn't you say that? Are you okay now?"

"Yeah, I feel fine now. But I couldn't write that exam. I was just too sick."

"Well, in that case…I suppose I could talk to the dean. Was it the flu?"

"Yeah! Yeah, it was the flu."

Remi's bullshit radar pinged. "Kyle, are you being honest with me?"

"Of course! Would I lie to you, Remi?"

"Yes. You would. You have. Many times." She sighed. She'd bailed him out of situations more times than she cared to remember. Helped him with homework. Loaned him money. Jase was right. He was eighteen. He needed to take responsibility for his actions.

"I'm busy right now." Jase turned away from the reception desk. "I'll call you back later."

He lifted a brow as she moved toward him. "Kyle again." She filled him in on this conversation as they rode the elevator to their room.

"He was hung-over and missed his exam," Jase said.

"He was not!"

Jase lifted one eyebrow and gave her a crooked smile as the elevator rose.

"You think?"

"I know. I know teenage boys. I used to be one."

She sighed. It wasn't beyond the realm of possibility. Then thoughts of Kyle scattered as she walked into their room.

"This place is amazing!"

Their room—or rather, suite—was immense. Sliding doors opened on to a balcony overlooking red tile roofs interspersed with green palm trees and, in the distance, the pale sand of the beach, the azure Pacific Ocean.

She trailed her fingers along the creamy duvet that topped the king-size bed and flopped down onto the chocolate brown couch facing the balcony. "Wow."

He stored their suitcases in the massive closet and went to shut the doors.

"Wait! I want to change." She extended her legs. "I can't wear these boots when it's so warm here."

But it took longer to change than she'd thought because once she started taking her clothes off, Jase attacked her. Or maybe she attacked him. Whatever. It didn't matter, they were hot for each other after a couple of days apart.

Down to her black lace underwear, she went to take the boots off and he said, "Leave them on." He knelt between her legs, admiring her in her bra and panties and stiletto boots. Her body heated up.

"Now that is a fantasy come to life," he said with deep satisfaction.

Her toes curled inside her boots.

"Very hot," he murmured, hands on her thighs. "Like a baby dominatrix."

"You want to be dominated?" Her heart hammed ferociously. She wasn't sure about…

"Not really." He bent over to lick the sensitive flesh of her belly and she shivered. "How about you?"

Oooh. Her breath sighed out of her. She moaned.

He lifted his head. "You do, don't you?"

She bit her lip and met his eyes.

"Oh, Remi, you naughty girl. My whips and chains are…uh…"

She laughed and pushed at his big shoulder. "You don't have any whips and chains."

"I can get some."

"That's okay." She kissed his shoulder. "I don't need that much dominating. I just need…"

"This." And he rolled her on top of him and laid a firm pat on her butt. She moaned and turned to liquid. "I know you like that."

She just moaned again and he pulled her face down for a blistering kiss. He gave he a couple more sharp little taps, sending heat shimmering over her buttocks, then rolled her to her back again. "And this." He clasped both her wrists in one hand and held them over her head while his weight pressed her into the mattress and he kissed her, his tongue sliding in and out of her mouth, so sexy. He sucked on her tongue, bit softly at her lips. Molten pleasure spread inside her as he rubbed his body against hers, mesmerizing her with his heat, his strength, pinning her there, helpless.

"I missed you," he breathed in her ear. Then he rose up and gazed down at her again and her breath caught in her throat at the expression on his face. "So pretty." He released her wrists and dragged a hand down from her shoulder, between her breasts, over her stomach. "Let's take these off." And he tugged the panties down over her thighs. She lifted her knees to her chest to help. The lace snagged on one sharp boot heel as he pulled them off and he freed them, then tossed them aside.

They exchanged a heated smile. "That's what happens when you wear boots to bed," she said in a breathy voice. "I'm just hoping I don't stab you in the balls."

He winced, but laughed. "Maybe we'll take them off." And he tugged the boots off too, one at a time, tossing them to the floor with one soft thud, then another.

Air on her bare legs felt so sexy and she kept her legs bent like that, feet crossed, and lifted her arms above her head on the bed. He kneed her legs farther apart, his own spread wide on the bed, his cock jutting long and hard over her. "Oh, Remi." His eyes devoured her and then he directed his cock into her, his index and middle finger on each side of it. He filled her so perfectly, so beautifully. Her eyes fell closed and he moved over her, one hand going to her forehead and tipping her head back. He kissed her mouth, her cheek, her ear, all the while rolling his body against her, inside her, in a drugging rhythm. "You feel so good." He rubbed his face against hers. "So hot and wet. So perfect."

Heat spiraled through her, flames licking over her body. "So good," she moaned. "Oh, Jase, it's so good."

He pushed up on his arms, then knelt between her legs. He reached for the lace cups of her bra and tugged them down, exposing her nipples, playing with them with his fingertips, his face intent, dark, aroused. Sensation shimmered from her nipples to her pussy and she lifted her hips up to him, whimpering with pleasure and need. God, he knew how to make her hot.

He pulled out then and she made a little cry of protest, but he rubbed the head of his cock over her pussy. Her clit throbbed and ached for more and when he pushed back inside her and reached for her waist, holding her steady with both hands as his thrusting grew harder, she slid her hand down over her belly and to find her clit.

"Oh yeah," he groaned. "So hot, baby. Do it, make yourself come."

"*You're* making me come." And it was true, the sensation of him inside her combined with the touch of her fingers on her clit threw her headlong into a hard, shuddering orgasm. She cried out, letting his thrusts prolong the ecstasy, drawing it out until he came too, falling over her again, sliding one arm beneath her shoulders and holding her tight.

After christening the king size bed with afternoon sex, they went for a walk on the beach and did a little shopping.

"I love this place." She did a little spin on the sidewalk. Jase laughed. "Seriously. I've never been anywhere. The ocean, the palm trees, the sun…I love it."

"You've never been anywhere?"

She shook her head and made a little face. "No. My parents were the ones who travelled. I've always wanted to see different places, but it just didn't happen."

"I get sick of travelling." His eyes danced though, as he took in her enjoyment. "But with you it's fun again."

"Where will we go for dinner?"

"The rooftop restaurant at the hotel is supposed to be good." He took her hand as they strolled back toward the hotel. "And the view is spectacular."

They went for a swim, a lazy, sexy swim, then showered together and changed for dinner. They were just sitting down at their table when Remi's cell phone rang again.

"Kyle, I said I'd call you."

She rolled her eyes apologetically at Jase, but he just laughed.

"Okay, so I wasn't sick sick," Kyle said. "But I still have to write that exam."

"If you weren't sick, why'd you miss it?"

A pause. "I was hung-over."

Oh, god. She met Jase's eyes, which crinkled with amusement. She sighed. "Kyle."

"I'm sorry, Rem, but we went out the night before…"

"When you should have been studying!"

"I did study! I swear I did. I was ready for the exam. I just went out for a while and a friend had some beer and…"

"Kyle. I can't believe you want me to bail you out because you got drunk and slept through your exam."

She caught Jase's eye and he made a face at her that brought a smile despite the serious conversation.

"Remi! You have to! Please."

She wavered. She sank her top teeth into her bottom lip and looked at Jase, whose face had grown serious. He slowly moved his head from side to side.

"What?" she mouthed at him, frowning a little.

"Don't do it," he said. "He needs to stand on his own two feet."

Torn, she still hesitated.

"Remi?" Kyle said.

Jase shook his head again. "Remi, you have to let go," he said.

"He's just a teenager," she whispered.

"What?" Kyle said. "Remi, come on."

"He'll never learn if you keep bailing him out."

Who was he to tell her how to handle her family? He was nothing but a big kid himself, with no responsibility whatsoever. What the heck did he know about being a parent?

He watched her, though, head tilted thoughtfully, his steady eyes full of intelligence and concern. Hell. He was right.

"No. Sorry, Kyle. You're old enough to be on your own at college, you either get yourself out of this or you face the consequences." Her stomach clenched. Even though she knew it was the right thing to do, it was hard, gut-wrenchingly hard.

"Good job," Jase said when she hung up.

She bit her lip and looked at him across the table. "I hate that. I know I have to do it, but…the stupid thing is, I'm the one who's going to pay the consequences of the extra tuition for him to do the course again."

"Make him pay it. Tell him to get a part-time job."

She nodded. "Yeah. I guess he could. But I want him to do well at school."

He shook his head, but smiled at her. "You love your brother and sister, don't you?"

"Well, yeah."

"And you like to be needed."

She eyed him warily. "I suppose."

"D'you ever think maybe you enable them by helping them out all the time?"

She frowned at him. "What are you saying?"

He lifted one big shoulder and turned his water goblet in his hands. "I'm just saying that you're not doing them any favors by bailing them out. Kids have to grow up and be independent and deal with the consequences of their actions."

"What do you know about it?" she snapped, stung by his words. "You're not a parent."

"Neither are you."

Her mouth dropped open. "Not technically! But I'm responsible for my brother and sister…"

"Remi, they're legally adults."

This was true.

"Hey, I know what family is like. I love my brothers. I'd do anything for them. I've fought for them when I had to. And just because I'm not a parent myself doesn't mean I don't know anything about learning how to take responsibility for my actions. I'm not always good at it, but I'm learning. I had to learn, when I was young, if I wanted to succeed in my career goals."

She studied his face, the intensity in his expression, the blaze in his eyes. There was no questioning his dedication to his sport and all that he'd achieved and she supposed she'd never really thought much about what he'd had to do to get there. Especially since his main goal off the ice seemed to be to have as much fun as possible. Her chest squeezed. "I'm sorry," she said. "I guess I just didn't like someone telling me how to deal with my family."

"I'm sorry too, then," he said. "For interfering. I care about you."

She sucked briefly on her lower lip. "I know."

"You're going to be an awesome mother some day."

She blinked at him and sat back in her chair. Her desire to some day be a mother with children of her own, was not something she was going to share with a guy she was having a fun little fling with. But his compliment pleased her and made her heart swell in her chest and her eyes sting a little. She shook her head and reached for her water goblet. "Maybe some day." She gave him a bright smile. "Thank you for the advice, Jase. Seriously, you're a smart guy."

His eye flickered but his lips lifted in a smile.

"And sorry for all the drama. This doesn't happen all the time."

"Uh…I beg to differ."

She tipped her head to one side.

"The first night we met you used tae kwon do moves on me and took me down. Then the cops showed up at your place. Then your sister had a meltdown and you had to go home to her. Now your brother's got a crisis. But at least your life's never boring."

She stared at him. Was he making a sarcastic joke? It didn't appear so. She shivered. Her life was nothing but boring compared to his! What was he talking about!

"Let's order," he said.

The night-time sex in the king size bed was even better.

Jase knew now what Remi liked and didn't worry about accidentally crushing her. Well, maybe just a bit. But now he knew what she needed. She was strong and feisty and she wasn't looking for soft and gentle. Which was fine with him. He was a physical guy, always had been, and sex was his favorite sport. And thank God, it was Remi's too, apparently.

They rolled across the bed together, mouths fused, bodies joined, sweating and panting and hearts hammering.

She reached for his cock, small hands closing around it, and her touch sent sizzles up his spine. His balls pulled up tight, ready to explode.

She squirmed against him, her little body all curvy and warm and rubbing against him as she moved down the bed, laying hot, wet little kisses over his chest, then his stomach. His abs quivered. Then she kissed his stomach below his navel, so sensitive, and he throbbed in her hands.

She made little moaning noises of pleasure as she combed her fingers through his pubic hair, then slid them down around and under his cock to stroke his balls. Delicate touches, making him groan and writhe.

She fisted his cock again in two hands and pulled, long firm strokes, just how he liked it, and when she bent her head he hissed out a breath. Her mouth on the head of his cock was like sweet heaven, hot wet heat and hungry suction. She swirled her tongue around and her teeth grazed the sensitive rim, making him jump.

"Fuck," he groaned, sliding his hands into her hair. He held her head as she moved up and down on his shaft, her mouth sublime. "Remi. God, your mouth. I love your mouth."

She murmured an agreement which vibrated a frisson of pleasure through him and then she let his cock release with a pop and licked her lips. She held his cock with her hands and looked down at it as if she was studying it. She smiled. He twitched. Hard.

She licked across the head, one long slow lick, then bent her head even lower and licked his balls. His hips lifted. Ah, fuck! He gritted his teeth, closing his eyes at the sensations that torched his nerve endings. He was so rigid and engorged it hurt, his cock leaping toward her.

Then she sucked one testicle into her mouth, tugged gently and released, licked over to the other and sucked it in too. He held her head, fingers tight and hard, trying not to explode, his whole body wracked with the need to come.

When her mouth closed over his dick again, he let go. He had to let go. He held her head, pulling her lower so she'd take him deeper. How much did she like to be dominated? Even like this?

His mind spun. Lots of girls didn't like that kind of aggression, but he just had a feeling…and he pushed Remi's head lower. He was big. There was no way she could take him all, but damn, she took him deep. The tip of his cock hit the back of her throat. He withdrew and she sucked ferociously, her mouth working.

He looked down at her and she looked up, all starry lashes and glittering eyes, and their gazes met and held. Joined in a tangible connection.

He lost it. He went over, pleasure racing from his balls outward, to his toes and up to his brain, body tense, balls tight, cock pulsing in her mouth.

She sucked him in, taking it all, holding his balls as they contracted. When she finally lifted her mouth off him, a trickle of thick white fluid escaped her mouth and ran down her chin. It was so fucking sexy he hardened all over again. Christ.

She wiped her chin with her forefinger, then sucked it into her mouth. He had to close his eyes, his body weak and trembling. His head buzzed, he couldn't think, couldn't hear, couldn't see. He reached blindly for her to lift her up over his body, lifting her right off the bed she was so little. He fucking loved that.

Who woulda thought.

He wrapped her up in his arms, curling his body around her. "Jesus, Remi, your mouth…"

"I loved that." Her nose pressed to the side of his neck. Was she sniffing him? He smiled. "You taste so good and I love making you feel good like that."

"That was more than just feeling good," he said on a groan, stroking a hand down over her smooth back, then the curve of her ass. He gave her a smack and she jumped.

"Hey! What was that for!"

He smiled. "Your punishment for being such a naughty girl."

When she squirmed against him, he hardened even more. Already. Wow.

Remi snuggled into Jase's body, throbbing with both need and satisfaction. The sharp salty taste of him lingered in her mouth and made her want more. His hands stroked over her body, sending humming pleasure through her nerve endings. When his fingers found her center, slicked through her wetness and rubbed over her clit, she shifted against him to allow him better access, opening her thighs to his delicious touch. His mouth on her breasts tugged a sweet path of delight to her molten center where she ached with a thick, liquid want. Electric sparks raced over her nerves.

She moaned and pressed her open mouth to the side of his neck, drawing the spicy male scent of him deep inside her.

The tingling around his finger grew, intensified, became fiery pleasure twisting up inside her all tight and hot. She felt it going higher, higher, everything inside her pulling up tight and then a cry ripped from her throat as she spasmed against his hand. She grabbed hold of his broad wrist to hold him there, pulsing against him, eyes closed, ears ringing.

"Beautiful." Jase kissed her forehead. "So beautiful. I love watching you come."

"Mmm." She softened against him, limp and languid. "Wow."

"Good?"

"Mmm. Not as good as when you're inside me, but yeah…so good."

They were both sweaty and Jase threw back the duvet to let the cool night air drift over them through the open sliding doors onto the balcony. Faint night sounds of traffic and music floated in on the breeze.

Jase hardened against her leg. She wiggled and reached down for him. "Already?"

"Hey. It's been a while since I came."

She choked on laugh. Truthfully she had no idea—it seemed like an hour, it seemed like a minute.

He moved over her. "I need to fuck you."

"Mmm. Yes."

She parted her thighs, still tender and quivering between them, but when he pushed inside her it felt perfect. Hot and tight, stretching her, filling her in a way that felt right and perfect.

He moved against her, this time slower and easier, not like their usual frantic hungry movements. He held himself over her on his arms, muscles bulging, and watched her face as he moved in and out. She lifted her legs higher to take him deeper, so deep she pressed a hand to her tummy, feeling him so far inside her it almost….almost hurt. And she loved it.

"Remi."

"Mmmm." She stroked his chest.

"I love you."

CHAPTER ELEVEN

She went very still. Her eyes closed, then opened. "What happened to just fun and games?"

He moved his head slowly from side to side. "It's more. Don't get mad again. I know it is for you too. Isn't it?" He moved his hips, his cock sliding in and out of her sweet pussy.

She blinked at him, her eye makeup smudged a bit, making her big eyes even bigger, hair tangled, lips swollen. She was so incredibly beautiful she made his heart stop.

"Yes," she whispered. "It's more. Ah, Jase. I love you too."

He kissed her mouth softly. "Thank you."

He thrust harder and she met him at each push, lifting her hips. He rose onto his knees, slid his hands under her knees and lifted them. He pushed her legs closed and she tightened around him, the friction intensifying as he thrust in and out. She gasped. Her eyes went dazed. Her lips parted, all shiny and wet and swollen.

He held her legs straight up with one hand around her ankles, lifting her ass right off the bed, and fucked her—long, hard thrusts, taking her, claiming her, owning her, until he tightened and a hard fiery wave of heat and pleasure swept over him, again, again, again.

He collapsed over her and then, mindful of his weight on her small body, rolled to the side, pulling her with him, chest heaving, lungs straining, heart thudding.

"I love you."

"I love you too."

Long moments later, she said, "I don't understand this. We hardly know each other."

"I know. I don't get it either. I've never really been in love before. I guess it just…hits you."

She pulled back to look at him. "You've never been in love before?"

"Nope."

"What about Brianne? You were with her for a long time."

"Yeah. But I didn't love her. Not like this."

"Why did you break up?"

"I thought I told you. She wanted to get married. I didn't."

"You were afraid of commitment."

"No." He paused, struggling for words. "Okay, yeah. I was. I was terrified." He squinted. "But I'm not any more. Not with you." He didn't understand it, but it was the truth. Miraculously, fucking weirdly, he wasn't afraid of a commitment—to Remi. He stroked a hand over her hair. "I'm more afraid of being without you."

"Oh, Jase." Her whispered words wrapped around his heart and squeezed.

After a long moment, he said, "What about you?"

"Hmm?"

Have you ever been in love before?"

"Yeah. Once."

His gut seized up. "You were?"

"Yes. I thought we were pretty serious." She laid her cheek back down on his chest and her hand slid up to his shoulder. "But he dumped me. Because I was…boring."

He choked on a laugh. "You? Boring? Sweetheart, he didn't know you very well."

"I…I thought he did. I thought my life was boring. I gave up a lot for my brother and sister. We had to plan…uh…things for when they weren't home. Which wasn't often. Lots of times I couldn't go out because I had to drive them to piano lessons or soccer games or parent teacher meetings."

"Oh, Remi." He envisioned her life at age twenty-two—all the responsibility she'd had and how she'd just done it. "That's not boring. That's…you."

He felt wetness on his chest and she sniffed. "I love you, Jase."

"You know when I knew I loved you?" He rubbed the middle of her back.

"When?"

"Last week at school. When you were talking to Ryan in the hall. And you told him he was smart."

"I…I don't get it."

He sighed and stroked a hand down her satiny back, over the firm curve of a buttock, lingering in the cleft there, making her squirm. "Ryan reminds me of me. I have ADHD too."

Her head swung up so quickly she almost knocked his chin. "You do?"

"Yup. I had such a hard time as a kid. People didn't understand it as much as they do now. I had some brutal teachers."

"Oh, Jase. " She cupped his cheek. "That's why you don't like teachers."

"Well. Not all teachers." He grinned, loving the feel of her small hand on his face. "But I sure didn't like Ms Wong in eighth grade. I struggled with reading and writing. Didn't do my homework. I was failing half my classes. She had no patience for me. Told me I was stupid and I'd never amount to anything in life."

Her eyes filled with horror and her mouth opened. "Oh my god. Oh, Jase." Her fingertips touched his mouth.

He smiled. "It's okay. If it wasn't for her telling me that, I might never have been so determined that I was going to amount to something. I was nothing if not stubborn."

"I can't believe a teacher would say that to a student."

"I know *you* wouldn't. And that's why I love you. *One* reason I love you. Even though you're a teacher."

Her eyes got glossy and her smile trembled. "Is that what you meant…when you found out I was a teacher…?"

"Yeah." He gave her a crooked smile. "I didn't want anything to do with a teacher. That's why sometimes I was such a jerk. But then I got to know you better. You don't make me feel stupid."

"Jase. You are *not* stupid." She paused. "Tell me about it. Tell me what happened when you were in school."

"Ugh." He sighed. "They didn't know as much about ADHD back then. It was in the nineties when it started to get more attention, which was when I was in school, but I had some bad experiences with teachers who didn't understand it. I had a hard time focusing and was easily distracted, and they'd get frustrated with me and yell at me to just still and pay attention. And I tried, but it wasn't that easy and I got frustrated too. I got angry. Then along with poor impulse control, I got in fights. Like I said, Ms Wong even told me I was stupid."

She rubbed his shoulder. "ADHD has nothing to do with how smart a person is. Some individuals with it have very high intelligence levels. Clearly you are an intelligent man, Jase."

"Well, I didn't feel like that and sometimes it still gets to me. My marks were shitty and I pretended I didn't care, but really I felt so inferior. Some kids thought I was stupid too, when we'd get tests back. When we had to do group projects, nobody wanted to work with me."

He felt her quivering breath.

"Hey, don't cry. I'm fine. I did okay. When we played sports, *everyone* wanted me on their team."

Her smile glimmered. "You're an amazing man, Jase."

He smiled. "Nah. I'm just a big kid. I don't even feel like I'm grown up sometimes. I play a game for a living. I can't believe my life, either, you know. Sometimes it's not real."

"You're talented and you work hard. It's real."

"Thank you. I was lucky I had hockey in my life. It actually really helped me and I had coaches who worked with me on things. I guess they could see I had some talent and I was worth putting time into…unlike some teachers." Yeah, there was still a little bitterness there.

"I'm sorry you went through that. But yeah…you've done great. When I watch you on the ice, I don't have a clue what's going on, but you think so fast out there it amazes me. You have to be smart to play like that."

He thought his heart might explode in his chest and swallowed hard, his eyes going foggy. She thought he was smart. "Next week, my parents are coming to Chicago. To watch the last home game."

"Yeah? That's nice."

"They're bringing my youngest brother. He's done for the season. And my other brother Logan is flying in too, to watch the game, because my *other* brother…" She grinned. "Is who I'm playing against."

"Oh!" Then she frowned. "Oh. This is your last game. This is do or die, isn't it?"

"Yeah."

"Who does he play for? Phoenix?"

"Yeah."

"If they lose…"

"They're out."

"If you lose…you're out."

"Yeah. We both need this win."

"Ooh. That's tough."

"I know." He gave a wry smile. "My parents will be having a heart attack. But they'll be cheering for me."

She frowned and then realized he was teasing and laughed, giving his chest a smack. "That has to be hard for them. Watching you two play against each other?"

He hitched a shoulder. "It's happened before. Anyway, we're all going out for a late dinner after the game. To celebrate. One of us, anyway. The other one will drown his sorrow. The whole family will be together."

"That's so nice."

"I want you to come."

"Really? Maybe you and your family should just…"

"No. I want you to meet them. I want them to meet you."

Her smile deepened. "Okay. I'd like to meet them too."

The morning sex was pretty incredible too. After a decadent breakfast in bed, they took a bath together in the huge jetted tub in the marble bathroom, surrounded by drifting steam and steamy sighs.

They played and splashed and laughed, shared long kisses and slippery soapy caresses. Remi's body felt incredible all slick and wet, and he drew his hands down the curve of her waist, the flare of her hips, back up to firm breasts with hard little tips. When his soapy fingers slid around to her ass, stroking between her cheeks, she daringly, boldly did the same to him, holding his gaze as she slipped gliding fingers over his butt, between his cheeks, making him clench and tremble with a forbidden pleasure.

She bit her lip, but didn't stop, and his cock hardened painfully against her as she played with his ass, teasing, tormenting, making his body draw up hard and hot. Then her fingers slid lower and cupped his taut balls. "I'm gonna come," he rasped out, lifting her hips, preparing to thrust inside her. But she shifted away from him.

Damn her, she was a tempting little wanton witch. Her fingers slid back to tickle his ass again while her other hand grasped his cock in a firm grip and pulled…once…twice…and then he erupted in her hand, hot semen spilling over her fingers. A long groan tore from his throat as he pulsed, spurted, again, and again, and again.

"Nice," she murmured, watching him appreciatively. And then she bent and licked him, her hot velvety tongue stroking over the sensitive head of his cock, making him twitch hard. "Mmmm."

She blew his fucking mind, every time. It just got hotter and more intense and now that he knew she loved him too, it meant even more. It meant…everything. Everything that was right and beautiful and shining, like a sheet of freshly Zambonied ice.

God, he was pathetic, comparing their feelings to ice. He choked on a laugh as he hauled her petite frame up against him and hugged her tight.

Somehow it turned into more than just dinner and Remi ended up at the Metro Center seated between Jase's mom and dad, whom she'd never met, near the same seat she'd sat in last time, six rows right behind the Wolves bench. The two empty seats to the left of Jase's dad waited to be occupied by Jase's brothers Matt and Logan, who were somewhere in the arena.

Remi clasped her hands nervously in her lap as they watched the warm-up. She breathed in the chilled air, that mingled scent of popcorn, ice and sweat.

"So," Laura Heller said. "How long have you and Jase known each other?"

Ack. She was getting the maternal inquisition. Remi turned to smile at Jase's mom, tall and elegant, her dark hair cut into a short spiky style. "A few weeks." It sure didn't sound long, even though she felt like she'd known him forever.

"How did you meet?"

"I picked him up in a bar." Remi clapped a hand to her mouth. "Oh, that sounds bad. It wasn't exactly like that. Neither of us was really interested in the other, but we both needed to pretend we were because…" She closed her eyes. She should just stop now, before she blurted out that they'd been so hot for each other they'd gone back to her place and then the cops had showed up and…she swallowed. "And then we met again when Jase came to the school I teach at, as part of the Stars for Reading program."

"Oh, you're a teacher?"

"Yes. I teach sixth grade. The kids really love having Jase come and work with them."

The horn sounded to end the warm-up and two hulking young men appeared in the aisle.

"There you are." Laura stood so they could squeeze by her. "Where did you disappear to?"

"Reporter from the CBC spotted us and wanted an interview." The younger of the two men smiled, his broad grin just like Jase's.

"Remi, this is Matt, Jase's youngest brother." Remi stood too, and Matt shook her hand, the charm in his smile tugging at her. There was a definite family resemblance between all the brothers, although she hadn't met Tag yet, who was still down on the ice.

"And I'm Logan," the other said with an equally engaging smile and a sparkle in his dark eyes. "The good looking brother. Matt's the baby."

Hardly a baby. Remi let Matt squeeze his big body past her to his seat and Logan shook her hand, towering over her, giving her an up and down look that made her feel warm and tingly. Those boys had good looks and charm just pouring off them, and how unfair was that, along with their mega athletic talent?

They settled into their seats.

"Does this feel weird for you?" Remi asked Jase's mom. "Watching your sons play against each other? Who do you cheer for?"

"It is hard, although it's happened many times. I just want them both to play well."

From down the row, Remi heard a snort. "Tag's too old and decrepit to play well," Logan said and Matt guffawed.

Laura rolled her eyes. "Do you enjoy hockey, Remi?"

"Sort of. I don't know much about it. I've only ever been to a few games."

"Hmm." Jase's dad Doug spoke up. A big, quiet man, he'd barely spoken since they'd arrived at the arena. "We'll have to teach you a few things about the game, then."

"Don't bore her." Laura leaned forward to look at her husband.

"No, please—I want to learn. The last game I came to with a girlfriend and neither of us knew what was going on."

"Trade places with me, Dad," Logan demanded. "I want to sit beside Remi. I can explain things to her."

"You stay in your own seat," Doug told him. Matt laughed.

Remi's cheeks warmed and she caught Laura's smile.

A sell-out crowd packed the arena tonight, the last home game of the regular season for the Wolves, and it was do or die. If they didn't win tonight, the season was over. All the fans—including Remi and Jase's family—wore white, thanks to a huge media campaign. Five guys sitting behind them had painted their faces like wolves and howled repeatedly. Remi found herself bouncing in her seat, the excitement in the air electric, energetic, galvanic.

The players skated back out onto the ice to thunderous cheering, blasting music and a blinding light display. Remi stood with the others and clapped until her hands throbbed. The crowd started whistling and cheering again halfway through the national anthem. Remi couldn't help but laugh, exchanging smiles with both Jase's parents at the exuberance of the fans. Compared to the last game she'd been to, this was way more intense.

Jase moved to center ice and she leaned forward, her body tense, as he prepared to take the face off. "That's Tag," Laura said in Remi's ear. Holy crapsicle. Jase was facing off against his brother. Nerves clutched at her stomach.

The referee paused with the puck in the air as the two centers appeared to exchange words. What were they saying to each other? Then the crowd went wild when Jase won the face off and one of his teammates took off with the puck.

"They both play center," Laura explained to Remi. "For a lot of years Jase played right wing, I think because he didn't want to try to compete with Tag, but he's so good at center."

Remi nodded. Sibling rivalry was a difficult thing at the best of times. She'd seen it with Jasmine and Kyle, despite her best efforts to treat them equally. What on earth would it be like in an intensely competitive environment like hockey?

She focused on the game, her eyes constantly seeking and finding Jase. The Wolves played well, attacking and keeping the puck down in the Phoenix zone, and it seemed like Jase was everywhere, all the time. And yet the other team was right there with him, constantly hitting him and knocking him around.

"Why are they doing that?" she asked in frustration, when once again he'd taken another brutal hit into the boards and lost the puck.

"Because he's the best player on the team," Jase's dad said dryly. "They gotta stay on him or they know he'll score."

Pride swelled in her, so big and warm she thought she might burst. That was her man down there. He loved her. She loved him.

Then Jase was smashed into the boards in a glass-shuddering, bone-jarring, head-shaking body check. Remi slid to the edge of her seat, trying to see if he was okay, while her heart went into a brief arrhythmia.

The crowd all yelled, demanding a penalty.

"That was a good check," Doug said to her. "There shouldn't be a penalty."

Like hell there shouldn't! Whoever had done that to Jase should be kicked out of the game! But there was no penalty despite the crowd's loud protests. Jase skated off to the bench, straightening his helmet.

Remi pressed a hand to her stomach and saw Laura's glance at her.

"Don't worry," Laura said. "He's tough. That's just part of the game."

Remi turned to her. "How could you watch that when he was little? You must have been so scared he'd get hurt."

"Yes, I was. Terrified. Every single game." Laura shook her head, mouth still lifted into a smile, eyes on the game. "When they're really young, of course, there is no body checking. But then they get older and the game gets a lot more physical. But there was no way I could stop any of the boys from playing. They loved it so much. Jase especially needed to play hockey."

Remi nodded, now aware of Jase's AHDH. Sports were a great way for kids to learn self-discipline and focus and he'd told her how good hockey had been for him.

And then Phoenix scored.

Although they were in the midst of a Wolves crowd, Laura and Doug cheered the goal because Tag had scored it.

Remi nibbled her lip as they announced the goal. "What does that mean when they say assisted by?" she asked Doug.

"Carver passed it to Romanov, who passed it to Tag," he explained. "So they get credit for assisting with the goal."

She'd seen all those stats—goals, assists and a whole lot more she couldn't figure out - GP, PIM, +/-, PP. ABCDEFG. Whatever.

The crowd was momentarily subdued by the goal, but the Wolves came back strong and peppered the Coyotes' goaltender with a series of hard, fast shots that had everyone in the arena screaming and groaning in unison.

"Damn!" Remi cried when another shot missed, her hands in fists. Oops. She slanted a grimace at Laura. Laura just grinned. And then one of the Stars got the puck and shot it all the way down the ice.

"Icing," Laura announced.

"What does that mean?"

The whistle blew. "If a player shoots the puck all the way down the ice and a player from the other team touches it first, it's icing."

Remi nodded. Okay.

The puck was brought back to the Coyotes' end for another face off. Jase skated around on one foot, then the other, waiting for the ref to crouch with the puck. Remi admired his grace on skates. She'd learned to skate as a little girl, but had never been so confident or graceful as he was and she could only admire the incredible skill it took to move that fast, stop that quickly, turn that sharply on those two razor-thin blades. Amazing.

The first period ended with the score one-nothing for Phoenix. "Going to get beers," Matt announced, standing up. "Remi, can I bring you one?"

"You're not old enough to drink here." Doug pushed his son back down into his seat.

Matt grinned sheepishly. "I could get away with it."

He probably could. He certainly looked older than nineteen with his massive size.

"I'll bring her a drink." Logan gave his brother a punch as he passed by him. Matt punched him back. Remi had to laugh. "Wanna come for a walk with me, Remi?"

The flirtatious gleam in his eye sizzled over her skin. "No thanks," she said with a smile and a shake of her head.

"Damn."

"Logan, she's Jase's friend," Laura scolded. He grinned and kissed his mom's forehead as he scooted past her and then bounded up the stairs to the concourse two at a time with his long legs.

"I'll go with him," Matt said.

"No beer," Doug said.

"Dad! I'm legal at home."

Doug rolled his eyes as if he knew he didn't have a hope of controlling his son. "It's true." He shook his head ruefully as he and Remi and Laura sat down again.

Laura shifted in her seat so she could talk to both her husband and Remi. "Jase is playing well," she said. "He won every face off."

How had she noticed that? Those face offs happened so fast.

"Yup," Doug agreed. "Maybe Tag's going easy on him."

"He would never do that."

Doug grinned. "Nope."

"But they're going to have to do better forechecking," Laura said.

A little lost, Remi listened to them analyze the game. God, Laura knew so much about the game, she sounded like a television commentator. After watching four sons grow up playing hockey their whole lives, Laura probably knew as much about it as they did. Remi sighed.

Jase scored a goal in the second period and the Wolves went into the third period with the score tied one-all. But despite intense pressure and a lot of end to end action, the Wolves could not put the puck in the net. The crowd was up and down with each opportunity, cheering, groaning, booing missed penalties.

"They need to change their lines up," Doug muttered. "Put Jase with Daviduk and Lalonde."

There were only three minutes left in the game.

"What happens if it's a tie?" Remi asked.

"They play five minutes of four-on-four overtime, and then if it's still tied, they have a shootout."

"They have to win." Tension gripped her, every muscle tight, her stomach in knots. She was getting a headache from biting her lips, her hands ached from clapping and her throat was raw from cheering.

And then the Coyotes took a penalty. The crowd went crazy.

"Damn," Laura muttered. "I mean, oh great."

Remi turned to her. "Tag just took a stupid penalty," Laura said. "The Coyotes play a man short now, with him in the penalty box." Her brow creased. "So for two minutes the Wolves have a power play—a man advantage."

Remi nodded. "That's good, though, right?"

"It's a great chance for them to score."

"Oh, hell," Doug sad. "They're gonna pull their goalie."

He nodded to the bench where the Wolves' goaltender had skated over to talk to the coach. The coach gestured wildly and the goalie nodded, squirted water into his mask, then skated back to the net.

"He's going back," Remi said.

"He'll come out when they get the puck down in the Phoenix end." Doug explained. "Goddammit, that's risky. Why the hell is he doing that? They've already got a man advantage."

They all sat forward to watch Jase take the face off and, damn, this time he lost. The Coyotes got the puck and immediately headed toward the Wolves net, tossing it back and forth with neat passes, the puck cracking against their sticks. But the Wolves defense knocked the puck away from Jase as he crossed the blue line. He and a Coyote raced into the corner and fought for the puck along the boards and Remi cringed at the bashing and crashing that went on, a vision of Jase bleeding on the ice flashing through her memory. She shivered.

Finally the puck came loose, but a Coyote slashed at it and sent it spinning down the ice.

"Icing!" Remi cried.

"Uh…no." Laura patted her hand. "They have a penalty so it's not icing."

Remi frowned. Mother of pearl. She wasn't used to feeling so stupid and uninformed. She wanted to slide under the seat. This game was more complicated than she'd realized. But then Jase swooped in and picked up the puck. The crowd screamed. Remi gripped her hands tightly together. Go, go, go, Jase! She sucked on her bottom lip as he deked around a defenseman, came to a fast stop in a shower of ice in front of another and slid around him, too, and then he was on his own, racing toward the Coyotes' net.

"Go!" Remi screamed with the crowd, the noise in the arena so loud it hurt her ears. She surged to her feet along with everyone else. "Go, Jase! Shoot!"

He lifted his stick, took a swing and blasted the puck at the net. Remi tensed, waiting for the red light—please, please—but the goalie snagged it in his glove and fell to the ice. The whistle blew and the play halted.

"Damn!" Remi realized she was clutching Laura's arm and hastily released it. "Sorry." She sagged and dropped into her seat.

"That's okay!" Laura flashed her a smile. "That was so close!"

Jase skated off the ice and another player prepared to take the face off.

Remi glanced at the clock. Only thirty-two seconds left in their power play. Only a minute and six seconds left in the game.

Do or die.

She so wanted this for Jase. She twisted her fingers together, gnawing her bottom lip again.

She looked down the ice. The goaltender was out of his net.

"He's out," she said to Doug and he nodded. "Why'd they do that? Isn't that just asking for Phoenix to score a goal on them? How can they play with no goaltender?"

Doug grinned. "They put another player on in his place. That means they have a two man advantage."

"But an empty net!" That seemed crazy dangerous.

Her heart leaping, fingers clasped so tightly they hurt, she watched as the puck was dropped. Wolves got the puck. Lalonde circled behind the net and paused. And waited.

"What's he waiting for?" Remi cried. She vibrated with tension.

"They're getting set up. Look at the players on the blue line."

Lalonde shot the puck from behind the net to one of his teammates, and the Wolves played with the puck like it was a pinball, passing it from one player to another, to another, and back again, back and forth, up and down, while the Coyotes whirled helplessly around in front of them, lunging with their sticks, trying desperately to get the puck.

"They need to shoot at the net!" Remi eyes darted back and forth to follow the puck.

"They will." Doug patted her shoulder. "Just…wait…now!"

Finally, the opening they'd wanted and Daviduk didn't even stop the puck, just slapped at it as it shot past him on the ice, directing it into the net.

"Yeah!"

The red light flashed, the horn blasted and the entire crowd in the Metro Center went wild. Remi pumped a fist in the air. She turned to Laura and they hugged, swaying back and forth.

Laura drew back, her smile wide and jubilant, and Remi collected herself. Dear god, she'd just hugged Jase's mom and she didn't even know her.

But the bubbly feeling inside her couldn't be repressed. Amid the noise of the still-cheering crowd, Jase took the next face off and won it, and the Wolves toyed with the puck while the clock ticked down the last seconds of the game. Then the roof nearly rose off the Metro Center as the game ended—the Wolves in the playoffs.

CHAPTER TWELVE

"The puck had fucking eyes, man!"

"No shit! With that traffic in front of the net, I couldn't believe it went in! You had horseshoes up your ass tonight!"

Jase grinned. His only goal of the game hadn't been pretty, but what the hell.

His brothers had greeted him as he walked into the lounge at the downtown hotel where they and his parents were staying, but although he accepted their back-slaps and congratulations, his gaze slid past them to Remi. She rose from her seat, her smile so sweet and generous, and he pushed by Matt and Logan and held out his arms.

She flew into them and he held her tight, lifting her feet off the floor as usual. "Congratulations!"

He kissed her, a long, hard, jubilant kiss.

"I knew you'd do it."

He drew back and met her eyes, smiling, his heart expanding, still buzzing from the adrenaline high of the game. Having his folks and Remi there just amplified the high.

His parents waited behind her to congratulate him too, exchanging amused looks. He blew out a long breath and greeted them while Matt and Logan went into the restaurant to get a table there.

"Good game, son." Dad clapped a hand on his shoulder. "Your plus-minus was great tonight."

They moved to the restaurant, him holding Remi's hand, and crossed the plush carpet to the large round table set up for the seven of them—where was Tag? Jase frowned and looked around. Tag must have got held up by the press even longer than he had.

At this late hour, few diners occupied the other tables in the posh restaurant and the quiet tinkle of piano music and subtle lighting steadied Jase's edgy nerves. It was hard coming down sometimes, especially after a game that mattered as much as this one had. He held Remi's chair for her as she took her seat, smiling up at him. Damn, she was pretty. He sat beside her, lifted her hand and kissed it.

They exchanged a heated glance. Adrenaline equaled sex for Jase, and much as he wanted to spend some time with the family, he wanted even more to take Remi back to his place and fuck her senseless. Fuck them both senseless. He shifted in his chair, then winced. That check into the boards had left a few bruises.

Ah well. It was worth it.

Then Tag arrived.

Jase rose to his feet to greet his brother, which was almost like looking in a mirror. Tag had an inch and a few pounds on him and Tag's nose was perfect and straight, but they shared the same eyes and mouth and chin. They stood in front of each other for a long moment. The tightness in the corners of Tag's eyes and mouth told Jase how his brother was feeling and Jase felt Tag's disappointment like a stone in his own gut. He wished he knew what to say, but neither of them was very good at talking about crap like that.

"Good game." Tag slapped Jase on the back.

"Thanks, man." Jase paused, then they gripped each other in a tight, emotion-laden hug.

Growing up as Tag's younger brother had never been easy. Competition, challenge and conflict had always been there. For most of Jase's life, he'd tried so hard not to compete with Tag, knowing he could never be as good as his big brother, that he'd gone in the wrong direction, lost his way, almost lost himself.

"Course you wouldn't have won if I hadn't let you win every face off," Tag said, cracking the tension.

"Bullshit." Jase rolled his eyes and grinned. "You're just getting so old your reflexes are slow." But when Tag's face tightened for a fleeting second, he wished he hadn't said that.

Hell. Tag wasn't old. He was only thirty-one, only two years older than Jase. In his prime.

Although hockey players did have a short career.

He shook his head. Tag was a great player, one of the best, and Jase only wished he could live up to his big brother.

He pushed that thought aside, determined to celebrate. And not only celebrate the game. He was celebrating Remi being there, celebrating that they were together and that his family was getting to meet her. He eyed them, hoping like hell they liked her.

He introduced her to Tag, the only one she hadn't met yet, and then they ordered dinner.

"So what do you think, Jase?" Dad asked. "Can you take St. Louis in the first round?"

"Hell yeah." It was the only answer. No doubt. No fear. "We'll take 'em in four."

"Morsey's injured," Tag said. "Probably done for the year. Helluva an advantage."

"Poor bugger," Logan said. "That sucks."

"Yeah."

"You're gonna have to improve your penalty killing against them," Tag said.

Remi's fingers curled around Jase's. He glanced at her. "Are you bored with all the hockey talk?" he murmured into her ear. "Sorry. This is what my family's like when we get together."

She shook her head and her big aquamarine eyes met his. His body tightened. "I'm not bored," she said with a small smile, then dropped her eyes.

"Yes, you are." He let go of her hand and slid his arm along the back of her chair, leaning closer.

"No. I just feel…stupid."

He reared back. "What?"

She gave him a wry smile and shrugged. "I wish I understood half the stuff you guys are talking about. Even your mom knows more about hockey than I do."

"Well of course she does. She used to play hockey too."

Remi's eyes shot wide. "She played hockey?"

"Yeah. What? Why are you looking like that?"

She shook her head. "Nothing. I'm just surprised."

"Lots of women play hockey. Didn't you watch the Olympics?"

"Well…yes. Okay, sure. I just never thought about your mom playing hockey. Wow."

Whatever. He'd never thought much of it, but he supposed it was kinda unusual.

Their low conversation was attracting interested, knowing looks from his family. He grinned.

"Sorry about all the hockey talk, Remi," Mom said with a smile. Jase watched her. She liked Remi. He could tell. Good, good. Warmth spread inside him.

"That's okay." Remi smiled too. Yes! They liked each other. Fucking awesome. He caught his mom's eye and her smile changed, softened and her eyes glowed. His chest tightened and he nodded, and then to his horror, Mom's eyes got teary. Ah, hell. He frowned at her and she blinked and gave a little laugh.

"So how are you going to like playing in Winnipeg next year?" Jase asked Tag with a smirk.

"Shut the fuck up. The team's going nowhere."

"There've been rumors that the Coyotes might be sold," Jase explained to Remi. "And lots of rumors about them moving to Winnipeg." He grinned at Tag. "You don't want to move back home with Mom and Dad? And hey, Winterpeg after living in the desert with palm trees and sunshine all winter."

Tag sighed. "What happens, happens." He looked at Remi. "So, Remi. How the hell did you hook up with a loser like Jase?"

"Shaddup," Jase said mildly.

Remi laughed. "It's a long story."

"How's business, Dad?" Jase changed the subject again.

"Great, great."

"Gonna retire soon?"

"Not until one of you comes home to run the store."

Jase met his brothers' eyes, one at a time. They all knew Dad wanted them to take over the sporting goods store. And maybe one of them would. One day. But not any time soon. His gut clenched.

His dad laughed. "Never mind, you buncha goons. I'm not waiting for you. I have no intention of retiring."

Jase regarded his father. Although sixty years old, he was still fit and energetic and certainly with it. Definitely still capable of running the store. And he had lots of help. The store had grown enough to hire a substantial staff. But still, guilt nudged at his conscience and he hoped Dad was being honest when he said he didn't want to retire until one of them came home.

"Excuse me."

They all looked up at the couple that had stopped at their table.

"Are you the Heller brothers?"

They all grinned and nodded.

"Our two sons are such big hockey fans. They would love it if you'd give us your autograph."

Jase and his brothers willingly signed their names for the couple who were all smiling and grateful. But when Jase looked at Remi, he saw her head bowed again. Shit. He knew she was still uncomfortable with the fame and the fans and the press. He reached for her hand again and squeezed.

He tried to keep the conversation away from hockey, at least part of the time, wanting his parents to get to know Remi.

When the waiter appeared with the bill in a discreet leather folder, Tag said, "Give the bill to him," and nodded at Jase. With an exaggerated sigh, Jase held out his hand. Tag grinned. "We made a bet. Just before the opening face off. Winner buys dinner."

"Now I know you let me win," Jase grumbled, reaching for his wallet. He slanted a glance at Remi beside him, loving the laughter that sparkled in her eyes.

He was on top of the world tonight. He had it all and having Remi at his side was the ultimate thrill. What more could a guy ask for?

That night, together in Remi's bed, he wanted to show her how he felt, all his love and desire and gratitude. He kissed her over and over, licked into her mouth, found her tongue with his and played, nipped at her lips all soft and pouty, consuming her with his kisses. She responded immediately, so sweetly, opening her mouth to him, winding her arms around his neck and pulling him down to her, closer. He lay on top of her, on his elbows, his hands fisted in her silky hair, kissing her, tasting her, sinking into her. Her fresh flowery scent filled his head, making him dizzy.

"I love you," he whispered, over and over. "I love you."

She whispered it back, the words so sweet on her lips. He kissed her jaw, her cheek, her eyebrows. He felt it right to his bones, his need for her. Heat slid down his spine and gathered in his balls and he pushed into her hot softness. Her fingers dug into his shoulders and she made the hottest little noises of pleasure. She tipped her head back and he kissed her throat, sucked gently there, then dragged his tongue over soft skin.

They drifted into another dimension, lost in the pleasure of each other, moving together, murmuring soft words, touching each other everywhere. Heat twisted inside him, pressure built, perspiration gathered on his body and he came inside her, hands in her hair, his mouth on hers. "I love you."

Remi woke up to Jase's furnace-like body wrapped around her in her bed. Saturday morning.

She had laundry to do. Grocery shopping. Her car needed an oil change and she needed to sit down and pay some utility bills. And then there was the marking of tests, preparing for a big project.

Later.

Jase was there, in her bed, big and warm and hard, and she wasn't going to let that go to waste.

She shifted against him and his hand went to her butt. "Mmm," he said.

"I love you, Jase," she whispered, not sure if he was even awake enough to hear her.

He was.

He flipped her onto her back, and smiled down at her. "I love you too. So much, Remi."

He bent his head and kissed her. "Oh, let me go brush my teeth," she begged.

He laughed and rolled to his back, taking her with him. "I don't care."

"I do."

She buried her face in the space between his neck and his shoulder and felt his cock harden against her leg. "I'll be right back."

She quickly used the bathroom and brushed her teeth, then slipped back into bed beside him. He pulled her on top of him and she gazed down at his face, the beard stubble darkening his strong jaw, eyes so deep and delicious, his beautiful mouth. She traced a finger over one eyebrow, brushed her fingertips across his lips.

"Last night..." she began and then emotion clogged her throat up. Last night he'd made love to her with such tenderness and devotion she'd cried after, pressed against him, her love for him so huge and engulfing.

"I know." He ran his hands down her back, over her butt, back up and into her hair. "I know."

She gave him a shaky smile, touching her mouth to his. His opened immediately to her and he tilted her head for a deeper angle.

The alarm pinged, announcing someone had just entered the house.

They both froze and lifted their heads.

It could only be Jasmine. No one else had a key.

"Remi?" Jasmine's voice called out.

What the hell was she doing there this early? Remi frowned and looked at her alarm clock. Okay, it wasn't early, it was almost ten-thirty. They'd had a late night with Jase's family and then they'd made love half the night, so they'd slept late.

She met Jase's eyes and hitched her shoulders, then smiled. "I met your family," she said. "Now it's your turn."

"I've met Jasmine."

"Bah. For thirty seconds."

"Uh...this isn't the best..."

The bedroom door opened. "Remi, are you still...oh my god."

Remi, on top of Jase, with her back to the door, froze. Then she glanced over her bare shoulder. "Jasmine."

"Sorry, sorry." The door closed.

A few weeks ago, Remi would have been horrified. Mortified. Distraught. Now—she laughed.

She rolled out of bed. "I better go see what she wants." Still smiling, nothing able to penetrate her blissful bubble, she slid her arms into the silk wrap she'd bought at Victoria's Secret the other day and tied the belt as she meandered down the hall.

"Are you still here?" she called out.

"In the kitchen."

Remi walked into the kitchen smiling. "Hi."

"Sorry about that." Jasmine grimaced. "I had no idea…is that Jase?"

"Yeah."

"I just never thought…" She blew out a breath. "Sorry."

"Maybe knock before you walk into my room." Remi smiled as she scooped coffee grounds into the filter. She brushed off her fingertips and pressed the button to start the coffee. She needed coffee.

"So you and him…"

Remi smiled, leaned against the counter. "Yes. Me and him."

"Oh. You seem really…happy, Remi."

"Yeah. I am." She tipped her head. "What are you doing here, Jas?"

"Oh. Yeah. I needed to talk to you about something."

Jase sauntered into the kitchen in his suit pants and the T-shirt he'd worn beneath his dress shirt last night, looking rumpled and sexy as hell. Jasmine's eyes widened.

"Hi. You must be Jasmine." Jase held out a hand and speared her with his charming smile.

Jasmine made a noise and shook his hand.

"We met before, but only briefly. I'm Jase."

"Uh. Yeah. I remember. Hi."

Remi put her fingers to her mouth. "Jasmine apparently dropped by to talk to me about something. So, what is it, Jasmine?"

"Maybe I should come back later." She couldn't seem to take her eyes off Jase.

Remi almost laughed. "No, don't be silly. What is it?"

Jasmine looked back and forth between them, watching Jase cross the kitchen and kiss Remi's forehead. Remi smiled up at him.

"I gotta go," he said regretfully. "To take my parents to the airport."

"Oh yeah. Okay." She went on her toes and he lifted her against him for a long, sweet kiss.

Jase kissed Remi, smiled at her sister, then headed back to her bedroom to get dressed.

See, this was the problem. His suit and shirt were wrinkled from lying in a heap on the floor where he'd left them last night and he had nothing else to wear. Saturday morning he did not feel like putting on a suit. He'd have to rush back to his place, change and then get to the hotel to pick his parents up. Everything would be easier if he and Remi lived together.

He waited for the familiar panicky feeling to claw inside him at the thought of committing like that, but it didn't come. He buttoned his shirt with fingers that didn't tremble. Huh. It was kinda weird, but they'd figure it all out later.

Remi followed him to her front door, holding her coffee mug. He bent and kissed her mouth. "I'll call you later, okay?"

"Okay."

He patted her cute butt under the silky robe, drawing a smile from her, and then he left, locking her door behind him. The early April morning held hints of spring, the breeze softer, the sun warmer as he strode down the sidewalk to his Jeep, parked at the curb.

It felt like a beginning.

As he drove downtown and thought about everything that had happened in the last twenty-four hours, an expansive feeling of well-being rose inside him. He smiled as he drove. They'd made the playoffs. Yeah, there was still a long road to the Stanley Cup ahead of them, but they'd done it after a long season that had handed them lots of challenges—injuries, trades, talk of financial problems with the team.

He winced a bit, remembering that Tag hadn't made it. But that was life.

His parents had been there, had been proud of him, had seen him play better than Tag. He didn't like to gloat, but he couldn't help a tiny feeling of satisfaction at that. It had been a long time coming.

Remi had been there and she'd been proud of him too. He loved that. And he liked knowing his parents had met her and liked her and now…the M word even popped into his head and didn't cause a panic attack.

In his apartment, he quickly showered and changed into jeans and a T-shirt, threw on his jacket and headed out again, over to the hotel.

Marriage.

He could see being married to Remi one day. Moving in together was a big step, marriage would really be rushing it, but the idea of one day taking that leap didn't scare the shit out of him. He grinned. Maybe he was growing up.

Or maybe he'd just found the right woman.

Maybe he'd been wrong when he said that to Brianne—maybe it *was* her. Maybe the reason all the hints about marriage and weddings had scratched away at his nerves was because he knew she wasn't the one for him.

Which could only mean Remi *was* the one.

He paused in the hotel lobby. Put a hand to his chest. His heart beat normally.

It was okay. It was really okay.

Wow. He laughed out loud.

His parents and Matt sat on couches arranged in a grouping on one side of the lobby, their luggage sitting on the floor beside them. They were all looking at him as if he'd walked in wearing his skates and equipment. He laughed again.

"Feeling pretty good today, huh?" Dad said to him, standing as he approached them across the expanse of gleaming granite floor tile.

"Yeah."

"You haven't won the Stanley Cup yet."

"I know."

As they walked out to his Jeep, Mom took hold of his arm.

"Jase."

"Mmm?"

She looked a little flustered, like she wanted to say something, but was afraid. "Are you and Remi…serious?"

"Did you like her, Mom?"

The two of them paused on the sidewalk while Matt and Dad loaded suitcases into the vehicle.

"Well, I just met her, but she seems very sweet. You looked so happy with her."

He nodded, throat constricted. "Yeah."

"She's um…different…than other girls you've gone out with."

He hesitated. He knew what she meant, but wasn't sure how to express it. "I know. She's…real."

Mom smiled. "Yes. She is."

He nodded, glad he'd somehow made his mom happy, even more glad that Remi was in his life, but he felt like a big dumb jock because he didn't have the words to express all that.

After seeing them off at O'Hare, he drove to the Metro Center where their practice had been moved to the afternoon for a change. The physical workout felt good. Much as they all wanted to take it easy to celebrate their win the night before, they also knew they had a lot of work to do. The playoffs were a whole new season. Mentally they had to get into a different place. Physically they needed to be at their peak.

He debated going straight to Remi's place after the practice, but glanced at his watch. It was early. She had things to do too. He'd go home, call her, they'd figure out what they were going to do tonight. They could have a nice celebration dinner, just the two of them, somewhere quiet and casual, then go back to her place and…

Well. Yeah.

In his apartment, he sat down in front of his computer. His Twitter feed was full of congratulations at the win. He went through emails, some things from his agent to look at, some stuff from his financial guy about his investments. He was glad he'd been smart with his money. His parents had drilled that into him over the years. His career could end tomorrow with a bad check or a puck in the face, so he had to be prepared for anything.

The security buzzer announced someone at the front door. He frowned, spun around on the chair, then went to the security system. Had Remi decided to come over instead of waiting for him to call?

But the security camera showed Brianne standing there. Huh? What the hell was she doing there? He paused, his finger on the button to let her in. She buzzed again.

With a sigh, he picked up the phone. "Brianne? What are you doing here?"

She looked into the camera. "I need to talk to you, Jase." She hugged a big purse to her like it was a security blanket or something. His frown deepened.

"What about?"

She glanced around, then looked pleadingly back at the camera. "Just let me in, Jase. We have to talk."

Hell. He buzzed her in, shoved a hand through his hair and paced while he waited for her to come up in the elevator. What the fuck was this about? If she was going to beg him to get back together, she'd picked the wrong time, with him just figuring out he wanted to spend his life with Remi. His gut still clenched, though, at the thought of having to tell Brianne that.

Maybe it was something else. Maybe she'd just realized she was over him and came to tell him that.

Maybe the Toronto Maple Leafs would win the Stanley Cup this year. Haha. Yeah right.

He moved to the door at her light knock, and opened it.

She walked in.

She actually didn't look too good. Which was weird, considering that she didn't like leaving her home without hair, makeup and clothes all perfect because you never knew when paparazzi could be waiting to take pictures of them and that was how she earned her living, after all.

Her hair was in a ponytail, she had no makeup on under the big dark glasses she wore and she was dressed in pair of stretchy black pants and a long sleeved grey T-shirt.

"Hey," he said. "What's up?"

She turned to him, biting her top lip in a way that was very unattractive. If she knew how she looked doing that, she'd never do it. Something was clearly wrong.

"Have a seat." He gestured to his black leather couch.

She sat and pushed the sunglasses to the top of her head. Blinked. "Congratulations," she finally said. "You made the playoffs."

He smiled. "Yeah. Thanks."

She sat there, saying nothing, her hands clutching her knees.

"Brianne?"

She swallowed, nodded, then looked at him, but her gaze was on his chest, not his eyes. "I have something to tell you."

"Okay." Get on with it, he thought. He resisted the urge to glance at his watch.

"I'm pregnant."

CHAPTER THIRTEEN

"So what did you want to talk about, Jasmine?" Remi sauntered back into the kitchen after saying good-bye to Jase, feeling soft and relaxed and happy.

"Well. Um. Ethan and I want to buy a house."

"Oh. Really." Remi's stomach rolled over. It had been a big step for them to move in together in Ethan's apartment. Buying a house together sounded serious. She still wasn't convinced their relationship was all that mature. She sat at the big oak kitchen table with Jasmine.

"We want to buy a house, but things have tightened up a lot because of the recession," Jasmine continued. "So we need a big down payment."

"Oh. I guess you do." Remi nodded, still not sure where this was going. She sipped her coffee, scalding hot, dark and rich. "Do you have some money saved up?"

"No."

"Oh." She waited.

Jasmine looked down at her coffee, appearing to struggle for words. Then she looked up. "If you sold the house, I could use my share of the money to buy a new one."

Remi shook her head. "What?"

"It's our house." Jasmine smiled. "All three of us. Right?"

"Uh…right." Remi's mind spun. What did she say? What?

"So if it belongs to all three of us, then one third of the value is mine and I want that money for a down payment on a house of our own. Me and Ethan. So you need to sell the house."

Remi stared at Jasmine. What was she talking about? "But I live here, Jasmine."

"I know. But you could find somewhere else to live. You'd have your third of the money."

"But..." Remi blinked, looked around her. This was her home. This was *their* home. Even though Jasmine had just moved out, she'd already moved back once. She needed a place to come home to when things didn't work out. Okay, *if* things didn't work out. *Think positive.* And Kyle—he lived in the dorm at college, but this was really still his home.

"I can't move out, Jasmine," she said slowly. "I don't want to sell this house."

"But, Remi." Jasmine leaned forward. "A third of this house is mine."

It was true.

Their parents had left everything to all three of them, including the house. It had to be split evenly three ways, somehow, some day. But Remi had never thought ahead to the day that might happen.

How could she leave here? The house meant so much to her. Stability. Security. Family. In a life that had her parents flitting in and out and then gone for good, it was the one constant. Home.

But that wasn't the only problem. Remi did not have faith that Jasmine and Ethan's relationship was strong enough to last. Buying a house together was a serious commitment.

She sighed. She knew how that was going to be received. Jasmine wanted to hear that as much as she wanted to have her head shaved.

Remi ran her hand through her hair, still tangled from an energetic night with Jase. "Jasmine. This is kind of sudden. I need time to think about it."

"What's to think about? You know you have to do it. Part of this house is mine."

"Jasmine. Think what you're asking. I can't just sell the house on whim. I need to find somewhere else to live. And besides..." She tried to stop herself, but the words came pouring out. "I don't know if you and Ethan buying a house together is such a good idea."

"I knew it." Jasmine pushed her cup away. "You just don't like Ethan."

"It's not that." Dammit, why had she said that? She needed to be careful here. "It's just what I said. You two have fights all the time. You don't trust him."

"Yes, I do."

Remi resisted the protest that sprang to her lips. Fine. "Okay. Could you just let me think about it? Maybe there's another way."

Jasmine stood up and crossed her arms. "There is no other way. We don't have enough money and we'll never have enough money for a down payment. The way the economy is now, we'll be lucky if we ever have a house. How are we supposed to have kids, living in an apartment?"

Remi stared at her, aghast. "You want to have kids?"

"Well, maybe some day."

Mother of pearl. Jasmine was only twenty-one. There was no way she was ready to have kids.

Or was Remi just jealous because that was something *she* wanted so badly?

Ugh.

Suddenly Remi felt the weight of it all pressing down on her shoulders deflating her earlier bubble of joy. She slumped a bit. "I'll think about it," she said slowly. "I promise."

"Whew. Okay, thank you Remi."

Jase squinted at Brianne. "You're what? Pregnant?" Is that really what she'd said?

"Yes." She twisted her fingers together on her lap, still looking at his chest.

Why was she telling him this? Did she think he'd be upset? He didn't care about Brianne's life any more, he'd moved on. She had to know that.

Suddenly his gut cramped. She couldn't be telling him this because…holy fuck. Did she think he was the father?

"Brianne." His voice came out sounding funny. "Why are you telling me this?"

She looked at him blankly. "I thought I should. You have a right to know."

"Are you saying…?" He felt his throat close up, paused. Tried again. "Are you saying I'm the father?"

Her eyes widened. "Of course you're the father! There hasn't been anyone else."

The room moved around him, shifted, faded away. He wasn't sitting, he was floating. He gripped the armrests of the chair to hold himself in place. His vision went foggy and he felt like his brains were spinning around in his head.

It couldn't be true. She couldn't be pregnant. It was a mistake. "You're on the pill."

She nodded, bending her head. "Yes. But…" She shrugged. "I guess we're one of those point-zero-one per cent where it doesn't work. For whatever reason. I don't know."

"Are you sure? How do you know? You could just be late."

Jase's fingers ached from clenching the upholstery and he tried to relax. His ass was almost lifting out of the chair, his body had gone so tight and rigid.

"I did two tests. Just to make sure."

He stared at her, the room still moving in circles like a bad case of bed spins after too much partying. And then he shook his head. Was this for real?

"Brianne. You're not just doing this to try to get back together, are you?"

Her mouth dropped open. "No!"

"Are you sure?" She'd been phoning him all the time, wanting to talk. This couldn't be true. "How far along are you?"

"Two months."

But…but… "Brianne. We broke up two months ago. Are you sure there hasn't been anyone else?"

"They start counting from the first day of your last period," she said, her voice low. "Which was two weeks before we broke up. It probably happened that last night…" Her words ended on a small sob and she pressed a hand to her mouth. "I'm not exactly happy about this either. There goes my Victoria's Secret job."

That did sound like Brianne, but…

He narrowed his eyes at her. It couldn't be true. It just couldn't. Anger surged inside him that she would stoop this low.

"You'd better go." He stood.

"What?" She stared at him. "You really don't believe me?"

He slowly shook his head. "No. I don't."

"Jase!" Her cry sounded distressingly anguished. "I'm telling you the truth! I wouldn't lie about this!"

He shook his head stubbornly, folded his arms across his chest and lifted his chin. "Just leave, Brianne."

"But…but…what do I have to do to make you believe me?"

He scowled. "I don't know."

"If I…show you the pregnancy test…?"

He pursed his lips. "That'll prove you're pregnant, I guess. It won't prove I'm the father."

"Jase!" Her eyes filled with tears. "I haven't been with anyone else! I love you!"

Fuck. He closed his eyes.

"I can get something from my doctor." She stood, her fingers twisting together. "My doctor can tell you how many weeks I am. Then you'll know."

He gave a jerky nod. "Yeah. You do that," he said. She wouldn't get anything from her doctor. Because it wasn't true.

He wasn't even going to tell Remi about it. Because it was just so crazy and there was no need for her to get all upset about it. Jesus! He swiped a hand across his forehead as he drove back to her place later. They'd decided to just order pizza and celebrate his win at her place.

When he got there, she greeted him looking a little like a goaltender who'd just been bombarded by fifty shots with no defense. Which was pretty much how he felt. He sucked in a breath as he kissed her.

"You won't believe what happened," she said. He followed her into her kitchen where she began to open a bottle of wine.

Oh, man. He could say the same to her. But he wasn't going to.

"My sister wants me to sell the house."

"You're kidding? Why?" He reached for the bottle and corkscrew she was struggling with. "Here. Let me." He popped the cork out and poured wine into two glasses while she told him about her earlier conversation with Jasmine.

But his mind drifted off, back to that horrifying conversation with Brianne. He still couldn't believe she would go that far to try to get him back.

"Jase?"

He looked up at Remi. "Yeah?"

"Are you okay? You seem…distracted."

He forced a smile, his body tight and twitchy. "Yeah. Fine. Go on."

He tried to listen, he really did, but his thoughts were all over the place and Remi was noticing. *Fuck.* He had to stop thinking about Brianne. He firmly pushed those thoughts aside and focused on Remi. "So what are you going to do?"

"I don't know." She looked around her. "I love this house. But it's true. Kyle and Jasmine are entitled to their share of the house. Even though I think they need this place to come home to. At least for a while."

He nodded and drank some of the wine. Then the words just popped out of his mouth. "You know…you could move in with me."

He couldn't believe he was sitting there calmly, steadily looking at Remi, inviting her to move in with him, and his heart wasn't racing, his gut wasn't heaving, his neck and shoulders weren't rock hard with tension.

He'd thought about it earlier and now the idea had slid into his head like a puck gliding into the net, and before he'd even had time to think about it, he'd said it. He wanted Remi to live with him.

She stared at him. "What?"

"You could move in with me." He reached for her hand. "I want you to live with me."

She moved her head slowly from side to side, pretty lips parted. "But we hardly know each other. We can't move in together."

"We know each other." He stroked his thumb across the back of her hand. "I love you, Remi. I want to live with you."

"Are you crazy?"

He remembered the last time they'd had a conversation like this and how heated and angry her question had been. This time her voice was soft, wondering. He grinned. "No, I mean it."

"Wow." She blinked at him. "That's a pretty serious step for a guy who just wants to have fun."

"It would be fun living with you. I know it."

She smiled and shook her head. "Jase, there's more to it than that."

"I know. I actually thought of it this morning, how much easier everything would be if we lived together. Just think about it. Maybe this thing with Jasmine will blow over. There's no rush. But you know…even if you don't have to sell the house…think about it."

She nodded, her eyes a little dazed. "Okay."

"Let's order pizza. I'm starving."

It took Brianne a week.

She showed up at his apartment the next Saturday, grim-faced and pissed. "Here," she said, shoving a paper into his hand. "Nine weeks. Now do you believe me?"

He stared down at the note on official medical stationery. It looked…real.

His stomach heaved, his mouthed filled with saliva and he swallowed repeatedly. He could not puke. He could not puke.

"And I brought this too," she snapped, pulling a plastic baggie out of her purse. She handed it to him too. He looked at the plastic stick inside. "That's the pregnancy test I took. For the third damn time." Her lips tightened into a thin line. She glared at him.

He wiped his mouth. The silence stretched out, long and thick.

A million questions backed up in his brain. He closed his eyes.

Jesus. A baby. Fuck.

Fuck, fuck, fuck.

"What are you doing to do?" He sounded like his voice was coming from far away, echoing in his ears.

"I'm…I'm going to have the baby."

He squeezed his eyes closed. He'd never been someone who believed in abortion but he'd also always believed in a woman's right to choose. Because they were the ones who got pregnant. But at that moment, he had to ask, why, *why* she would do that when her career and his life would be so hugely impacted by this.

But he knew why. It was a baby. Their baby.

Jesus Christ. How could this have happened?

How could he be a father? He felt like a kid himself. And what was he supposed to do about Brianne? They'd broken up. He didn't love her. But she was going to be the mother of his child.

Nausea rolled again. He fought it down and looked at Brianne standing there, arms folded across her chest, hip cocked.

He had to ask it. "What do you want from me, Brianne?"

Her face crumpled and her eyes filled with tears. "You know what I want."

Did she want them to get back together? To try to make something work for the sake of their child? The questions ricocheted around inside him, but he was a coward, too afraid to speak them aloud in case she said yes, that's what she wanted.

Remi.

Oh, Christ, *Remi*. How was he going to tell Remi about this?

He'd just asked her to move in with him.

The idea of hurting her sliced through him with such a sharp jagged pain he made a noise. He cleared his throat, glancing at Brianne. She watched him with sad glossy eyes and a shaky mouth.

He turned and walked into his living room, rubbing the back of his neck. "I don't know what to say."

"Neither do I." She followed him and perched on the edge of his couch. He lowered himself into a chair.

"D'you...do you want us to get back together?"

She blinked at him. "I still love you, Jase. You know I do."

Fuck. That was not what he wanted to hear. That jagged pain inside him intensified.

"I don't know if I can do this on my own, Jase."

He moved his head slowly up and down. He got that. He wasn't sure if he could do it either. A baby! Christ!

He leaned his head back, trying to imagine his life with a child. With Brianne. Terror clawed at him, long talons dragging through his intestines, panic bubbling up inside him with that familiar feeling of being caged, trapped, noosed.

Like marriage, he'd always figured parenthood would come some day. He wasn't a confirmed bachelor, sworn to stay single forever. Nah. His parents had created a great family and he wanted that too. Some day. Some very far-distant day.

A son to teach how to play hockey.

Maybe a girl. But girls could play hockey too.

But not now. Not now. *Not now.*

He lifted his head and looked at Brianne.

"I can't do it alone," she whispered. "I need you, Jase."

She held out a hand.

He ached. He hesitated. But the despair and pleading in her eyes tugged at something inside him. They'd done this together. Created a baby together. He rose up, walked over to her and sat down beside her. She turned into him and he hugged her, holding her against him, her face pressed to his chest, his cheek to her hair.

Guilt weighted heavy on his shoulders—a feeling like he was cheating on Remi. But Brianne needed him. Man, did she need him. More than he wanted to be needed and a battle raged inside him over who he owed more to, over what he was supposed to do, over whether he had it in him to do the right thing—or whether he had it in him to even know what the right thing was.

His life was so fucked.

CHAPTER FOURTEEN

Remi looked at her watch again. Seven o'clock and Jase still hadn't called. She'd assumed they would spend the evening together, as they had been lately. Where was he?

She rubbed her neck and shoulders. She'd spent the afternoon grading papers and planning a big class project she was going to get the kids working on next week. Her mind kept veering off, though, thinking about selling the house, thinking about moving in with Jase... Pinwheels spun in her stomach every time she thought about that. God. Live with Jase. Could she do it?

She was in love with him, wanted to be with him. But how hypocritical was it of her to tell Jasmine she shouldn't buy a house with Ethan and then move in with a man she'd only known a few weeks? She pressed her fingers between her eyes where tiny hammers had started thumping.

She got up from the kitchen table where she'd been working and stretched, then sighed. Maybe she should call Jase and see what had happened to him. She hoped everything was okay.

Her heart stuttered. Maybe he'd been hurt in practice that morning. God. He could be sitting in a hospital right now.

She punched in his cell phone number. Waited. "The cellular customer you are calling is not available."

She looked at her phone with a frown. He had his cell phone off? That was unusual. She called the number at his apartment, but it rang and then went to voice mail.

Should she leave a message? Sure, why not. "Hi, Jase, it's me. It's just after seven, just wondering what happened to you. If you get this, give me a call and let me know you're okay. Bye."

She hoped that sounded casual enough.

She walked to the front window to look out on the dark street, as if Jase might just drive up at any minute. What if he regretted making that impulsive offer of moving in together? Was he avoiding her? She rolled her eyes. Even if he did have second thoughts, surely he was mature enough to just tell her. She could take it. All he had to say was, "Hey, let's not rush things" and she'd be fine. She didn't want to rush things either.

In fact, she wasn't even sure if she'd do it. If she had to sell the house—and that was just one more thing she was undecided on—it would probably be better for her to get her own apartment or something. It would be the sensible, responsible thing to do.

She'd always been sensible and responsible.

Since she'd met Jase, she'd done things she'd never have dreamed of—picking up a guy and taking him home, hot sexual adventures, flying off to California for a sexy weekend. Crazy. Moving in with him would be the craziest thing of all.

But there was no denying how much she wanted that. How much she wanted to wake up with him every morning, to go to bed with him every night, to cheer him on and share his triumphs and yes, his losses, because he would have those. To be there for him.

She'd come a long way from wanting nothing to do with him because of paparazzi stalkers, aggressive female fans and a huge paycheck. Now—she loved him. None of that mattered.

She also had to admit she liked how he was there for her. How supportive he'd been when Kyle had been freaking out, even though she'd been annoyed at him. How steady he'd been when she'd been ambushed by Jasmine's request. She'd been thinking about it all week and she longed for him to be there so she could share all her confused feelings about selling the house. How it was more than just a house, it was their home. But yet, if Jasmine and Kyle didn't live there any more, there was no real logical, rational reason not to sell it. Truthfully, the cash would help pay for Kyle's tuition. Or she could insist he invest it and save it as a down payment on a home of his own one day. And was she being selfish by wanting to stay there, when truthfully Jasmine had a valid point that the house belonged to all three of them.

But Jase wasn't there to talk to about it.

She moved away from the window to wander around her house, straightening things, wiping the counter that was already spotless, staring into space.

Maybe she could find a movie on TV to keep her occupied for a while. She sat down on the couch and flicked through the channels, finding a chick flick she'd already seen, but hey, without Jase there, it was a good time to watch it again.

She fell asleep with the television on and woke up feeling groggy and disoriented. She still hadn't heard from Jase. And she didn't hear from him all day Sunday either, until her cell phone rang at nearly ten o'clock when she was getting ready for bed, heart heavy and aching, stomach cramped with worry.

"Hello?"

"Hi." It was Jase. She recognized his voice even in that one word.

"Jase. Where are you?"

"St. Louis."

"Oh."

"I…" He stopped. "I'm sorry I didn't call you yesterday. Uh…something came up and…I'm really sorry, Remi."

"Is everything okay, Jase? You sound funny." She pushed her bangs off her face. Something clutched at her heart and squeezed, sending scary feelings through her, shivery, worried feelings.

"I'm okay. I just wanted to call you. I wanted to…" He stopped again. "Fuck. I'm so sorry."

"It's okay."

"Listen, I'll call you when I get back."

"Sure. That's fine." Her stomach churned. Something felt wrong. He did not sound like himself. "Good luck tomorrow night. I'll be watching."

"Thanks, Remi." There was a long pause, then he said, "I love you, Remi."

"Oh." Her heart squeezed. "I love you too."

She hung up with trembling fingers, closing her burning eyes. She'd go to bed, get a good night's sleep and in the morning everything would be fine.

But Monday morning she discovered how *not* fine things were. Skimming through the morning paper while she drank coffee, she flipped the page and her eyes were immediately drawn to a small headline—"Chicago Wolves player arrested for disorderly conduct."

She leaned forward, frowning. "Saturday night, Chicago Wolves center Jase Heller was arrested at Sage Restaurant. According to restaurant manager Brian Smythe, Heller had arrived at the restaurant with a group of teammates at about nine o'clock. When advised of the dress code by the hostess and told that he could not enter the restaurant wearing blue jeans, Heller became angry and argumentative. When Mr. Smythe reinforced the restaurant policy and again told Heller he could not enter wearing blue jeans, Heller stripped off his jeans and walked into the restaurant in his underwear. Restaurant personnel asked Heller to leave, but he refused. Police were called and Heller was arrested and charged with disorderly conduct, public intoxication and resisting arrest. He was later released on bail."

Remi sat frozen in her chair, her coffee forgotten. It was a wonder her eyes hadn't popped right out of her skull and rolled across the floor. What the hell? Arrested? He'd taken off his pants in a classy restaurant and made a scene?

At least he'd been wearing underwear.

She wanted to disbelieve that this could have been Jase, but the black letters on the page popped out at her as if they were in big bold font.

She shook her head. There must be some mistake. This was not possible.

The coffee she'd drank burbled in her stomach and threatened to come back up. She shook her head. What was going on? This was insane.

April fool's day had passed days ago. This couldn't be a prank. But he hadn't said a word of this when they'd talked last night and her sense of unease and dread grew.

She had to go to work.

As if she could concentrate on thirty energetic kids. But she had no choice. In fact, she was going to be late.

She drove to school in a daze, thoughts tumbling around in her head like laundry in a dryer. Nothing made sense. She felt lost, like she was wandering through a maze, not sure which way to turn, smacking up against walls, desperate to get out.

What had she gotten herself into? Had she fallen in love with a nut job? Had he fooled her that well?

No. No. They loved each other. She had no doubt about the depth of their feelings for each other, which only made the situation more bizarre. In her wildest imaginings, she could not come up with something that reasonably explained this.

All day it took monstrous effort to stay focused enough to teach, to keep things under control with a group of pre-teens who looked for any weakness, any small crack that would give them the advantage, because once they started it was even harder to bring them back.

By the time the bell rang at the end of the day, she was exhausted.

And worried sick. She hadn't been able to eat lunch and certainly wasn't interested in dinner.

She had to talk to someone, so when she got home she called Delise and told her what had happened. Delise hadn't seen the newspaper article, but sounded as shocked and confused as Remi felt.

"Don't even say I told you so," Remi said fiercely. Delise had been gradually more accepting of her dating Jase but still had reservations about it.

"I won't. Do you want me to come over?"

"Um...maybe. I'm going to watch the game on TV." Seeing Jase on television would at least reassure her that he was alive and functioning.

"I'll come over. I'll bring popcorn and beer."

She didn't want popcorn and beer, but didn't say anything, letting Delise think she was helping.

"Thank you for coming," she said later, as they sat side by side on the couch, a bowl of popcorn between them. Delise was munching and Remi'd picked up a few kernels, but they tasted like she was eating dog kibble. One beer on an empty stomach had her a little woozy. She kept her eyes glued to the television, watching for Jase.

He was there. She caught sight of number twenty-five in the line as the national anthem played, but the cameraman apparently wasn't as interested in him as she was and passed right by him.

"He's there," she breathed.

"So, that's good."

"I guess." Maybe she would have felt better if he'd still been in jail or if he'd actually been hospitalized with a head injury and amnesia.

Jase did not take the opening faceoff. In fact, as the game progressed, he didn't play a lot, and when he was on the ice he seemed sluggish and slow. Was he sick? Icy fingers squeezed her insides painfully. "Oh, Delise." The words came out shaky. "Something's wrong."

Delise glanced at her and patted her leg, but Remi could tell she didn't know what to say. Had she been rudely dumped? Or was there really something wrong? She nibbled her bottom lip until it was raw. The Wolves were not playing well as a team, and going into the third period, the score was three-one for St. Louis. Not a good start.

Even she could tell the Wolves were frustrated.

Then they got two quick goals and tied it up. They both cheered, but it didn't make her feel much better. Gut-gnawing anxiety still chewed away inside her.

Another nail biter, the clock ticking away time. She wasn't sure if the same thing happened in a playoff game, if they did a shoot out or if they kept playing, but she knew it couldn't end in a tie.

The Wolves got a few more great shots on the net, but the St. Louis goalie made some heart-stopping saves. She watched as Dominic smacked his stick into the boards with frustration. Where was Jase? Why weren't they playing him much? They needed him!

And then, with only a minute forty-three seconds left in the game, there he was, circling on the ice, ready for a face off. He crouched, alert, poised. The camera zoomed in on him and the St. Louis center, who said something to Jase. Jase said something back.

Remi had a feeling they weren't making a bet on who'd pay for dinner after the game.

The ref dropped the puck and Jase smacked at it, but didn't get control. The camera followed the puck, but then the crowd was screaming, the whistle blew and the television screen filled with an image of two players going at it, gloves off, fists flying, shirts wrenched.

"Oh sweet baby Jesus." She felt her eyes go wide and her mouth hung open. She covered it with her hands. It was Jase in a fight.

Delise and Remi both sat forward, the popcorn forgotten. Remi couldn't breathe and her heart accelerated.

The two men continued to hammer at each other and she swore she felt every punch that landed on Jase as if they struck her own body. She flinched and tensed. The refs circled them, the other players drifted over to the boards near their respective benches.

Then Jase dropped the other guy to the ice and fell onto him, punching at his face with fierce, frenzied blows.

"Jesus!" She pressed her hands to her mouth, wanted to cover her eyes, look away. She couldn't stand it. "What are you doing?" she shouted at the television, as if he could hear her. "Stop, Jase. Stop it!"

The refs finally pulled Jase off the other player and dragged him away, bleeding from his face, chest heaving, hands still in fists.

They went to a commercial.

She shook her head, beside herself. She wanted to teleport herself to St. Louis, find him and ask him what the hell was going on. She just did not get it.

She knew fighting was a part of hockey, a big part. She and Jase had talked about it, how he didn't condone fighting just for the sake of fighting, but with high adrenaline and intense competition it was going to happen sometimes, and it was okay if it was for some noble purpose like defending another player or protecting the goalie. Although she didn't exactly get what was noble about beating someone up.

She'd never seen Jase fight, but then she'd only seen a couple of games. He wasn't known as a fighter. He was known as a smart player, big, but quick-thinking and intuitive, a player who used finesse rather than his fists.

Delise looked at her, her lips rolled in. "Are you okay?"

She shook her head. She didn't even know what to say. She stood. She walked back and forth in front of the television until the game came back on, arms wrapped around herself.

Jase had, of course, been given a penalty. She didn't understand it all, apparently he got more than one penalty, but in the end, the Wolves were shorthanded for the rest of the game. And guess what? St. Louis scored.

And won the game, thanks to Jase Heller's stupid penalty.

"Think, Remi, think."

She replayed everything over in her head. "He asked me to think about moving in with him." She met Delise's eyes. "That shouldn't have been enough to scare him into panic-mode and send him running the opposite direction, but…that was why he broke up with his old girlfriend, so maybe he *is* regretting that." She bit her lip. "For some reason he ended up out with his hockey buddies Saturday night. He must have had a lot to drink for him to drop his pants in a restaurant and create a scene like that."

"Maybe he was celebrating making the playoffs," Delise suggested, her face somber.

Remi paced around her living room, not really seeing anything.

"No." She shook her head. "The playoffs already started. I can't imagine why he'd do that. But clearly, he got carried away, drank a bit too much, got arrested…" she rolled her eyes, "and was too embarrassed to tell me. But that doesn't explain why he played so little tonight or why he got in that fight that cost the game."

"I don't know, Remi."

"Something's wrong." After examining all the facts, she concluded that something was definitely wrong. Clammy-hands, heart-freezing, gut-churning wrong. And if he wasn't going to tell her what it was, she was going to go to him and make him.

Except he was in another city. Dammit. And he wouldn't be back in Chicago until Thursday.

Jase sat down in his coach's office, his insides a mass of twisted nerves.

"Okay, Jase. What's going on?"

He was getting tired of that question. Tired of hearing it, tired of trying to talk his way around it.

"Nothing."

"Bullshit. You go out and get wasted last weekend, act like an asshole, get arrested, show up for practice the next day so hungover your face was green and you could barely skate. Then you get in a stupid fight and take a dumbass penalty that cost us our first playoff game. Last night you didn't play much better."

Jase slumped in the chair, unable to meet Dan's eyes.

"You're saying that's nothing?"

He shook his head.

Dan waited. "Fuck." He shook his head, his mouth tight. "Okay, then. If nothing's wrong, get your shit together and act like the professional you are. We've got another game tomorrow night, and if we lose, we only have one more chance. We need you, Jase, but I won't hesitate to make you a healthy scratch if you aren't able to get your head in the game. This is not the time to be out drinking and partying and acting like an irresponsible teenager."

Jase winced.

He rubbed his forehead.

"You're better than this, Jase," Dan continued, his voice easing.

Shit. Jase's stomach rolled over.

"Are you sure you don't want to tell me what's wrong? Maybe I can help."

And that did it.

Jase leaned one elbow on the armrest of the chair and covered his eyes while he tried to get his tight throat to relax enough to speak. He tried and nothing came out. Cleared his throat. Swallowed.

"I found out on Saturday that my ex-girlfriend is pregnant."

Silence. Then, "Jesus."

"Yeah." Jase took his hand away and met Dan's eyes. "It's not that…I don't want…fuck." He swallowed again. "I don't know what to do. I've been seeing someone else—someone I really care about. Christ! I don't want to hurt her."

Dan nodded and leaned back in his chair, arms folded across his chest. "Yeah, I guess I see the problem. So she's pretty upset about this?"

"She doesn't know."

"Oh. Jesus, Jase. You gotta tell her."

"I can't tell her." Anguish slammed into him like a body check. "I don't know what to tell her, because I don't know what I'm supposed to do. Am I supposed to break up with her so I can be with Brianne? So we can get back together and be parents to this baby? Am I supposed to ask Brianne to marry me?" His voice cracked.

"Oh, man." Dan rubbed his eyes. "I don't know the answers to those questions, Jase. I can't tell you what to do. But a couple things I can tell you. First of all—you have to deal with this. We're in the playoffs. We need you here and present, mind and body and soul, every game, all sixty minutes. You can't let your personal life interfere with your professional life."

Jase nodded. "I know." He felt like dog crap on the sidewalk about how unprofessional he'd been. He tightened his mouth.

"And I can tell you that you're a good man. You've got a good solid background—your parents brought you up right. Yeah, you're young."

"I'm twenty-nine." Not a kid. Not like Remi's younger brother wanting her to bail him out of missing an exam. Jase was old enough to be taking responsibility for his own mistakes, just like he'd urged Remi to make her brother do.

Dan waved a hand. "From where I'm at, you're young. But you're right. You're a grown man and you need to figure this out. You need to do the right thing."

"I don't know what the right thing is. The right thing for me is different than the right thing for Brianne. And for our child. And for Remi." He rubbed the ache in his chest. "I don't want to be selfish, but…I just don't know."

"Go," Dan said. "We're done with our practice. You've got the rest of today and tomorrow to figure this out. Go do what you need to do, but I expect you here tomorrow night for the game, a hundred per cent ready to play."

Jase nodded and stood. He felt like a teenager in trouble for staying out past curfew, except this was a way worse infraction than that. He left Dan's office, trying to keep his head up. He got what Dan was telling him. They paid him big bucks to play hockey, not to mope around with his head up his ass pouting because things weren't going his way.

Yeah. He had to deal with this. He still didn't know exactly what he was going to do, but one thing he knew—he had to tell Remi.

CHAPTER FIFTEEN

Usually Remi loved having kids visit her after class. Some of her current students stayed and some of her former students, now in grade seven or eight, often came after school to hang out in her classroom, sometimes helping her mark spelling tests or clean up, good kids who she enjoyed talking to and laughing with.

But today she had to get out of there, like now.

"Sorry, everyone." She shoved papers into her briefcase. "I have to leave early today."

Well, it wasn't early, but it was early for her since she usually stayed late.

"Aw, Ms Buchanan. Not already."

She smiled at them. "Go home. Go play video games and eat junk food or something. Go bug your parents."

They all laughed, knowing she was kidding. Slowly they started to make a move to leave, but not fast enough for her. She tapped a foot and resisted the urge to get up and drag them out.

Then a big shadow appeared in the door of the class room and the kids all yipped. "Hey! Jase!"

Her heart stopped. Then thudded fast and hard, making her dizzy.

God, he looked rough. Dark beard shaded his jaw and tension drew down the corners of his mouth. He clearly hadn't shaved since she'd last seen him. His tousled hair stuck up in all directions and he wore the most faded, ripped and ragged pair of jeans she'd ever seen, along with his expensive lamb-soft leather jacket. Most impressive of all was the black eye.

His eyes met hers, but he gave the kids smiles and talked to them for a minute.

"What? It's not Wednesday?" he asked. "You mean I'm here on the wrong day?"

"Stars for Reading is over!" they told him.

"Oh no!"

They all laughed. His eyes met Remi's across the room.

Thank god it was over. Dropping his pants in a restaurant and getting himself arrested wasn't exactly being a good role model for the kids. They would have kicked him out if the program was still going.

"Hey, I need to talk to Ms Buchanan, so scram." He grinned at them, a strained grin, but they listened to him better than they'd listened to her, which made her want to pout briefly, and in only seconds the classroom was empty and she and Jase were alone. They looked at each other. She had a hard time getting air into her lungs.

"You're probably pissed off at me," he finally said.

She debated how to play this. Like a mother whose child has disappeared while shopping, found safely moments later—should she be furious at the disappearance? Or happy and relieved he was okay? Emotions churned inside her.

"Should I be pissed off?" She tried to hold his gaze, but he let his eyes drop.

"Yeah. You should."

"Why?"

"Because I'm a big stupid jerk."

She felt a fist squeezing her heart.

"No, you're not."

He moved toward her and put his hands on her waist and she let her briefcase drop to the floor. Then he bent his head and kissed her. Much as she wanted to kiss him back and never, ever stop, she couldn't just pretend nothing had happened. She put her palm on his chest and pushed.

"What's going on, Jase?"

He lifted his head and gazed down at her, his mouth a straight line of grimness, eyes dark.

"Nothing."

She shoved harder at him and he took a step back. "Bullshit. Something's obviously wrong."

"I should have called you on Saturday." He pushed his hands into his pockets and elevated his shoulders like a little boy. "I'm sorry."

"That's it? You're sorry?"

"Yeah."

She stared at him. That wasn't good enough for her. How could he think it was?

"Wanna get some dinner?"

She felt her eyebrows descend and set her fingers to her temples. "Dinner?"

"Sure. Something quick." He moved toward her again and traced his fingers down the side of her neck and over her collar bone in the opening of her blouse. She shivered. "And then we can go back to your place and I'll make it up to you that I didn't call on Saturday."

She lowered her chin and looked up at him through her lashes. He was going to do this—act like nothing big had happened.

Jennifer appeared in the door of the classroom with some papers in her hands. She stopped short upon seeing Jase. "Oh, hi Jase. I didn't know you were here."

He shot her his most charming grin, made especially bad-boy sexy by the shiner, and she smiled in return. Remi wanted to roll her eyes, but didn't. "Just came to talk to Remi."

Jennifer eyed them. "Well, I can talk to you about this tomorrow, Remi."

"Okay. Thanks. We're just leaving."

This was not the place to be discussing Jase's problems, whatever they may be, so she grabbed her coat and purse and briefcase and they walked out of the school together.

"Let's just go to my place," she suggested. "If you're hungry, I'll make you something, but I don't want to be having this conversation in a restaurant."

He frowned. Good. Just so he knew they were having a conversation.

He followed her home and once the door had closed behind them, he reached for her again. His mouth was warm and delicious on hers, then he kissed his way over her cheek and jaw and the side of her neck, sending shivery delight over her body. It was so hard to resist his potent sexual charm, but she grabbed hold of his big biceps and tried to push him away.

"Stop, Jase."

He muttered something against her neck and didn't move. "You're so sweet, Remi," he murmured. "God, I missed you. I had to see you. Even…"

Even what? She ached for more of him, longed to arch against him and throw her arms around his neck. She almost did. Then she used some of the moves she hadn't used for a while and slid out of his grip with a fast bend of her knees, then grabbed his arm and twisted it up behind his back sharply.

"Jesus Christ!"

She gave his arm a hard wrench, not to hurt him, just to remind him that just because he was big didn't mean she couldn't protect herself from him. Then she let him go and stepped away, putting space between them.

"Do not think you can just show up and get me all hot and bothered and I'll just forget about whatever is going on," she said, her jaw so tight it hurt. "Don't think you can use sex to distract me from everything else." Standing up for herself was hard, but she knew it was important, important to their relationship and important for her own self-respect.

He stared at her, then rubbed his face. The lost look on his face almost did her in, but she straightened her shoulders and lifted her chin.

"Sit down." She pointed to the arm chair. "And talk."

"Uh…"

"Oh, god, Jase. I saw the newspaper article. You were arrested! You barely played half of the game Monday night and then you got in a fight and took a stupid penalty and cost your team the game."

He winced.

She was just getting started. "So you didn't call me. Fine. We don't owe each other anything. Really. All I wanted to know was that you were okay. Then you call and don't say a word about what happened. Then I see that in the paper and watch you blow the game—I was worried about you!"

She pushed her bangs off her forehead and blew out a long breath. That had actually felt pretty good. Except she was still worried sick about him.

Jase sat in the chair, not saying a word, hands on the armrests.

"What's this all about? Tell me. Did you freak out after you asked me to move in with you?"

He stared at her.

"'Cause if you did, just stop. We didn't even talk about it. I don't know if I even *want* to move in with you. It was no reason to go nuts."

"That's not it," he said in a low voice.

His shoulders slumped and again she went all soft and warm inside, wanting to throw herself into his lap and hug him and make him feel better.

"Then what is it?"

"You were worried about me?"

"Of course I was!"

She shook her head.

His lips pressed together he nodded and sat forward, head bowed. Then he lifted his head. "I never thought you'd be worried about me."

She sank down onto the couch, legs feeling woolly soft. "I love you, Jase. Of course I'd be worried about you."

"Oh, fuck." He closed his eyes and leaned his head back. "Sorry, Remi. I should've called you, but I didn't. I'm sorry you read about that in the paper. I was an idiot. But it's done."

She shook her head, not convinced this wasn't some major crisis.

"That's it," she said slowly. "Were you celebrating that night? At Sage?"

"Celebrating?" His laugh cracked. "Hell. Yeah. Sure. Celebrating."

All she could do was sit there and look at him.

"C'mere, Remi. Please." He held out a hand and despite her practical, sane, sensible nature, she rose off the couch and went over to him. He tugged her down onto his lap and she snuggled in against him, so big and warm and strong. His hands tightened on her body and he buried his face against her hair. She felt his chest rise and fall with his breathing, faster than usual, felt his heart thudding beneath her palm.

"I need you," he whispered. "So much."

She nodded against him, then lifted her head. She didn't realize she was crying until his mouth touched hers and they both felt the wetness. He groaned and used his fingertips to wipe away her tears as they kissed.

"Don't cry, Remi. Please don't cry. I'm not worth it."

How could he say that? More tears squeezed out of her eyes, despite the kisses he laid on her mouth, his hands holding her face.

The kisses grew hotter, their need for each other accelerated. Their hands roamed over each other's bodies, sliding beneath clothes to find skin, his finding her breasts, hers gliding over the satiny muscles of his back.

He shoved up her skirt and cursed at the black tights she wore beneath it, but he hooked his fingers into the waistband and dragged them along with her panties off over her hips and legs, leaving her bare to him. He unzipped and pulled out his erection, long and hard and, then he groaned. "Fuck," he muttered. "Need a condom…"

"It's okay," she whispered. With crazy wild thinking, she didn't want him to use a condom. She wasn't going to get pregnant, being on the pill, but if she did…it'd be okay. She trusted him.

But he lifted his hips off the couch and shoved a hand into his pocket. He quickly sheathed up and then, still dressed, he pushed inside her and she loved it.

He buried his face against her hair as his big body jerked and heaved over her, filling her, stretching her. She tightened her thighs on his hips, squeezing him inside her, every thrust pushing the air out of her lungs and leaving her breathless. She gripped his shoulders and hung on tight, he rode her so hard, just how she liked it, hard and fierce and fervent.

She cried out, holding on tighter, lifting into each push of his body, her clit bumping against his pubic bone, each drive pushing her higher and a long, low noise escaped her as she came, holding herself against him. He groaned too and she felt him come inside her.

She wrapped her arms around his big body and they held each other for long moments, their labored breathing the only sound in the room.

"Now are you going to tell me what's wrong?"

CHAPTER SIXTEEN

She loved being held by Jase in bed after sex, his arms around her, sinking into his voluptuous body heat, her legs twined with his, her cheek on his chest. But they weren't in bed and their clothes separated them in a way that was more than just fabric.

"Yeah," he said in a gravelly voice. "I do have something to tell you."

"Okay."

He paused and she waited, playing with his chest hair.

"You remember Brianne?"

Her stomach clenched and her fingers stilled. "Your old girlfriend Brianne?"

"Yes."

She waited again.

"She's pregnant."

Jase's heart thudded steadily beneath her cheek. Her heart, on the other hand, had stopped. Her body felt hot and tight. She couldn't move. She couldn't breathe. Her thoughts blurred and the room shifted around her, closed in on her, then faded out.

She wanted to say, so what? Who cares about her anymore? What's the big deal?

But she knew what the big deal was. Jase wouldn't be telling her this if it didn't matter hugely to him. And it could only matter to him for two reasons—either he was still in love with Brianne and this fact devastated him or...he was the father.

And she knew which one of those it was.

She knew.

Her heart probably started beating again, she didn't know, but it hurt. It hurt so bad she almost cried out with the agony of it.

She rolled away from Jase and sat up on the edge of the couch, her back to him. Her eyes burned, but no tears came. Her stomach tightened so much she felt nausea rolling over her. She still fought for oxygen, the room shifting around her as if she was on a slow moving merry go round.

"It happened just before we broke up," Jase continued in that low, barely audible voice. "Before I met you. I haven't been with her since, Remi. It's not like that."

She gave a jerky nod, but although that did take care of the foremost question in her head, that assurance did not make her anguish any better. Not at all.

She stood, but her knees were like butter and her vision went dark and she had to sit back down quickly. She sucked a breath into constricted lungs.

Then questions flooded her brain, clogging up and confusing her. She couldn't get words out. "What…" She swallowed, tried again. "How did you…"

"Remi, come here. Please." He tugged on her arm, trying to pull her back to him, but she twisted out of his grasp. Fury blazed inside her suddenly, fury at him for doing this to her.

"Get out," she snapped at him. "Get out of my house."

"Remi, we have to talk."

"I can't. Not right now." She couldn't look at him. She pressed a hand to her eyes. "I just can't."

He was still and silent. Then he stood. She still couldn't look at him. She heard him putting himself back into his pants, the rasp of the zipper. The crushing pressure in her chest had her gasping.

"Remi, I don't want to leave you like this."

"Just go! Leave me alone! I can't talk about this right now."

"Should I come over tomorrow?"

"No."

"Remi…"

She couldn't look at him. She didn't know if she'd want to see him tomorrow or the next day or ever, for that matter. She felt the weight of his gaze on her, even though she sat with her back turned to him, his semen seeping out of her, sticky and wet between her legs. She listened for the clap of the door closing behind him. And then she fell apart.

She had never called in sick when she wasn't sick, but Friday morning she did. Well, she *did* feel sick. She hadn't slept more than a couple of hours and that sleep had been restless and disturbed. She could not function in the classroom and it was better that she'd found a substitute teacher and just stayed home. She had three whole days to try to deal with the mess her life had suddenly become.

It was almost too painful to even think about, but she made herself do it, like picking at a scab or worrying a sore tooth.

Brianne was pregnant. With Jase's baby. The baby Remi had always wanted, with the man she loved, the man she now wanted to have babies with. She stood and kicked a chair. Hard. Ow.

She sat on her bed and buried her face in her hands.

She was in love with Jase. She'd actually been considering moving in with him. She thought she'd met the man she wanted to be with forever and he loved her too. Their future had stretched ahead of them, bright and shining and forever, maybe with…babies. Children. A family of their own.

And now this. She and Jase were done. How could she be with a man who'd gotten another woman pregnant? She started to cry yet again. You'd think the tears would have dried her right out, but somewhere, somehow her body was able to produce more and she cried and cried again until she lay down, exhausted.

She hated how she felt after a big crying jag. She hadn't had one for so long, not since her parents had died. She hated the stuffy nose, the swollen, stinging eyes, the puffy lips, the feeling of being on the edge of starting all over again.

She sat up slowly on her bed and dragged her hands over her cheeks, shaking her head. The pregnancy had happened before she and Jase had met. It wasn't as if he'd cheated on her.

So he said.

No, Jase wouldn't lie. She knew him better than that. He hadn't cheated on her, hadn't planned this. When she thought about it logically, she realized it was just an awful mistake that happened to people sometimes.

Only she'd never thought someone else's unplanned pregnancy would affect her.

She was responsible, used birth control. Why hadn't Brianne? Why hadn't Jase? It was both their responsibility. Anger at both of them flared up in her so hot and furious she couldn't breathe. How could they have been so stupid and irresponsible? How many lives had been impacted by something so careless?

With a small burn of shame, she recalled how she'd been willing to forego a condom the last time they'd had sex, how she'd been willing to take the risk. And the burn turned into a shaft of agony remembering how she'd almost hoped she'd get pregnant.

When Jasmine called to see if she'd done anything about selling the house, Remi wanted to yell at her. Didn't she know she had other bigger problems right now? But she bit her tongue and quietly told Jasmine she would have to talk to Kyle about it. It was his home too and he needed to be part of the decision. The school year was almost done for him. He'd want to come home for the summer.

"Actually, I want to go to Australia for the summer," Kyle told her when she called him a while later. She sat down heavily on a chair. "A bunch of buddies are going and I want to go with them."

She stared across the living room, the phone to her ear. "How will you pay for that?"

"Well, I thought you might help me out. But we're going to work when we're there. Some odd jobs or something."

"But Kyle, I don't have a lot of extra money for that. What about tuition for next year?"

"I'll try to save enough when I'm working to help pay for that. It'll be fine."

She told him about Jasmine and her wanting to sell the house.

"That would be perfect!" Excitement colored his voice. "I could use my share of the money for the trip and there'd be enough to pay for the rest of my college. Then you wouldn't have to worry about it."

True.

"But you'd have no home to come home to." For some reason that seemed so important to her—to have a place her brother and sister could come home to if they needed. To be there for them if they needed her.

"I know. But I'm older now, Remi, I'll find a place in the summers. I'll have enough money for that."

Apparently she was the only one who wanted to hold onto the house.

Was she being overly emotional about it? Perhaps she was. Was she being selfish wanting to keep the house? Maybe.

So she called a realtor and arranged for him to come over and look at the house. She might as well do it all—sell the house, give up their home, find some little apartment to live in by herself for the rest of her life. She got so agitated, she started packing things in boxes, decorative things that served no purpose, clothes that were out of season, anything left behind in Kyle and Jasmine's bedrooms.

So much for redecorating the house, like she'd wanted to.

Pain stabbed through her like a knife as she threw stuff into boxes, blinded by stinging tears.

And wasn't this just the way it always was. Her sacrificing everything for everyone else.

Oh for heaven's sake. She paused over one of the boxes she was filling. She sounded like the biggest martyr in the world, all sorry for herself. *Get over it, Remi.* This wasn't just her house and she needed to accept that. She rolled her eyes at herself and straightened her shoulders, then went to find the newspaper. She had a life to get on with.

She scanned the classifieds for apartment listings, looking for something near the school. Two bedrooms would be good, in case Kyle or Jasmine did in fact need a place to stay. But she bit her lip when she saw prices in the neighborhoods she'd like to live in. Eep. She'd had it pretty good, living rent-free in a house that was paid for. Maybe it was going to have to be one bedroom. If Kyle or Jasmine needed a place to stay, they'd have to figure things out.

The next day, the realtor was enthusiastic about the house. Remi knew it would sell easily. Her parents had bought the house many years ago and since then the neighborhood had become very desirable and house prices had escalated to the moon. They'd get good money for it. So she signed the papers and the For Sale sign went up in the front yard.

She cried when she looked at it, her emotions all ragged and shaky. But she swiped the tears away and pressed her lips together and returned to shoving stuff heedlessly into boxes. And while she did that she tried not to think about Jase.

Then the doorbell rang.

She froze with her hands in a box of sweaters, tears dripping down her cheeks.

It was Jase.

He eyed her face, which she knew only too well looked atrocious, then her baggy yoga pants and faded T-shirt. "Hi."

She stood aside and held the door open for him to come in.

"I have a game tonight," he said.

Oh, yeah. Life did go on. And he had to go play a game while their lives fell apart.

Then a hot wave of shame swept over her. That wasn't fair. Jase's career may be a game, but he was talented and dedicated and serious about it. So were a lot of other people, including a lot of fans who counted on him being there and winning. It really was a big business, despite being just a game.

"Oh. Okay."

They walked into the living room and stood facing each other. He actually didn't look much better than she did. His face too was tight, with lines grooved around his mouth and eyes. He still had greenish and yellow bruises around one eye, still hadn't shaved and now had dark circles under both eyes.

"Can we talk about this now?" he asked in a rough voice.

She nodded and put her hand out for him to sit on the couch.

"I want to tell you what happened."

She sat at the far end from him and picked up a cushion to hug against her like a shield. "Okay." She needed to hear it. Painful as it was, she needed to hear it, needed the answers to her questions, like, *how could you be so fucking stupid*? She bit her lip.

"Brianne came to see me a couple of weeks ago to tell me. I didn't believe her. She's been phoning me ever since we broke up and I thought she was making this up so we would get back together."

Hope flared in her as she listened. Maybe that was true!

But he extinguished that hope with his next words. "She got something from her doctor to prove how far along she is." He bent his head. "The timing worked out. It must have happened the last time we were together."

Shit.

"I told you, Remi, I haven't seen her since we broke up. Other than that night at Rouge. We were done."

"Birth control?" She managed to squeeze the words out between tight lips.

"She was on the pill." He looked at her, anguish in his eyes, and she believed him. "She doesn't know what happened either. It just…did. She's not happy about this either, Remi. She'd just been offered a job by Victoria's Secret and now she won't be able to do it."

Oh, that was really too bad. But again, a hot wave of shame washed over her. Modeling was also a perfectly legitimate career choice.

"So she's going to have the baby."

"Yes." Jase nodded. "She wants to have the baby. I can't…I…"

"What do you want?"

He lifted shiny eyes to hers. "I don't know, Remi. This messes up my life so bad, but…it's a baby. I can't tell her to have an abortion."

"It's her right to choose," she murmured. "Whatever her choice is."

"Yes."

"But it affects you too. You'll be a father, Jase."

"I know." He groaned and tipped his head back. "God, I know. I've been thinking about this so much."

"So Saturday you found out, you…what? Went out and got drunk?"

"Yeah." He bowed his head, hands on his knees, his knuckles still scabbed from the fight he was in. "I did. Not proud of that. Not proud of how I acted. All I can say is, I was hurting. Like I've never hurt before."

"It's not that bad." She tried to play it cool. "Most people become a parent at some point, Jase. It's not like you're fifteen or something."

He frowned. "It's not that. Well, it's partly that. Being a father scares the hell out of me. I don't know if I can do it. But I was more upset because…well, because of you."

Her eyes went wide. Her insides knotted. She clutched her pillow tighter. "Me."

"Yes." Again, agony filled his dark eyes as he stared at her. His hand moved on his knees, like he wanted to reach for her, but held back. "I just found you, Remi. I love you. After what we went through—I was so happy. Yeah, I was afraid of commitment and marriage—until I met you. When you're with the right woman it's not scary any more. You're the right one. I love you. And I was fucking *dying* thinking about telling you about this, knowing how hurt you were going to be. This is the worst thing in the world that could have happened."

Oh. She stared back at him, her stomach flipping around inside.

He rubbed his eyes. "I should have just come and told you right away. I acted like an idiot and I'm sorry. My coach is pissed off at me, the team's pissed off at me, my parents are pissed off at me, you're pissed off at me. Shit."

She nodded, but was softening inside, her heart thawing just a little.

But fear still held her in an icy grip.

"What are you going to do?" she asked him, voice shaky.

"I don't know." He swallowed. "I knew I had to tell you about it. That's why I came to see you the other day. But I still don't know what I'm going to do."

"Do you still care about Brianne?"

"No. Well…" His hesitation was like a slap in the face and she flinched. "I care about her as a friend. We were together a long time. But I don't love her, Remi. I love you. Please, please believe that."

She drew in a long shaky breath, and nodded.

"But I do care about my child," he continued, his voice so low and deep she had to listen carefully. "I know I have to do the right thing for my child. I just don't know what that is. Is it being with Brianne?"

She jerked and blinked. He shrugged his big shoulders.

"I just don't know." His voice caught, and wonderingly, she watched the big brute hockey player's eyes grow glossy. "I want to be with you, Remi, more than anything in the world, but I have an obligation now to someone else that I have to live up to. I have to be a man. I have to be responsible." He paused. "It's time for me to grow up."

She nodded as her heart splintered and cracked inside her ribcage. She understood that. She truly did, because she'd had to be responsible her whole life and she knew what that felt like.

"I don't want to keep you hanging while I figure it out," he continued. "That's not fair to you."

She would wait. She wanted to say it, but held the words in. Tears blurred her vision yet again.

"I love you, Remi." He shifted along the couch cushions and she lifted a hand to push him away because if he touched her, she'd be done, but he just moved her hand aside and pulled her onto his lap. She held onto him, wrapped her arms around him, buried her face in his neck and inhaled the warm male scent of his skin. For the last time. She dug her fingers into the softness of his hair. Tears wet her cheeks and his neck and his arms wrapped around her too, squeezing her so tightly she almost couldn't breathe. She felt his big body shudder and knew…he was crying too. "I love you, Remi. But I can't be with you. I'm sorry. I'm so sorry to do this to you."

She squeezed her eyes shut at the pain, like a knife dragged from her sternum down through her intestines. She knew. She couldn't speak to say the words, but she knew.

CHAPTER SEVENTEEN

He'd done it. He'd told Remi. He'd broken her heart and his along with it. Now he had to go see Brianne.

He'd made a decision. Now he had to tell her.

His insides churned.

Last night's game had been another disaster, but at least it hadn't been entirely his fault. Or maybe everyone just sensed that he was still messed up and that's why Arnette had let in three goals that should never have happened, why Griff and Frenchy had taken stupid penalties. They'd been fighting their way from behind the entire game and although Jase had played with everything he had, it hadn't been enough to pull out a win. They'd now lost three in a row and were up against the wire again. Sunday's game was either the end of the road or bought them time. At least it was a home game.

Jase hadn't been to Brianne's apartment since that night he'd broken up with her. She'd dropped off the few things he'd left at her place shortly after that and he'd never been back. He wiped sweaty palms on his jeans as he waited for her to let him in.

"Hi." She stood there, looking more like her usual self. Since she earned her living with how she looked, it wasn't surprising that she'd managed to get herself back on track fairly quickly. She didn't even look pregnant, dressed in low rise jeans and a snug T-shirt. "Come on in."

He walked in, legs rubbery as if he'd just skated a few hours of drills, and he rubbed his palms on his jeans.

"How are you feeling?" he asked politely.

"Tired." She made a face.

"You haven't been sick or anything?"

She shook her head. "No. Thank god. Just really, really tired. All the time. And hungry. It's hard to keep myself from eating."

He frowned. "You have to eat, Brianne. For the baby."

"I still have to watch what I eat. I can't put on weight too fast."

"But…that's what happens when you get pregnant. You put on weight."

"I know that." She pressed her lips together. "I just don't want to use the pregnancy as an excuse to eat everything in sight. I can't put on weight right now, I have jobs— contracts I have to fulfill. Don't worry, Jase, I know I'm going to gain weight. I just want to make sure it's not too much, too fast."

He knew nothing about pregnancy. "How much is too much? How much are you supposed to put on? Like, the baby's going to weigh seven or eight pounds, right?"

She shrugged and motioned for him to have a seat. "They say twenty to thirty pounds is healthy, but I would die if I put on thirty pounds. If I can keep it under twenty pounds, I should be okay."

His brows drew together. Twenty or thirty pounds? No wonder she was freaked out. "But thirty pounds is healthy. What if you…" Jesus, he was going to have to do some studying up on this. He needed to know these things. "What if you starve the baby and he doesn't grow properly?"

She just waved a hand. "I said, don't worry, Jase."

"Well, I am worried. It's my baby too, remember?"

"I know, I know. That's why you're here. You wanted to talk."

Brianne walked across her living room to a book shelf and picked up something. When she turned to him, she was shaking a cigarette out of a package.

Jase jolted to his feet. "What the hell are you doing!"

She blinked at him, then looked at the cigarette. "Uh…having a cigarette."

He strode across the room and yanked the slender cylinder out of her fingers, then grabbed the entire package. He crushed the package in one fist, the cigarette in the other. "You can't smoke when you're pregnant!"

She took a step back, her perfectly groomed brows rising. "When did you become such an expert on pregnancy?"

"Jesus, Brianne! Everyone knows that!"

"I can't quit, Jase. I've tried before."

He rolled his eyes. He'd never liked her smoking. She'd tried not to do it around him, so it bothered him less, but he knew she did. He could smell it on her clothes and sometimes her breath. He knew how terrified she was of putting on weight, and every time she'd tried to quit, a couple of pounds on the scale had her breaking open the tobacco again. He'd put up with it, didn't bug her about it, because—it was her life

But now it wasn't just her life. It was their baby's life.

"Yes you can. We'll talk to your doctor. Maybe there's something they can do to help you." He shook his head. "I can't believe you aren't putting the baby first."

"I am!" she cried. "I do care! It's just not that easy."

"That's what being a parent is," he said shortly. "It's not easy, but you give up things for the sake of your children. Because you love them and they're the most important thing in the world." *Remi...*

She nodded slowly. Jase went into her bathroom and crumpled the cigarettes into the toilet and flushed them. There.

When he returned, Brianne was sitting on her couch, leaning back, arms folded across her chest, her full lips even fuller in an angry pout. "So what did you come to talk about? Other than my smoking and eating habits."

"I will not let you endanger our child by putting nicotine in your body when you're pregnant," he said through clenched teeth. "You're going to quit, Brianne, and I don't care if you put on fifty pounds in the next week. I don't care about your goddamn contracts. I'm here to help financially, I'll make sure you're okay, but you are not going to smoke."

She stared at him, hands on hips. Her bottom lip trembled. "Financially?" she asked. "That's what this is about?"

He closed his eyes. What did she expect from him?

"Well, I guess that's one more good thing about sleeping with a jock. Not much intellectual stimulation, but you've got a great body and at least you've got lots of money."

His stomach bottomed out at her careless words and he stared at her. What the fuck did she just say? She did not just call him a stupid jock. His head whirled.

Stupid. He was not stupid. Remi knew that.

But he wasn't irresponsible, either. Not anymore.

"I wanted to talk about how we're going to do this," he said heavily, sitting down in a chair across from her. "I'm the father of this baby and I have a responsibility to the baby and I want to do the right thing."

Jasmine woke Remi up Sunday morning, later than she should have slept, but once again her night had been restless and agitated, with bad dreams that had her waking up sweaty and shaky. Her head throbbed, her eyes felt gritty from crying and her stomach ached.

This time Jasmine knocked on her bedroom door, but this time there wasn't any worry about interrupting anything.

"I saw the For Sale sign outside! So you're going to sell the house, that's fantastic!"

"Yeah." Fanbloodytastic. Remi yawned and walked to the kitchen to make some coffee, shuffling in her flannel pants and bare feet. "The realtor seems pretty optimistic that it will sell quickly."

"That's so great!" Jasmine clasped her hands in front of her. "I can't wait to get the money. Ethan and I are going to look at some open houses this afternoon."

"Maybe you should just hold off until we've actually sold it. It will take a while before things go through." She didn't even know how that all worked. She'd never bought or sold a house before.

Jasmine just waved a hand. "We can look. This is so great. And you can put conditions on the sale to make it go through quickly."

Remi leaned against the counter, arms folded across her chest, and looked at Jasmine. "And what about me?" she inquired quietly. "Where do you think I'm going to go if we get things 'through quickly'?"

Jasmine frowned.

"You know, I wish once in a while you'd think of someone other than yourself."

Jasmine's brows flew up and a hurt expression creased her forehead. The coffeemaker sputtered and hissed behind Remi on the counter. "What?"

At first, Remi'd been proud of herself for speaking her mind, but then regret filled her at her hasty words. She rubbed the back of her neck and let out a long breath. "I'm sorry, Jas. I'm kind of not in the best mood today."

"You don't look so great."

Remi bit her lip. "Jase and I broke up."

"Oh no! I'm sorry, Rem." Jas studied her. "You two weren't together that long though."

"That's true." She pasted on a smile. "I'll be fine. But I feel like I'm being pushed to sell this house without thinking it through."

Jasmine stared at her, then bent her head. "You're right. I'm sorry, Remi. Ethan's pushing me and Kyle agreed with the plan and…we weren't thinking about you."

Whoa. Okay.

Jasmine lifted her head. "Is it…possible…you don't want to sell the house because you think I'm going to come running home again?"

Remi blinked.

"And you want Kyle to come home in the summer, don't you? So you won't be alone?"

Remi's mouth opened, then closed. She stared at her sister. Her head throbbed and she put a hand up to her temple. "That's not true." Was it?

"You should be happy for me and Ethan," Jasmine continued. "And Kyle has his own life to live. He's going to travel, which will be awesome for him, right?"

"Uh. Yeah, right. And I do want you and Ethan to be happy together." She still had her doubts about that, but yeah, she knew they'd have to work things out themselves. "And I know Kyle has his own life now. I just…want to be here for you. If you need me." That was all she'd ever wanted. It was important to her.

She'd been there for them since the first time their parents had taken off on one of their mission. She'd been there for them when Mom and Dad had died. She'd made the money that paid the bills and bought the groceries. She'd paid Jasmine's college tuition and now Kyle's. She'd spent hours of her life driving them both around to lessons and activities and appointments, not even having time for a real relationship, as Darryl had pointed out to her when he'd given her the choice between him and her family.

She'd done it because she loved them, because it was the only thing to do.

Darryl hadn't been the right guy for her anyway. At the time it had hurt like hell, but that now seemed like nothing. Now…a violent rush of pain thinking about Jase almost had her doubling over. Dense silence filled the kitchen while she struggled for control, swallowing through a tight throat so she could speak. She turned away from Jasmine and blinked her stinging eyes. Jase was a whole other issue.

No, Darryl hadn't been the right man for her. She'd been devastated when he'd made her choose, telling her she was boring and had no time for him, but she knew now, after what she'd felt for Jase, that she would never have ended up with Darryl anyway. Her feelings for him had been like flat water compared to her bright and sparkling champagne feelings for Jase.

Jase. Oh Jase. It so wasn't fair this happened to her again, only this time…

"Remi. Are you okay?" Jasmine's voice behind her sounded hesitant, confused.

"I'm okay." She certainly didn't want to talk about Jase. "It's no big deal." She forced a smile and turned around. Jasmine was right. Painfully, eye-openingly right. The house was just a place to live. What she was really struggling with was the fact that Kyle and Jasmine didn't need her like they used to. She had to face the fact that they were adults. Like Jase had pointed out. God, he'd been right too. They were adults and she needed to let go. "So, buying a house will be exciting for you and Ethan. Where are you looking?"

They chatted for a few minutes about neighborhoods and prices.

"I'd better go," Jasmine eventually said. "I'll talk to you later."

"Sure. Bye."

Remi poured herself cup of coffee and sat down at the table. She stared blankly at the dark steaming liquid.

They didn't need her any more. That was okay. That was what happened when kids grew up. That was the goal of parenthood—to raise adults who were independent and strong. She remembered Jase asking her if she'd ever thought she was enabling them by being there for them every time something went wrong. She'd thought she was doing the right thing, because she loved them and being there for them after their parents had died was the most important thing in the world to her. But maybe she'd needed to be needed more than they needed her. If that made any sense at all.

So Jasmine might get a reality check when she and Ethan bought their house and moved in together, but that was life. Kyle might get a shock too when he didn't have anywhere to go between terms, but he'd have to figure it out. They were both adults and needed to make their own decisions and take responsibility for their lives.

And she had to take responsibility for her own life too. Yeah, being on her own had been an adjustment, and selling the house and moving into an apartment wasn't going to be easy. On the upside, it would be lot less work…no lawn to mow in the summer, no snow to shovel in winter, no furnace to replace when it broke down. A place all her own could be exciting. And instead of lonely she'd feel free.

Delise had tried to tell her to change her attitude and she'd been working on it. She'd probably still worry about Kyle and Jasmine, but being without all that responsibility was actually liberating. She'd only have herself to look after, and when it came right down to it, looking after herself was really the most important thing she could do. At one time she might have thought that was selfish, but now…she felt a need to do this, do find out who she really was, to be her own person.

Now she was free and Jase was the one being saddled with a huge responsibility. Huh. She could almost laugh at that, except…it really wasn't funny.

She understood responsibility and she got why Jase had to step up. She wouldn't love him as much if he had done anything else, if he had tried to ignore the baby, pretend it wasn't his, deny his duty. He would never do that. Because it was his child and he was doing the same thing she had—anything he had to for that child. For love.

Her heart squeezed painfully and she took in a shaky breath.

But how much should Jase sacrifice for the sake of his child?

When Darryl had given her that ultimatum—him or her family—she hadn't even considered it. Now she knew that was because she hadn't really loved him , not the way she loved Jase—with her whole heart, her soul, her mind and her body. So she'd let Darryl go, continued on with her life, doing what she had to do.

She wandered into her bedroom and looked at the boxes half full of things. She stood in front of her dresser, staring at her watch, a pair of earrings and…the bear Jase had built for her, that day at Navy Pier, in his little Chicago Wolves uniform. A sharp stab of pain pierced her heart as she reached for the bear, remembering that day, the crazy fun they'd had. She'd probably fallen in love with him that day.

She hugged the bear, pressing her cheek to the soft fur, aching inside as memories of that day rolled through her head. She'd been so happy, so carefree. "Remi is beary beautiful." Jase's voice spoke from inside the bear and the tears fell harder and the ache intensified.

Why did she have to let him go? Why did *he* have to let *her* go? Parents together "for the sake of the children" was a huge mistake. Nobody these days expected a man in that position to ask the woman to marry him—did they? Wasn't that the worst reason to get married? Especially if the relationship had ended and they didn't love each other anymore? Wouldn't that just be doomed to failure? And what kind of life would that be for their child if they stayed together and were miserable?

The questions bounced around in her aching head until she felt it might split open. She rubbed her temples. Think, Remi. Think.

She'd sacrificed a lot in her life. And she didn't regret it. But she wasn't going to let Jase sacrifice his whole life. There was more than one way to take responsibility for something.

She surged to her feet, then stood there for a moment, mind racing. She had to talk to him. She had to talk to him *now*.

She glanced wildly at her watch, but she wasn't wearing one. The alarm clock beside the bed said nearly one. Where would he be? Practice? At home? She had to find him.

She grabbed her purse and was fishing for her keys when she realized she was still dressed in pajamas. With a growl of annoyance, she dropped her bag to the bed and reached for some clothes.

When the phone rang, she dove for it, somehow the idea that Jase might be calling her implanted in her mind. But it was the realtor, calling to tell her there was an offer on the house.

"A great offer," he said.

"Wonderful," she huffed, trying to get out of her pajama pants with the phone tucked between shoulder and ear. Just what she needed. "That was fast."

"I can come over right now."

"No. No. I have to go out somewhere. I'll call you later."

"Remi, you don't want to lose this offer."

"I...I have something important to do. Please. I'll call you later."

She had to talk to Jase.

CHAPTER EIGHTEEN

She called his cell phone, but he didn't answer. She drove to his apartment, but he wasn't home. Remi stood on the street in front of his apartment building, biting her lip, wondering if he was with Brianne. She had no idea where Brianne lived and she didn't think she had the nerve to go there anyway. The other place he could be was the arena. They were likely practicing for tomorrow night's game.

When she walked in the front doors of the arena, she gazed around in wonder. The cavernous, empty building was such a contrast to the way it was during a game, packed with people, buzzing with noise and energy. A few of the food places were open, but only a couple of people sat drinking coffee near the donut shop. As she crossed the concrete floor, she could hear noises from the ice, the crack of a stick against the puck, the duller thud of the puck hitting the goalie's pads, the scratching of sharp skates on ice, echoing voices.

"Go, go, go!" a voice yelled, presumably the coach. She approached one of the entrances and stood there looking down at the ice through the mesh that closed off the ice from the concourse. Sounds echoed in the arena, bouncing off empty seats and the rafters high above.

The players skated around in some kind of drill, taking turns with the puck racing to the net. They weren't wearing their uniforms, so she couldn't find Jase.

She knew where the only entrance was to the bowl, and walked around the concourse to it. She'd briefly met the security guy once when Jase had introduced her, and he smiled and nodded at her as she walked past, holding her breath.

She descended the steps, right behind the bench in the section she'd sat in during the games she'd attended. A few seats were occupied in the arena, sports reporters from the newspapers, one guy she recognized from TV who called the Wolves play-by-play.

She searched out Jase on the ice, her eyes finally lighting on one of the biggest guys in the practice jerseys, who'd just skated to the bench and stood talking to the coach, his hands resting on the top of his stick. There he was.

She blinked, clasped her hands together and watched him. She couldn't hear what he was saying, just the animated tone of his voice and the coach nodding.

And then he looked up at her.

She froze. Her fingers tightened around themselves and she held his gaze.

He'd stopped talking and then the coach turned his head to see what Jase was staring at. He said something to Jase, who nodded, eyes still on Remi.

Her stomach flipped and flopped and her hands shook.

"Okay we're done!" the coach yelled. Some of the players ignored him and kept skating around, one of them gave another a playful body check and another fell to the ice as if exhausted and lay there spread-eagled. Remi smiled faintly.

Jase took his gloves off and beckoned to her. She slowly stepped down the wide concrete steps, watching him, until she was right at the boards beside the bench.

"What're you doing here?"

"Looking for you."

"Oh."

He was even huger than usual, the skates adding inches to his height, the equipment adding bulk to his body.

"I wanted to talk to you, but this probably isn't a good time." Seeing the intensity of the practice reminded her of the importance of the game tomorrow night. She probably should have just left him alone until the playoffs were done.

"We're done."

"Yeah, but the game tomorrow…I don't want to distract you…"

A glimmer of a smile passed over his mouth. "Yeah. That's what Coach just said to me. Don't get distracted."

"I'm sorry." She turned to leave.

"Wait." She paused and turned back to him. "I'll be more distracted if I don't know why you came here. Gimme fifteen minutes to change and shower." He lifted his arms and his mouth quirked up. "You don't want to come near me until I shower. Trust me."

She nodded.

"I'll meet you on the concourse. By the donut shop. Okay?"

His eyes regarded her watchfully and she noticed his fingers were shaking too when he stuffed his gloves under one arm to skate off the ice.

What was she doing? She might be crazy. But she had to tell him some things. Some important things.

She ordered a coffee that she didn't want and sat alone at a small table sipping the tasteless liquid. She heard the Zamboni rev up and drive onto the ice, its motor humming as it circled the surface. A couple of guys walked past, bearded and damp. Looked like nobody shaved during the playoffs. That wasn't a tradition she was completely in favor of, but oh well.

Then Jase came out, his face darkened with his beard, longer than stubble now. On him, it looked good. Remi shook her head. His hair too was damp from shower. He wore his leather jacket and a pair of jeans and sneakers.

She watched him look for her, then spot her, and she swore he was relieved when he did. He started toward her with his long athletic gait. Her heart swelled in her chest so big it hurt. God, she loved this man.

Her eyes smarted and she blinked hard. She was not going to cry any more. Dammit.

He stopped in front of her so she had to look way up in to his face. "D'you want to stay here and talk? Or go somewhere else?"

"Um...maybe we could go somewhere else."

"My place is close. We can walk."

"Okay." She'd just leave her car. She could come back for it later.

They emerged into afternoon brightness, blinking a little after the gloomy arena, the downtown streets busy with traffic and pedestrians. They started down the sidewalk toward Jase's apartment building, only a few blocks away.

The sun warmed them with increasing strength and the breeze that lifted Remi's hair felt gentle like spring.

"So what did you want to talk about?"

Their hands swung at their sides as they walked and she wished he would take her hand and hold it. But he didn't. She pressed her lips together, stomach a mass of twisting nerves. "Let's just get to your place." She paused. "How did your practice go?"

"It was okay. Everyone's kinda tense. We lost again last night."

"I know. I watched."

"Oh."

"But you played well."

"Yeah, I did okay." He shook his head. "But we gotta get our shit together tomorrow night or we're done."

"You can do it."

He looked at her and smiled. "Thanks. Maybe you should come to the game. Last time I think you brought me luck."

She laughed. "I doubt I did."

They rode up the elevator in his high-rise building, her remembering the first time she'd been there and they'd been all over each other. Her stomach did a little flip low down. Her breathing shallow, she tried to focus on drawing air into her lungs.

Jase led the way in. Sunlight flooded through the wall of windows, the view beyond spectacular, all the way to Lake Michigan in the hazy distance. She smiled at all his exercise equipment taking up half the space, the other half filled with leather couch and electronic equipment.

"Have a seat," he said, his jaw tight.

She sat on the couch and set her purse on the floor. "So."

He sat beside her, but not touching, eyeing her as if she was alternately a bomb that might explode or a meal he wanted to devour.

She twisted her fingers together again. "I wanted to talk to you."

"Uh-huh."

Hell. She'd already said that.

"I've been doing some thinking. About you and…Brianne." She forced the name out through stiff lips. "And the baby."

He leaned back and lifted a brow. "Really? Me too."

Was that sarcasm? She licked her lips. "Maybe this is none of my business, but I don't want to see you make a big mistake."

He frowned. "Like what?"

"Like…I know you want to do the right thing and I know you're going to take responsibility and be a father to your child, but…oh shit." Her throat closed up.

"What, Remi?" Now he leaned forward and reached for her hands. His were big and warm on her clammy ones.

"Dammit." She swiped at a tear. "All I do is cry lately. I hate this!" She drew in a shuddering breath. "I know you want to take responsibility and man up to the consequences of your actions and all that, but Jase, I don't think getting back together with Brianne is the right thing for you. For any of you, even the baby." She bit her lip. "I'm sure Brianne is a lovely person," she continued. "But don't you think it would be a big mistake to get back together with her for the sake of your baby?"

"Yup."

"Because I…what?" She stared at him.

"Yup, that would be mistake," he agreed, regarding her soberly. "I already figured that out, Remi."

"You did?"

"Hell, yeah. Big mistake. *Huge* motherfucking mistake."

"Oh."

He smiled at her. "You telling me this because you still want me for yourself?"

She snuffled out a laugh. "Actually, no."

"What?" He scowled.

"I do love you, Jase." She touched his cheek. "You told me you couldn't be with me, and if that's how you feel, I respect that. I've done a lot of thinking too. But my main reason for coming here and talking to you was just to keep you from making that mistake, from sacrificing too much. Not to try to hold on to you."

"I was coming to see you after the practice."

"You were?"

"Yeah. To tell you I'd realized I couldn't get back with Brianne. To see if you still wanted me." Her heart expanded in her chest, stealing her breath as she watched his face. "But…big 'but'…" He paused. She met his agonized gaze. "I don't know if I can ask that much of you."

"Ask what?"

"Brianne has to be in my life," he continued, voice low. "She's going to have my baby. It's not what I would have chosen, but it's there. Somehow we're going to have to be parents to this child together. Not married. Not as a couple. But somehow. We talked about it today."

"You did?"

"Mmm." He let out a long sigh. "I couldn't go back to her. I just couldn't. I knew how miserable we both would be. That wouldn't be right. It wouldn't be fair."

"I know! That's just what I was thinking too!" She palmed his beard-roughened cheek. "That's what I came to tell you!"

"You came to save me from that?" His eyes twinkled.

"Yes."

"Oh, Remi. Love you so much."

She looked down at her hands, then up. "I love you too, Jase."

"I don't want to lose you, Remi," he said quietly. "I told you we couldn't be together because I hadn't figured things out, but now I have, I…I want to be with you. But my life is so screwed up. It's a lot to ask, but d'you think you could still be with me?"

She let the words play out in her head. It *was* a lot to ask. She loved him so much and wanted to be with him, but she hadn't come here for that. She'd just decided that being on her own would be good for her. But maybe she could do both…she and Jase could take their time, letting their relationship grow while they dealt with their personal challenges.

She nodded, lips quivering. "I do love you, Jase. And yes…I want to be with you. But we need to talk about what that will look like. I know this won't be easy. Not for any of us. I hate it— I fucking *hate* it—that she's having your baby. It makes me feel *sick* when I think about it. I'm not going to deny that."

He nodded somberly. "I hate it too," he said. "Because I wish it was you who was pregnant."

"Oh." Her heart missed a beat, then accelerated unevenly. Oh god, she wished that too. But she'd come to some other realizations lately too. "Oh Jase."

Their eyes met and held and then he hauled her onto his lap and she melted against him as he kissed her, tipping her chin up and slanting his mouth across hers. She pressed into him, held on tight to him, kissed him back hungrily, desperately, deeply.

When they drew apart, breathing heavily, he rested his forehead against hers.

"You said this was the worst thing that could happen," she said. "But it's not. I know that now. It's really not."

"Yeah. I know" He cupped the back of her head and she felt his hand trembling. "But it's going to be hard. I'm going to want to share custody of the baby. I'm going to want to spend time with him or her. I have a weird job and I travel a lot and I'm not sure what that's going to look like. I'll help Brianne financially of course, not that she needs it, but I will."

"Of course."

"That's not an issue, but…being a father…I don't know how the hell to do that."

"I don't think anyone does." She stroked her fingers through his hair. "Until they're doing it. You just do it. And do the best you can."

"I can do it if you're with me. If you're sure. Like I said, it's a lot to ask of you." He drew back to look at her and uncertainty darkened his eyes. "I've already asked so much of you. Putting up with puck bunnies and paparazzi and injuries."

"I'm sure."

He hugged her tightly again. "Thank Christ. I can't wait until we have babies of our own."

Her heart stuttered. "Well, I hope you're not in a hurry for that." She smiled and met his eyes. "The funny thing is, all I've ever wanted is to be a mother. I love kids. I love babies. I love looking after people. As you know." She gave him a roll of the eyes and he smiled back at her. "But…you made me see it, Jase. I…" Her throat tightened. "I've been holding on to Jasmine and Kyle, protecting them too much, doing too much for them…because you were right." It was hard to say the words out loud never mind admit them in her own head, but she did it. "I liked being needed. When they both moved out, it was devastating for me, because my whole life was wrapped up in them, looking after them. That's who I was. But I've decided I need to find out who I really am before I become a mother."

"Oh." His eyes filled with understanding. "Remi. You're an amazing person. You have so much love inside you, so much caring. I told you before, you'll be an awesome mom."

"I will." They both laughed. "But first I want to do things for me. I want to have fun. I want to have love. With you." She kissed him. "I want to ride Ferris wheels and build teddy bears. I want to travel. Will you take me places, Jase?"

"I'll take you anywhere you want."

They kissed again, long and sweet and clinging. Remi shook and burned inside for him, a huge swelling of relief and love and longing for him inside her.

"I've been acting like such an idiot," Jase murmured against her hair long moments later. "So unprofessional—letting my personal life interfere with my professional life. Dan had to ream my ass the other day to make me see straight. I was letting everybody down."

"Yeah, you were kind of acting stupid."

"I hope I haven't fucked up my Stars for Reading for next year. I love doing that. Helping those kids."

"People will have forgotten by then. Or you can help kids some other way."

He grimaced. "And I almost lost you."

"Almost." She smiled, trailing her fingers down the side of his neck and under the collar of his shirt. "I'm sorry I wouldn't talk about it. I had to think things through. I was upset when you told me and I had to calm down and get rational again. It's hard to be rational when you're all emotional. It hurt so much, Jase. It still does. That she's having your baby when that's all I wanted." Somehow telling him that, sharing that with him, made the pain lessen just a bit. Not much, but a bit.

"It will happen, I promise you. Whenever you're ready."

Her throat closed up again and she nodded.

"And *I* wasn't exactly rational when I went out and got stupid drunk and then dropped my pants in a restaurant." He smacked his forehead. "Fuck me. Just when I thought I'd gotten my crazy impulses under control."

"Please don't do that again."

"I won't." He gripped her tightly. "I promise, I won't. That was the last time I ever act so irresponsibly. Without thinking through the consequences of my actions. I've been such an irresponsible idiot."

"No you haven't." She grabbed hold of his shirt and gave it a sharp tug. "I don't want to hear you say things like that. You were under a lot of stress and you got drunk and did a stupid thing, but you are not stupid. And you are not irresponsible. You didn't blame anyone else for what you did that night, you took responsibility for your actions. You showed up every week to help those kids read. You take responsibility for every loss your team has. Yes, your job is a game, but you take it seriously—you know you have responsibilities to the team, to the owners, all the businesses that depend on you and especially the fans. And you're taking responsibility for your child."

She took a breath and let it out, long and slow. "I was ready to let you go," she said softly, breathing in the fresh masculine scent of his recent shower. "Because I knew you had to look after your child. I know parents have to make sacrifices for their children. But there are some sacrifices you shouldn't have to make. And I didn't want you to do that."

"I'm glad you realize how special I am."

She swatted his chest, but laughed. Then her cell phone rang. She leaned down to grab her purse from the floor and dug around in it for the phone. It was the realtor.

"We have to get together to go over this offer," he said.

"Oh, yeah." She sighed, not wanting to move off Jase's lap. "Okay. I'll meet you at my place in an hour."

"Who was that?" Jase asked as she ended the call.

"My realtor. I listed the house and there's an offer already."

Jase had gone very still. "Uh...Remi..."

Regretfully she slid off him and stood, straightening her sweater.

"The offer..." He stood too. She looked up at him, tipping her head to one side. "The offer is...from me."

She gave her head a shake. "What?"

He held her gaze.

"You made an offer on my house? You want to buy my house?" She squinted at him.

"Yeah." He smiled, showing lots of white teeth, and shoved his hands into the front pockets of his jeans. "I saw the For Sale sign and realized you'd decided to sell. Uh…are you okay with selling it? 'Cause I kinda had the feeling your sister was pressuring you to do it."

"I'm okay with it now." She sighed, pushing her fingers through her hair. "I'm sad about it, yeah. I love that house. It was our home. But I realized you were right and I need to let them deal with the consequences of their decisions. If things with Jasmine and Ethan don't work out, I'll be there for her, sure, but she'll have to deal with it. And Kyle too. He wants to go away this summer. If things don't go well at college, he'll have to figure out what he wants to do with his life." She straightened her shoulders. "And I already started looking for an apartment near school. But Jase…" She frowned. "Why would you buy the house?"

"So you can live there." He stepped toward her. "I didn't know if we'd ever be together at that point, but I hated to think of you being forced to leave your home. I know you love that house. So I just had the crazy idea that I'd buy it and you could live there."

Her breath stuck, her heart pattering, feeling very warm and dizzy, she just stared at him. She could not believe what she was hearing. He wanted to buy the house? For her? That was crazy.

Crazy nice.

"You can't do that." She tried to get air into her lungs.

"Why not? I can afford it. It'd be like an investment. Real estate's supposed to be a good investment, that's what my financial guy tells me. Plus there's some tax benefit or something." He waved a hand. "Which I definitely need. Don't worry, I ran this all past him, so it's not *that* crazy an idea."

"I…I don't know what to say." Her mind wobbled, words clogged up in her tight throat. Nobody'd ever done anything like that for her. She was always the one looking after everyone else.

He shrugged. "You don't have to say anything. But…" He looked endearingly uncertain, big shoulders up at his ears.

"Maybe…if you think it's rushing, you can just stay living there and I'll keep my apartment, but maybe one day…I could move in with you there. When you're ready."

Her heart expanded, ready to burst out of her chest. "Oh, Jase."

He pulled his hands out of his pockets and took one giant Jase-sized stride toward her and set his hands on her waist. He kissed her, a slow, gentle kiss. "I want to marry you. I want you to have my babies. I want to live together even though I know I'm asking a lot of you. My life's not easy—lots of travel, lots of stress—"

"Lots of injuries," she murmured, remembering how nervous she got for him every game. Would she ever get used to that?

He made a dismissive face. "And on top of it we're going to have a child who's not always with us and you're going to have to put up with my ex being in our lives…fuck, Remi, that's a lot to ask. But it's what I want."

"Lots of women do it," she murmured. "People divorce, have blended families. It's not easy, but it's not like we're the only ones it's ever happened to."

"Yeah." He breathed out a long slow exhale. "After all you just said, though, I don't want to pressure you or rush you. I understand. I'll wait until you're ready."

"Thank you, Jase. I would like to wait a while before we live together. And I know it won't be easy sometimes. But we'll make it work. Right?"

"Right." He hugged her close.

CHAPTER NINETEEN

Jase drove her to pick up her car and followed her back to her house to meet with the realtor.

"Are you sure you want to do this?" She peered up at Jase as she looked at the papers.

"I'm sure." He was absofuckinglutely one hundred percent sure.

She paused and lowered the pen. "Okay. But I've been thinking about this and I'm not going to live here."

"What?" He frowned.

"I think it's important for me to live on my own and I think having a place that is just mine, totally mine, will be good for me. Even if it's a little one-bedroom apartment. I wanted to redecorate the house—well, now I'll decorate my apartment, and it will be just the way I want it. And I'll have my girls over for makeup parties when you're on the road and stuff like that."

He lifted his eyebrows.

"So, *you* can live here." She studied his face with those beautiful turquoise eyes. "But if you don't want to do that, then don't buy the house."

The realtor made a choking noise that might have been panic at the thought of losing the sale. Jase ignored him.

He thought about this. He liked the house. It wasn't as convenient to the arena as his apartment, but it was a helluva lot more homey. And he knew it was important to Remi. He tapped his chin.

He got that she wanted independence. Living in a little apartment might be going too far, in his opinion, when she could just stay here. Financial independence also seemed unnecessary.

Paying rent was a waste of money when he had tons of it. But it seemed important to her, so fine. He'd give her that. And maybe, if he was patient—not one of his strengths, but hey, he'd spent most of his life working on that—eventually she'd agree to move back in with him.

Or not. Who knew, maybe they'd find their own place some day. Meanwhile, this would be an investment.

"Okay," he finally said. "I'll live here. Sign the damn papers."

She smiled and bent her head.

The deal was done.

When they were alone, he pulled her into his arms. "I want to look after you," he said. "But I respect your independence."

"Thank you."

His cell phone rang. He pulled it out and looked at it. "Brianne."

Remi made a face.

Jase silenced the phone and shoved it back in his pocket. "I'll need to tell her about us. Set her straight on a few things, some boundaries. Don't worry." He brushed his mouth over Remi's. "I won't be taking calls from her while we're banging our brains out."

She choked on a laugh. "Good to know."

"Speaking of which…let's go do that." He kissed her again, this time more deeply. His blood heated. "I've missed you so much, Remi."

"Oh, me too. Jase." She stroked her fingers through his hair and over the back of his neck. His dick hardened and a sizzle zipped up his spine as she kissed him back with hot, open-mouthed kisses. He lifted her little body against him and started for the stairs. She wrapped her legs around him and held on tight.

In her bedroom, he paused. His body burned with need for her and yeah, he wanted to bang her brains out. But his chest was filled with a huge swelling of relief and gratitude and love for her. He thought he'd lost her. He'd been trying to be a man, to sack up his responsibilities like he'd never had to before, but letting her go didn't have to be part of that.

So he laid her gently on the bed, with careful reverence. He knew she wasn't delicate and fragile. He knew they were well matched physically despite their size difference. But like he'd said, he wanted to look after her and care for her. Forever, if he was that damn lucky.

"I'm so sorry, Remi." He gazed down at her. "I never wanted to hurt you."

"I know." She held her arms out. He moved over her, settling between her thighs to hold her head and kiss her again. He pressed his aching dick against her softness, their jeans between them as he kissed her over and over. His tongue licked into her mouth and sucked on hers so gently. He nipped at her bottom lip, then her top one, then slid his tongue inside again. She moaned into his mouth.

He rolled to his back, bringing her with him, mouths still fused, one hand in her silky hair the other on her ass. She ground against him with needy demand and his palm on her ass cheek urged her on.

His breathing quickened and his heart slammed against his ribs. "Oh yeah, missed you so much, my hot girl."

She pushed up and reached for the hem of her sweater. Then it was gone, leaving her in a tiny black lace bra that had his balls tightening. She fell to the side and managed to kick off her leggings. He got rid of his own shirt and undid the buttons of his jeans to release his throbbing cock, then watched as she slowly tugged them down over his thighs.

Once they were gone, he lunged up and reached for her, spinning her beneath him again. "You are so fucking sexy," he growled. "Look at you." He hooked a finger in the front of her bra. "You know this makes me hot."

She smiled, slipping her hands behind her to unfasten the bra. He whisked it away, and the sight of her pretty tits was even better. "Gorgeous. Perfect." He bent his head to take a nipple into his mouth.

Her soft whimpers filled his ears as he sucked, reveling in the taste of her, the way her abdominal muscles tensed and quivered. Her hands filtered through his hair again, holding his head at her breast while he played there, cupping her soft flesh and squeezing, tasting her sweet nipples.

"Your beard is scratchy," she murmured. "Is this going to last through the playoffs?"

He lifted his head to smile at her. "Yep."

Their eyes met and hers gleamed with amusement. "Ah well. It is kind of sexy, in a rough, redneck way."

He spluttered. "Redneck?"

"Teasing. Kiss me."

He was happy to do that.

Then he stripped off the little black thong underwear she wore. Lying beside her, he slipped an arm beneath her shoulders. His other hand slid down to cup her pussy. "So soft." His fingers slipped deeper. "And so wet." He sucked her nipples again while he fingered her, sliding fingers inside her, then out, rubbing over her clit, making her gasp and purr.

"Oh yeah, Jase…right there…"

He tugged harder on the bud he was sucking, using the edge of his teeth and she twitched against him. "Need to fuck you, baby. Need to be inside that hot, wet pussy."

"Do it. I need you too."

He rolled over her again between those smooth thighs, lifting them up and back. Then he paused. "I don't have a condom."

"I have some." She pushed up onto her elbows. "But we don't need them."

Their eyes met, and the trust and love shining in hers nearly made his heart explode. "Sure?"

"Sure."

He closed his eyes briefly and plunged into her body. She cried out, falling to her back, cupping her own breasts. "Oh Christ, Remi. That feels so fucking fantastic."

"Y-yes. God yes."

He pumped in and out, found her clit again and settled wet fingertips over it. Her huffs of breath and whimpers grew faster. He gazed at her with rapt attention as a flush swept from her breasts over her chest and into her face. Close.

"Yes!"

Her back arched. Her clit swelled against his fingertips and her pussy squeezed him. "Fuck yeah," he growled. "Beautiful."

He stretched out over her and kissed her. With his nose resting alongside hers, he continued to slide in and out of her tight pussy. Tingles raced up the backs of his thighs and his ass clenched. He gazed into her eyes, the connection intimate, full of worship and wonder.

"Aw yeah," he groaned. His orgasm burst deep within him, shooting sparks up his spine, white-hot electricity searing his dick as he exploded. "Fuck yeah. Love you, Remi."

"Love you too." Her hands darted up and down his back, then clutched him as he went still on top of her, pulsing inside her. "So much."

His heart was a pounding drumbeat, his breathing harsh. He inhaled her sweet floral scent and tried to gather his scattered wits. Eventually, he rolled off her, but kept her with him again, keeping them joined, as close as they could be. Her thigh on his, he caressed her back and hip. Nose to nose, they smiled into each other's eyes.

"We'll be okay," he whispered, now stroking her hair off her face. "I promise. It might be hard, but we'll be okay."

"Yes. We will.

"I feel bad dragging you into a mess like this. All you wanted was fun."

"No." She touched her lips to his. "All I wanted was you."

AUTHOR NOTE

Thank you so much for reading Breakaway! Make sure you're on my mailing list for news about my next releases. If you enjoyed Breakaway, please consider leaving a review at the retailer of your choice or at Goodreads to help other readers find my books. You can also contact me at **info@kellyjamieson.com** to tell me what you thought of it or ask me any questions!

**And please turn the page for a sneak peek at
Heller Brothers Hockey Book 2,
FACEOFF**

Tag Heller smiled and answered questions, acknowledging how happy everyone was about the team coming back to Winnipeg, acknowledging the team's abrupt ending to their season without even making the playoffs and the rebuilding they hoped to do in the coming year. He smiled but his temples throbbed and he really, really wanted a beer.

Since he'd arrived back in Winnipeg, it had been a nonstop whirl of promotional activity. Never mind finding a place to live or even unpacking in the bedroom at his parents' home. A thirty-one year old guy living with his parents. Nice. Really nice.

He'd looked at a few houses the realtor had shown him, but he had no idea what he was looking for and didn't want to make a rash decision out of desperation. He hadn't even sold his condo in Phoenix yet. The real estate market was still tough there after the recession. Luckily he had money and didn't have to rely on selling his old place, but still…it was a huge pain in the ass.

This press conference was wrapping up, thank god. One of the new team owners, Mike Glendower, was there, as was Brad Boscoe, the new coach. And this was only about the hundredth press conference he'd been at since arriving back in town a week ago. Okay maybe a slight exaggeration.

"Thrilled to be back in my home city," he said for the thousandth time. There was a lot of truth to it, but picking up and relocating was never easy, even when it was coming home. And there was a helluva difference between Phoenix and Winnipeg. Sure, it was summer now and the weather here was great, but in the dead of winter in forty below temps and the wind howling down Portage and Main, he'd be missing the desert sun something fierce.

He knew how much this meant to the city, more than any other player on the team since he'd grown up there and was fully aware of how devastating it had been to lose their NHL team. He'd been seventeen at the time, on the brink of embarking on his own pro hockey career. His home town Jets hadn't been the team he dreamed of playing for, but still, losing them had been a huge loss for the city. So this was monumental.

Even though the team had played crappy last year.

As the conference wrapped up, he rose from his chair and shook hands with some of the team personnel who were there. Everybody looked as happy as pigs in shit. None of the other players were there yet and Tag knew *they* weren't feeling so happy. Even as much of a pain in the ass it was for him, a single guy, to pick up and move, a lot of the guys had wives and families, kids in school with friends in Phoenix, and they were not so happy about moving. And especially to Winnipeg.

Which was why the team and the league were counting on him so much to put a positive spin on this for everyone—the league, the city, team personnel and the players. He'd always been a leader on the team, captain for the last five years, but now they'd told him he was the face of the new Jets.

Great. Just what he didn't want.

He just wanted to play hockey.

But it was July, and training camp was still a long way off. Meanwhile there was all the business part of hockey that had to be attended to, especially at this important juncture in the team's existence.

When he walked into his parents' home an hour later, his mom was in the kitchen making dinner. He headed straight to the fridge and helped himself to a beer.

"How did it go?" she asked him, rinsing some green beans in a colander in the sink.

"The usual." He drank deeply. "I'm tired of it already."

"I know." She smiled. "But you're doing great."

He grunted.

"I have some good news for you though," she said. "Scott MacIntosh is coming home next week with his new baby."

"Cool." He and Scott had been best friends pretty much their whole lives, although in the last ten years they'd only seen each other a handful of times. Scott now lived in Vancouver and their paths rarely crossed, although they kept in touch by email and on Facebook. Tag had only met Scott's wife at the wedding and one other time.

"I know! So Jenn MacIntosh and I were talking. Scott and his family are heading straight up to the lake when they get in. Jenn and Greg are going to be up there for the next three weeks on holidays. And we decided that we should all go up to the lake for a week. All our boys are home right now. All their kids are home. We could have a big family party up there. Doesn't that sound great?"

It did sound great. A week of chillaxing at the beach sounded like heaven. But he wasn't sure if that was possible right now. "I don't know, Mom. The team has all kinds of shit planned for me."

She gave him a look. "The season is months away. You can tell them to just back off."

He laughed. "Sure. I'll do that."

"Seriously, Tag. One week without you there isn't going to hurt them that much."

True. "Our golf tournament is in three weeks. We have to be back by then for sure."

"Of course. I already talked to Matt and Logan. Jase and Remi fly in Monday and I know Jase wants to take Remi up to the lake to show it to her. But you don't have to come until next weekend."

Huh. Jase and Remi. His little brother had gotten serious about a woman, and it wasn't the model he'd been dating for a couple of years, it was some little school teacher. But, in a bizarre twist, the supermodel ex-girlfriend was pregnant with Jase's baby. Tag had no doubt that the model had gotten knocked up on purpose in an attempt to hang onto Jase and his fame and fortune, and this new girlfriend would probably be next. Although Mom and Dad seemed impressed by her from the time they'd met her in Chicago.

No, Tag didn't envy Jase and his messed up life. He much preferred his single, no strings attached life.

"Okay, I'll see what I can do. Maybe we can rearrange some stuff."

She smiled. "Thank you. Can you imagine? It's been years since both our families were all together."

"Yeah. It has." Seeing old friends like Scott was good. Scott's younger brother Michael was the same age as Jase and they'd probably be happy to see each other again. And then there was Scott's little sister, Kyla. Tag couldn't help but smile at remembering her, how she'd trailed after the six boys, trying so hard to be one of them and how hopeless it had been. Poor little Kyla. Totally outnumbered by the boys. Totally outdone by them. All six boys had been athletic and energetic and she had been…not.

"Michael still lives here, right?"

"Yes that's right."

"Still single?"

"Yes."

"And how about Kyla?"

His mom looked at him with a smile. "You be nice to her."

He laid a hand on his chest. "When was I ever not nice to her?"

"You boys used to torture her unmercifully."

"She loved us."

Mom shook her head. "Maybe so, although I have no idea why. Anyway, yes, Kyla still lives here. She works at a big law firm."

"Oh, yeah. She did want to be a lawyer. She always was kind of geeky-smart."

His mom grinned and bent her head to the salmon she was sprinkling fresh dill over. "Geeky. Well. I guess you haven't seen her for a while."

He drank more beer, leaning against the counter. "Yeah. How long has it been? I don't even remember." Totally not true. He shrugged. "When's dinner?"

"About an hour."

"Okay. I'm going to take a shower. Matt and Logan and I are going out tonight."

"Ah." She nodded. "Behave yourselves."

"Mom. We're adults."

She gave a soft snort. "So's your brother Jase and that didn't stop him from getting into trouble."

Tag repressed his grin, remembering Jase's arrest a few months earlier. Really, getting arrested was serious stuff. It shouldn't be funny. Jase had caught hell from all directions for that little mishap. He couldn't wait to rib his little brother about it, though.

"Just remember," Mom continued. "The whole city is watching you now."

He sighed and clunked his empty bottle down on the granite counter. "Yeah. Thanks for the reminder."

Tag leaned against the bar at Harmony, loud music thumping in the darkness, strobe lights pulsing over the crowded dance floor. He lifted his beer to his lips.

"I'm too old for this," he muttered to his brothers.

"Yeah, you are," Matt said. "It's embarrassing, actually."

Tag's lips twitched. He shifted position and caught the eye of a girl at the end of the bar who was blatantly giving him the eye. She stood with two other girls dressed in skimpy halter tops and short skirts who were also looking at him and his brothers. She looked like she was barely out of high school. And she probably was. After living in the States where the legal drinking age was higher, coming to a bar here at home, where eighteen-year-olds were of legal drinking age, was a little disconcerting for Tag. The girl smiled seductively at him. Tag sighed.

Matt, at age twenty, fit in better with the crowd in the bar than Tag did. Even Logan, a few years younger than Tag, fit in better.

"I'm here to keep an eye on you youngsters," Tag said. "Mom was worried about you."

"About us? Bullshit."

Tag grinned. "Remember what Jase did a few months ago. Getting arrested isn't a good move. I think she's a little paranoid."

"No shit. What the hell got into him, anyway?"

"He was obviously hammered," Matt said.

"Obviously. But that's not like him," Logan said. "He's never been one to drink too much."

"He'd just found out that Brianne was pregnant," Tag said, remembering those phone conversations. Christ, Jase was going to be a father. Holy shit. Tag could barely wrap his mind around that concept. "We can give him a hard time about it when he gets here," he added, smiling at the prospect. "He flies in Monday."

"We can also bug him about losing the Cup to the Sharks."

"All the way to the finals and then couldn't do it." Matt shook his head.

One of the girls Tag had noticed earlier appeared beside him.

"Hi." She fluttered her mascara-laden eyelashes at Tag. "Can you guys settle something for me and my friends? I keep telling them that you guys are famous hockey players and they don't believe me."

Tag sighed inwardly and nodded. Matt smiled at the girl. "I'm not famous," he said. "But I am a hockey player."

"Oh." She looked confused, then looked at Tag. "But *you're* famous, right? You're Tag Heller."

"I am." He resisted the eye roll and smiled. "These are my brothers, Matt and Logan."

"I knew it! I saw you on TV the other day! You play for the Jets, don't you?"

"Yup."

Tag had no intention of flirting with girls, buying drinks or dancing. But apparently Matt did. The next thing Tag knew, the three girls had joined them, introducing themselves, batting their eyelashes and giggling. He couldn't bring himself to be rude to fans, even though these girls were probably more puck bunnies than true fans who'd be buying season tickets. He recognized the type after many years in the NHL.

He really was getting too old for this. Why had he agreed to come out to a bar tonight? He was tired and grouchy and that week at the lake away from all the attention and the need to always be "on" was sounding better and better.

OTHER BOOKS BY KELLY JAMIESON

Heller Brothers Hockey
Breakaway
Faceoff
One Man Advantage
Hat Trick
Offside

Love Me
Friends With Benefits
Love Me More
2 Hot 2 Handle
Lost and Found
One Wicked Night
Sweet Deal
Hot Ride
Crazy Ever After
All I Want for Christmas
Sexpresso Night
Irish Sex Fairy
Conference Call
Rigger
You Really Got Me
How Sweet It Is

Power Series
Power Struggle
Taming Tara
Power Shift

Rule of Three Series
Rule of Three
Rhythm of Three
Reward of Three

San Amaro Singles
With Strings Attached
How to Love
Slammed

Windy City Kink
Sweet Obsession
All Messed Up
Playing Dirty

Three of Hearts

Loving Maddie from A to Z

ABOUT THE AUTHOR

Kelly Jamieson is a best-selling author of over thirty-five romance novels and novellas. Her writing has been described as "emotionally complex", "sweet and satisfying" and "blisteringly sexy". She likes coffee (black), wine (mostly white), shoes (high heels) and hockey!

Subscribe to her newsletter for updates about her new books and what's coming up, follow her on Twitter @KellyJamieson or on Facebook, visit her website at www.kellyjamieson.com or contact her at info@kellyjamieson.com

CPSIA information can be obtained
at www.ICGtesting.com
Printed in the USA
LVHW02s1758040318
568600LV00039B/2410/P